Jill Paton Walsh was educated at St Michael's Convent, North Finchley, and at St Anne's College, Oxford. Her adult novels are *Lapsing* (1986), *A School For Lovers* (1989), *Knowledg[...]* shortlisted for the 1994 Booker Prize, and *The Serpentine Cave* (1997). She [...] her children's literature, including the [...] Prize and the Smarties Award. Her lat[...] *Bohemia*, is now available as a Doubl[...]

She has three children and lives in Ca[...]

www.greenbay.co.uk

'I read *Knowledge of Angels* straight through one night: it was the best read of a novel I have had for years'
SUNDAY TIMES

'If I were a Booker judge, I would select this [*Knowledge of Angels*] as most worthy of the prize'
DAILY MAIL

'My favourite [book] this year. The book I would have most liked to win the Booker. It reworks ancient legend to tell a modern tale'
SUNDAY EXPRESS

'*Knowledge of Angels* has the pace and velcro-grip of a whodunnit. It is no surface-skimming thriller, rather a profound and subtle book of contemporary allegorical significance'
SCOTLAND ON SUNDAY

'A novel that tests the intellect yet also excites the imagination. Paton Walsh's novel grips the mind and the heart. It ought also to grip the Booker Prize'
THE ECONOMIST

'Although *Knowledge of Angels* is about questions of faith and intolerance, it is never boring. This is thanks, in part, to the compelling nature of its various stories. It is also thanks to Jill Paton Walsh's beautiful spare language'
NEW STATESMAN AND SOCIETY

'Jill Paton Walsh's passionate fable, a novel about the extremes to which adherents of faith will go to attack those who differ and a search for meaning in an age in which faith has lost much of its edge. It is an important book because its subject touches all of us'
EVENING STANDARD

'Paton Walsh draws sparkling dialogue from the bare bones of mediaeval theologians and her apparently simple tale is alive with multiple ironies'
DAILY TELEGRAPH

'Clarity of line and tone, intelligent sensitivity to the human condition, graceful, beautifully balanced prose'
THE TIMES EDUCATIONAL SUPPLEMENT

www.booksattransworld.co.uk

'Jill Paton Walsh's mediaeval historical novel did more than stick in my memory. For many days the book's powerful mixture of vividly clear writing, strong characterisation and intense theological argument haunted my daylight hours and troubled my dreams'
THE TABLET

'An incandescent novel . . . a mesmerising story populated by provocative characters in vivid atmospheric landscapes'
BOSTON GLOBE

'*Knowledge of Angels* is several different kinds of novel that come together astonishingly well. It is a philosophical argument in a line that stretches from Swift to C.S. Lewis's *The Screwtape Letters*. It is as if she has set her text down on parchment and illuminated it. As a mediaeval courtly manuscript displayed trees, rabbits, hilltop villages, swooping angels, knightly processions and peasants reaping or making love, *Knowledge of Angels* – by means of writing alone – is a series of brilliant illuminations. They do not outshine the text so much as place it in a more spacious human context'
LOS ANGELES TIMES

'[The author's] lapidary prose leads the enchanted and unsuspecting reader from escapism to self-scrutiny'
NEW YORKER

'An illuminated and illuminating book . . . [that] advances to a brilliant and relentless conclusion'
NEWSDAY

'An immensely powerful and intelligent novel, beautifully written and filled with resonances for the dilemmas of our own time'
SUSAN COOPER

'A disturbing and beautiful novel of ideas'
URSULA LE GUIN

'What a marvellous and arresting fable! . . . I was reminded of *The Name of the Rose* and I suspect this novel will have an equivalent success'
ANNE STEVENSON

'Rather like looking at a mediaeval illuminated manuscript recreated by a clever modern artist . . . luminous'
INDEPENDENT

Also by Jill Paton Walsh
A SCHOOL FOR LOVERS
GOLDENGROVE UNLEAVING
THE SERPENTINE CAVE

and published by Black Swan

A DESERT IN BOHEMIA

and published by Doubleday

Knowledge of Angels

Jill Paton Walsh

BLACK SWAN

KNOWLEDGE OF ANGELS
A BLACK SWAN BOOK : 9780552997805

Originally published in Great Britain by Green Bay Publications
in association with Colt Books Ltd

printing history
Green Bay edition published 1994
Black Swan edition published 1995

12

Black Swan Books are published by Transworld Publishers,
61–63 Uxbridge Road, London W5 5SA,
a division of The Random House Group Ltd.

Addresses for Random House Gorup Ltd companies outside the UK
can be found at: www.randomhouse.co.uk
The Random House Group Ltd Reg. No. 954009

Printed and bound in Great Britain by
Cox & Wyman Ltd, Reading, Berkshire.

The Random House Group Limited makes every effort to ensure that the
papers used in its books are made from trees that have been legally
sourced from well-managed and credibly certified forests. Our paper
procurement policy can be found at: www.randomhouse.co.uk/paper.htm

Mixed Sources
Product group from well-managed
forests and other controlled sources
www.fsc.org Cert no. TT-COC-2139
© 1996 Forest Stewardship Council
FSC

For Jane Langton,
and to the Aclaridians, wherever they may be found,
especially J.R.T., B.H., P.M.H.W., B.L., P.D.,
Margaret, Edmund,
and Clare

This story is based very remotely on the true story of the Maid of Chalons — *vide* Rousseau, *Epitre II sur L'Homme.*

It is set on an island somewhat like Mallorca, but not Mallorca, at a time somewhat like 1450, but not 1450. A fiction is always, however obliquely, about the time and place in which it was written.

Suppose you are contemplating an island. It is not any island known to you. You are looking at it from a great height – you see fig orchards, vineyards, almond orchards, and apricot orchards. There are little towns topping the gentle rises on the ample plain, the houses with their pantiled rooftops like so many tiny ploughed sloping fields clustered round the naves and towers of churches. If you looked for rivers, you would see courses of tumbled stones, with exhausted water lying in discrete pools – the hallmark of a Mediterranean land watered by intermittent violent torrents, and both parched and fertile. You see the wooded cliffs of the shore, the beaches of bright sand, the principal city, ringed by walls and rising from its harbour. You see along the northern and western shores the great mountains, the complex of ridges and green, well-watered valleys, the woods and rocks, and the high pastures, and above the tree line the towering summits, so tall that they keep their thick mantles of snow all through the heats of summer.

At this height your viewpoint is more like that of an angel than that of any islander. But after all, the position of a reader in a book is very like that occupied by angels in the world, when angels still had any credibility. Yours is, like theirs, a hovering, gravely attentive presence, observing everything, from whom nothing is concealed, for angels are very bright mirrors. Hearts and minds are as open as the landscape to their

9

view, as to yours; like them you are in the fabled world invisible.

The time of your contemplation is as mysterious as its place – it is a strange translation of the time known to the islanders, it is the time of the angels, to whom everything is always present. You have only to open a book to find Hamlet eternally bracing himself to murder his uncle, when from Hamlet's point of view he has done the deed, and lost his life and been laid these many centuries beside Yorick, whom he knew. You are looking long ago – at a time before large ships, or tarmac roads, or any of the deep scars on the land made by more than muscle power; you are looking some time in the eternal present, in the long slow centuries of the deep past.

You see now a party of young men, a line of donkeys, slowly and laboriously ascending a mountain path, while on the deep-drift clefts and buried ridges far above them another young man struggles, wrapped in the dark fleeces shepherds wear, descending towards the same destination. Their climb is present to your quiet observation, present to their struggling bodies as they painfully ascend. They will climb as often as you or anyone opens this book and reads; but the climb is to them irrevocable; each footfall as they make it vanishes into the past.

Knowledge of Angels

1

Once they had climbed through the woods of pine and holm oak which covered the lower slopes of the mountain, the *nevados* would be visible from the town all day. Above the woods the mountain was almost sheer for thousands of feet, and they moved slowly on the narrow shelves that served for paths. They had donkeys with them, bearing rolls of reeds, and simple food for their sustenance in the snows. At midday, under a pale clear sky, they climbed through a ragged strip of cloud that hung across the peak, well below the shining summits. From below it appeared a soft and narrow scarf of cloud; to the *nevados* it was a region of blurred footholds, and sudden chill – they could feel how high they were as soon as the sun was veiled – which took an hour to climb through. Still another hour scrambling on the nearly bare rocks of the crest, where the scrubby vegetation of rosemary and thorns had given place to lichens and tiny plants shrinking in clefts and crevices, and their destination was in view.

They had reached the snows. The fall was late in the year – it was April already, and in the valleys the almond blossom was over and the figs were slowly unrolling pale green fingers of foliage on the tips of their skeletal branches. But the fall was heavy and had blanketed a wide sweep of the summit. The sharp crenellations and broken cliffs of the mountaintop were softened and smoothed; the deepest shadow on the sunlit snows was paler than the grey rocks underneath.

The snow was lying forty feet lower than it usually extended and had engulfed their workplace. The snow-house itself was covered over, and the treading platform could never have been found had they not known exactly where it was. The mountain hut was half hidden in a deep drift, and they had to dig their way into it. The youths unloaded the donkeys' burdens, excavated the hut door, and drove the donkeys within. Half the hut was a byre; the animals' body warmth helped to soften the biting cold. A copper brazier stood on the floor between byre and sleeping platform, and they filled it with the charcoal that had been carried up in the summer, when the journey was easier. Outside, the men had already begun to work.

They linked arms and danced on the treading floor, their stamping feet packing the snow down hard. As soon as it looked translucent they stopped, and began the harder task of cutting it into blocks and putting the blocks into the snow-house, spreading reeds between one layer and the next, to make it easier to lift in summer. While three of them, hands wrapped in rags, lifted and packed the blocks of snow, the others shovelled more snow onto the treading floor, and the dance began again. Warming up as they worked, the dancers began to sing. Their voices dispersed in a vast silence. They were sustained by the thought that a little straw basket of ice, the size of a man's fist, would sell for a king's ransom in the towns, in the heat of summer.

By and by they were interrupted by a call, a cry like a gull's, far off, drifting down to them. They stopped work at once, and listened. They shaded their eyes. The sun had begun its descent, turning a mellow gold, and blazing on the brilliant slopes of snow. And a young man was coming down to them, moving as fast as he could. His snowshoes seemed clumsy – great baskets on his feet – but he moved steadily towards

14

them on the snow face; they could not ascend towards him themselves. Long before he reached them, they could see from his fleecy cloak that he was one of the shepherds.

The flocks had been driven up into the high valleys earlier than usual, the spring having been soft and warm until this unseasonable heavy fall of snow. But the shepherd should not have been above the snow-gatherers. Trouble.

The confabulation began as soon as he came within shout of them.

'Something is taking the sheep. We need help.'

'A wolf?'

'No. Something . . . It doesn't kill like a wolf. We are afraid. Bring your cutting tools.'

'Of course it's a wolf. What else could it be?'

'Come and see. Come at once – it will be dark.'

'How far are you?'

'An hour, along the foot of the snows. We are roasting a lamb for you. You can eat, and then help us watch.'

They left fodder for the donkeys and went with the shepherd at once. It would delay the work of taking snow but it was something new. Their lives were starved of surprises or events; the island was remote.

The shepherds would stay in the high mountains all summer long; they had made themselves comfortable. They lived in a large cave, across the mouth of which they had built a rubble wall with a door and windows. A cleft in the cave roof had been used to make a chimney for a charcoal fire. There were only three of them, two old men and a very young one. They had sent the youngster to fetch the *nevados*.

'Old Luis is beginning to see the other world, admit it,' said Galceran to the messenger as they went. It was well known that thin air and solitude drove the shepherds crazy after months aloft. By September

15

they would come down burned as brown as walnuts and barely able to speak, flinching at the racket of the streets. Their wives and mothers would comfort them with basins of hot water, with clean clothes and fresh fish baked in crushed lemons and sun-dried apricots from the little gardens behind the simple houses. By and by they would recover, and begin to shout and drink, and cavort with their friends again. But now, of course, they had been in the mountains only a fortnight or so.

'Not a wolf?' Galceran asked. 'What's your name?'

'Jaime.'

'Ah, Esclamonda's son. Aren't you too young for the mountains?'

'My brother is just married. I'm taking his place for a month.'

'Good lad,' said Galceran, grinning. 'How can Old Luis be sure what it is? Have you seen it?'

Jaime shook his head. 'It bites very deep,' he said, shivering. 'Luis says it must have fangs so long . . .' He placed his hands inches apart.

'We'll kill it for you, never fear,' said Galceran, cheerfully.

It was warm in the shepherds' cave. The promised lamb was roasting on a spit; the bread the *nevados* had brought from the valley that morning was not yet rock hard; Galceran had a flagon of wine in his pack. It felt like a holiday, but the old men were afraid.

'A large wolf,' Galceran insisted. He imagined himself felling it with a titanic blow from his snow spade and being acclaimed as the hero of the hour.

'Our troubles are with eagles now. They can take a new born lamb,' Old Luis said. 'There are hardly any wolves left. They are dying out. They've mostly finished up as pelts in the tannery at Ciudad.'

'Those that remain are the strongest, the most cunning,' said Salvat, 'like the one we killed last

16

week. We wouldn't have got her if she hadn't been old. I thought our troubles were over for the season. And now this.'

The shepherds had made a trap. They had staked out a weakling lamb as a lure and spread out a bale of fishing net. Someone had watched all night, with a cord in his hand. When the lamb cried, pulling the cord would engulf the predator in the net, and they would be able to bundle it up without getting near it. But it had not worked. The thing had come; the net had been cast. Jaime – it was he who had watched – had shouted; the others came swiftly with axes and lanterns. The thing growled and heaved in the trap. Then it had gone, leaving the lamb dead behind it. They showed the *nevados* the hole in the net, the slashed strands breaching it widely. They showed the stiff little carcass, its head nearly severed at the neck. The thing had left tracks in the snow; strange tracks.

'Whoever heard of a wolf with spoor like that?' Salvat asked. He pointed out the impression of the front paw, divided into four pads, the mark of the claws behind, not in front of the footprint. 'I am nearly eighty. I have heard a lot, seen a lot. Never anything like this.'

'We can track it to its lair now the snow is lying here,' said Old Luis. 'But we don't know what it is. We thought it best to get help.'

'At first light its time has come,' the *nevados* promised. 'Whatever it is.' They were strong men, and numbered nearly a dozen. They were therefore only a little afraid, with that pleasurable thrill that comes from mystery and a promise of excitement. The shepherds' cave was warmer and drier than the snow hut, and the roast meat better than their own salt fish and olives and stale bread would have been. The prospect of killing, of letting rage triumph, and of reaping admiration, not loathing, was as heady as

17

Galceran's wine. In the warmth of the night cave, the mysterious creature could not have been too large for them, or too appalling. The hugest wolf that ever walked would have disappointed them.

In the morning the tracks were clear to see. The thing had taken another lamb in the night, as expected. About every three days it was raiding the flocks; but the night before last, when it had bitten through the net, it had left its prey behind. That it would be hungry was predictable. And though the shepherds had searched for it in vain for nearly the whole of their two weeks in the high pastures, the snowfall had entrapped the creature better than the net – it could be followed easily now. The trail led up to the top of the hanging valley, climbing the stark rock-face, ribbed with clefts and riddled with caves, where anything could hide. For the first half mile or more the trail was unreadable, because the creature had been dragging its kill, obliterating its footprints as it made them. Then in a snow-filled cranny made filthy with blood it had left the larger part of the lamb, dismembered and horribly torn, taking the left hindquarter onwards. Now the trail was marked with a line of blood drops, and the haunch had been carried in the creature's teeth, leaving the strange trail clear.

There was a marked difference between its front paws and its back paws – the back paws had long claw marks in front of the paw mark, only the front footprints had the strange inverted claws. Like a hare it left leg-marks as well as footprints from time to time, and now and then its bloody burden dangled low enough to scrape and stain the sunlit purity of the ground.

'Look,' said Old Luis, as they rested, nearly a thousand feet above the grazing grounds. 'What kind of creature has a gait like that?' The leg-marks, long and narrow, extended behind the prints of the thing's front paws, and in front of its rear paws. They shook their heads and moved on. In a few more minutes they came round a rock bluff and saw the trail making straight across a level facet of rock, and into the mouth of a cave. It was a small cave. The finely balanced mixture of excitement and fear which had driven them urgently till that moment shifted suddenly towards fear. Jaime trembled. But it would be Galceran, surely, who went first?

It was. They moved as quietly as they could, and they fanned out, in case it rushed out of the cave and escaped them. They could hear it snarling and growling.

'Perhaps it has young,' said Salvat. 'It is feeding its young . . .'

They closed in. Then, suddenly they could see into the hollow in the drift in front of the creature's lair. The melt-cave at the door of the rock cave was abominable with scraps of slaughtered things – with blood and feathers and bones. Even on the nearly frozen air, a stench reached them. The thing held the stolen haunch of meat between its front paws, and was worrying it, snarling like a dog as it ate. It had a mantle of matted black fur over its head and shoulders, and bluish bald hindquarters. It did not hear or smell them coming, for it did not cease to drag off strips of meat from the bone.

Galceran let out a bloodthirsty yell. He raised his snow-mattock high above his head and swung it murderously. It was Jaime who stopped him. He jumped forward with a wail and, grabbing Galceran's sleeve, deflected the blow. Then he lurched backwards, doubled over convulsively, and vomited. He had seen, just in time, that the monster was a human child.

* * *

A child. It had hair matted into a thick pall that spread over its back and shoulders – that was what they had taken for fur. Otherwise it was naked. The terrible fangs with which it had slaughtered lambs and cut free from the entrapping net were only an old, rusty knife. It held the knife between its teeth. It ran away on all fours, zigzag in the space left by the line of men. It tried to run between two of them. But they were armed with nets and poles and caught it easily. Holding it by the hair, and beating it till it howled, they forced it to drop the knife. Then they bundled it up and carried it, slung from the longest pole, and dumped it into a sheep-pen made of wattles outside the shepherds' cave. It fought them all the way.

In the pen it ran from corner to corner, round and round, with a loping four-footed gait. It ran on the bent back knuckles of its hands and on bent forward toes. Huge hardened overgrown nails protruded from its hands and feet. They watched it in silence for a while and then retreated, averting their eyes, occupying themselves with making supper. At first light the *nevados* would return to the treading floor.

'Shall we feed it?' said Salvat, as they ate.

'Feed it?' said Luis. 'It's full of our lamb already!' But Salvat sliced a length of meat from the bone on the spit and took it on the end of his knife to the penned and running child. It sniffed at the offering, recoiled, and trampled it untasted, in the dirt. They tried bread, with a like result. At last, gagging slightly, Galceran took it the bucket of raw offal left from the evisceration of the roast carcass, and it ate.

'How old is it?' Juan asked.

'Hard to say. Nine? Younger? Older? It's all skin and bone and rage,' said Galceran.

'How has it survived?' another of the *nevados* asked.

'A wolf has suckled it,' said Old Luis, wiping his knife on a hunk of bread.

'Is such a thing possible?'

'It might be. There have always been stories.'

'What are we going to do with it?' Galceran asked.

'Don't ask me,' said Luis. 'To my mind your first thought was the best.'

'I would have killed it . . .'

'You should have done.'

'But that would be murder!' cried Jaime. 'Murder . . .'

'It would have been merciful,' said Luis. 'But it's too late now.'

'Is it?' said Salvat.

'How many are we?' asked Luis. 'Twelve *nevados* and three of us. Could we be sure that not one of fifteen people, as long as any of us live, would breathe a word to a wife, to a bishop, to a priest in the confessional, to a mother, a sweetheart by moonlight? Never, when living, drunk, or dying?' Glancing meaningfully at Jaime as he spoke, Luis made very clear where he thought the dangerous member of the party was sitting. 'There was just that one moment, when Galceran could truthfully have said that he did not know what it was – and the moment is gone. One whisper from any of us if we kill it now, and we would all hang.'

'You're right, of course,' said Salvat. 'A pity.'

'It would be murder!' Jaime insisted. 'God would know, even if we all kept mum for ever!'

'Holy Catalida!' said Old Luis. 'Do you think there could be a God – supposing that there is a God – with no more common sense than a bishop? Do you think that . . . *thing* is one of us?'

But the older men looked at one another. Luis was right. Something which they might have risked doing if they had been alone – grizzled heads only, in the mountains – was far too risky with a mawkish youth as witness, one with a tender conscience, the smell of his mother's piety still hanging round him.

Just then the thing began to howl. It set up a blood-curdling baying, that rang round the summits above them.

With the hairs prickling on their scalps, they rose from the circle round the fire in which they had been sitting and went outside. A half-moon cast barely perceptible shadows, and the child sat on its haunches in the middle of the pen, just visible, its head thrown back, howling full-throated. Far, far off, the cry was answered, faintly. A brother brute had heard it, from a distant cave. Someone lit a torch. The child cowered away from the light, as if afraid. In the flickering light it looked more terrible than ever – covered with blood from the offal bucket and hiding its face in its hair.

Galceran drew his knife and vaulted over the fence into the pen. 'I'm going to cut its hair,' he said.

'Don't, Galceran, you'll spoil it!' said Juan.

'*Spoil* it?' Galceran paused, amazed.

'We could earn a pretty penny taking that round the markets and charging for a look,' said Juan. 'The wolf-boy. Think of it!'

'Pah!' said Galceran. 'You disgust me.' And he advanced on the child. Terrified, it fought back. It took four of them, in the end, to hold it down, small though it was, while Galceran hacked through the pall of hair, cutting it off at the neck. They held torches to light the struggle. Before it was done, Jaime retired to the back of the cave, and curling up on his pallet wept bleakly and silently. He was thrown into the pit of dejection by the knowledge that a child could become no more than a wolf – worse – less than a wolf, for a wolf at least is natural. He gagged on his own tears at what he had seen under the bright torches, as Galceran tore away the masking hair. The child was a girl.

The *nevados* were three more days on the mountain, treading and cutting snow. They kept the wolf-girl tethered and staked on a leather thong. She refused their food and howled at night. When the time came to descend, they had trouble. The donkeys were terrified of her and refused to carry her, baring their teeth, and stubbornly resisting. She would not run on a lead, but would have needed to be dragged over every stone on the paths. When Luis tried to carry her, she bit his hand to the bone. They got her as far as the pine woods slung on a pole, bound wrist and ankle, like a carcass for the butcher, and stopped at the first band of trees to cut branches and make a cage. She seemed terrified of the cage, and they had to beat her unconscious to get her into it. After that they took turns, carrying the cage on poles. Before they reached the first farms, Galceran had had enough of it. There would be no glory in having captured a child. He let Juan take her in exchange for the promise of a bottle apiece, and a basket of olives to share.

2

As you saw, as well as mountains the island contained
an ample undulating plain, assiduously farmed by the
inhabitants of the little hill towns scattered across it.
Each had its splendid church and its square planted
with trees for shade. The lines of round or square
towers that clustered on the margins of the towns
looked from a distance like fortifications but were
actually disused windmills; built not to forfend a
flow of blood but to obtain a flow of water, of which
the plains were usually short. When a well ran dry, the
farmers built new towers to support the spinning
wheel of sails, leaving the old ones standing. Only
the towns very near the coast were actually fortified;
all through the island's history there had been danger
from pirates. Here and there on the plain were steep
hills, each topped with a sanctuary, and in the south
there was a second range of heights, which would
have counted as mountains in another country, but
here were reduced to hills by comparison with the
precipitate, spectacularly towering range of mountains
in the north, on which the snow shrank into ragged
patches but never vanished, even at the height of
summer.

The coastline was alternately rugged and incurved
by shallow, sandy coves, and the only large, safe har-
bourage was in the south, where Ciudad, the principal
town, had a fortified and defended anchorage. Elsewhere the coastline was resorted to only by fishermen,
a cheaper defence than walls being merely to build

24

settlements a little inland and out of sight from the sea. On the shore itself the fishermen sometimes built themselves little shelters, though more often they simply pulled their boats up the beaches to the margins of the pine woods and slept, if they were not going home, in makeshift tents of spars and sails. Fish were plentiful and, except for the storms at either equinox, the waters were usually calm, so the fishermen were somnolent fellows, plying their trade in leisurely fashion. The islanders had a passion for fish, and whatever was caught could be sold.

On one of a thousand fine days, Miguel and Lazaro sat under the pine trees, mending nets. It was very early in the morning, and the light shone levelly below the branches. Later there would be shade. Later it would be welcome. The nets were dyed with indigo, in a forlorn hope of catching the colours of the ultramarine and turquoise waters beyond the line of soft surf breaking on the sands. The men sat cross-legged, heads bent over the work, raising the shuttles of cord to pull the knots tight. Now and then they straightened and looked vacantly out to sea for a moment. Nothing was to be seen except the iridescence of the morning light on the silken expanse of water.

And then there was something to be seen. Something floating, far out. Lazaro frowned into the rising sun, and was dazzled. A drifting lobster-float, no doubt. What else could it be? Then, when he looked up again, a time-span later, for the sun had risen enough to enlighten rather than obliterate sight, it was much nearer, and moving. He pointed and spoke to Miguel. They got up and walked to the water's edge, watching. Soon they could discern clearly what they were seeing – a swimmer, slowly and wearily struggling from the far horizon towards the golden shore. He seemed to be failing as they watched; he seemed to be drifting offshore again. They ran to the little white-painted boat that bobbed in the shallows beside a rocky jetty and rowed out to bring him in.

He had been in the water a long time. His skin was swollen, softened, pallid and wrinkled like the hands of their womenfolk on wash days. His lips were cracked. He was naked, except for a sodden loincloth. Tumbled into the bottom of the boat he lay, eyes closed, face upwards, for a while. Then he groaned and rolled over and tried drinking the brackish slops in the bilge. They grounded the boat and carried the half-dead stranger up the beach. They laid him in the shade of the sailcloth tent and stared at him. He was a splendidly built man of middle age, bronzed-skinned and dark-haired, fully bearded. He reached for the water-flagon, but they withheld it. Instead Lazaro dipped a sponge and held it to his lips, letting him suck and sip a little at a time. Miguel brought the oil jar – olive oil was plentiful on the island, and they would have cooked their fishes in it at supper time – and rubbed oil into the waterlogged skin of the man's feet and hands. Then they pulled a sail over him and left him to sleep; his eyes were closed already in the utmost weariness.

They rowed far out – not as far as he had been when Lazaro first saw him, yet as far as they ever went, bundling the pile of nets over the back of the boat and rowing gently to trail it in the deep behind them. The bobbing floats and the weedy line of the floating edge of the nets broke the sparkling surface, and below the fish were gathered in unfailing plenty. It was so ordinary a day, the unchanging and endlessly recurrent aspects of rocky headland and swirling waters and soaring birds so completely like yesterday and tomorrow, that they thought they must have dreamed the swimmer. They scanned the shores behind them for any sign of a wreck and the horizon for any sign of a ship, but not a scrap of explanation for the swimmer could be found. Not even a drifting spar.

Nevertheless, they had not dreamed him; when they returned in the afternoon for the invariable siesta, he was still asleep where they had left him under the trees. At their approach, the swimmer woke. He tried to sit and failed, groaning. Lazaro offered him the water flask, saying, 'You can drink now.'

'He won't understand a word,' said Miguel. But the swimmer understood enough to take the flagon and drink deeply. Lazaro offered bread, and Miguel rubbed on more oil. Then at last the stranger spoke. He said, with a musical and marked accent, but perfectly intelligibly, 'I will reward you.' It was so unexpected, and so preposterous in the mouth of a nearly naked man lying helpless and wholly destitute, that the fishermen laughed. They roasted fish on a little driftwood fire and shared the bread and olives three ways.

'You shall have gold and rubies,' he said, and they laughed again.

At six the swimmer could still hardly stand unaided, let alone walk. They put him on the donkey, sitting him awkwardly on the fish panniers, but they had to unburden the beast first of the huge pile of green that usually topped its load, for it carried its own fodder home each evening. That evening Miguel hoisted the bundle of grasses onto his own shoulders for the trudge to the village. It was a small village – a church dedicated to St Anne, a little square, a few narrow streets of plain houses, gardens behind them, orange trees in every nook and cranny. At dusk the shopkeepers opened their doors and shutters again, the simple tavern was ready to serve the habitual customers, a scatter of lanterns at doorways lit the square. Throwing off the lassitude of the afternoon

27

heat, the people woke up and took a turn in the open air, strolling and chattering under the stars. Every day was the same, except that now and then a wedding or a funeral party brought a little joy, a little change. The appearance of the rescued swimmer was a sensation.

The sensation was increased when Lazaro helped him from the donkey, and he at once collapsed. The two fishermen stood over his supine body, telling their story volubly to the rapidly gathering crowd. His plight, especially since he was handsome, touched hearts at once. In caring for him the fishermen had a superior claim, and since Miguel had a noisy brood of children, while Lazaro lived with his widowed mother, it was to Lazaro's house that the swimmer was carried. But Lazaro's mother could not possibly be allowed sole possession of such a treasure – the women of the village crowded into her little room and drove out the men.

A great coming and going followed. Every nearby kettle was raided for hot water, and ewers were carried at a run down the street. The women from nearby houses fetched clothes for him. Hardship made them thrifty, and most families had old clothes laid by, neatly mended and laundered. An hour later he was washed, oiled, and decently clad in humble clothes. He emerged to be led to the tavern with uncertain steps by a crowd of triumphant women and girls, every one of whom knew more about the stranger than their menfolk by the width of a loincloth; unfavourable comparisons would be made for many years.

While he ate, ravenously, sitting at a table outside the tavern door, half the population of the village looked on, and he was surrounded by the buzz of voices like a lily in flower by the hum of bees. 'See how hungry he is!' the women told each other. 'Poor soul, poor soul, however long was he in the water?'

The men, meanwhile, were discussing the question of where he could have come from. On one thing they were agreed: he could not, as the farmers were suggesting, simply have swum round the jutting headland from a nearby cove, because the ferocity of the currents would have prevented it. He would have been swept straight out to sea.

'Well then – so he was – and you saw him swimming back again. Why not?'

The fishermen shook their heads. They knew what they had seen – a man swimming from the most distant horizon, making directly for land.

And now the stranger had finished eating. He could be questioned.

'What is your name?'

'Palinor.'

'Where are you from?'

'A country very far from here. Aclar.'

'Where?'

'You have never heard of it?'

'Never. What were you doing in the sea?'

'Swimming. Hoping for landfall.'

'But why were you in the sea?'

The stranger shrugged and spread his hands in a deploring gesture. 'I fell in,' he said, and laughed. Laughter filled the square.

'Hard luck, friend!' said the tavern-keeper.

'Could have been worse, after all,' said Palinor, smiling. 'There was no land in view. I was lucky in the direction I chose.'

'And there isn't enough luck in the world for all of us, at the best of times,' said the tavern-keeper. 'We'll celebrate for you. I'll fill a glass for everyone free tonight.'

The tavern-keeper became the hero of the hour. By and by Palinor said to Miguel, 'I am going to have trouble getting home, I fear. I shall need to find a money-lender, and passage on a ship . . .'

'We will take you to the citadel in the morning,' said

29

Miguel. 'Perhaps the prefect will help you.' Help with moneylenders and passage on ships was beyond the competence of anyone in the village, he well knew.

That night when the stranger was asleep in Lazaro's bed and Lazaro was lying on a bale of straw borrowed from the donkey, on the floor beside his mother's bed – all three sleeping in the only room of the house – Lazaro said softly to his mother, 'He offered us gold. He without so much as a shirt on his body!'

His mother said, 'I hope you accepted, son. Did you notice his hands?'

'Hands?' said Lazaro. He turned his head. The stranger's hand lay on the rough blanket of the best bed, barely visible in the dark room, though moonlight fingered through the shutters of the window that looked towards the garden.

'Not a callous on them, and the nails cut neatly and unbroken,' the woman said. 'They are not working hands. They might belong to a prince . . .'

Each of the four corners of the island had a citadel; a fortified acropolis, dating from the period of danger from pirates. In this north-easterly region the citadel was small – a simple ring of battlemented walls, containing an ancient church and the prefect's house, and commanding a view over the furrows of the earth-red, earth-gold roof tiles of the town to the surrounding plains and distant mountains. It was an hour on foot from the village.

The prefect was not impressed. He saw standing before him a man in working clothes, with no shoes on his feet and an attitude he at once sensed to be insufficiently respectful, asking for money. 'What are you doing here?' he asked. 'Are you an islander? If you are a native here, you should remember the punishment for an able-bodied beggar.'

'I am not an islander of this island.'

'Do you have permission to be at large here? You need a warrant for any journey outside the port at Ciudad.'

'I did not disembark at Ciudad; I swam ashore to save my life.'

'Nobody is allowed to land here. You should have come through Ciudad, and applied for a warrant.'

Palinor regarded the prefect coolly. He said, 'I had not the strength to swim round the perimeter of your island looking for the usual port of disembarkation. Since I have never been to Ciudad, I have no warrant to travel out of it. Do I need a warrant to go there now?'

'Foreigners need warrants to move about the island, in any circumstances.'

'Then I apply for one. To whom do I apply?'

'I can give you a temporary one, if your answers are satisfactory,' said the prefect grudgingly. 'Name?' He reached for a sheet of paper, and took up his pen.

'Palinor.'

'Port of origin?'

'Aclar.'

'Where?'

'Aclar.'

The prefect had never heard of it, but was unwilling to show ignorance. He was, truth to tell, unnerved by the unusual experience of dealing with an applicant who looked him straight in the eye.

'You are a citizen of that country?'

For the first time the man hesitated. 'I suppose so.'

'Answer yes or no,' said the prefect.

'Yes.'

'Religion?'

'None.'

The prefect stared. 'You can be Christian, Saracen or Jew,' he said.

'I am none of those,' said Palinor.

'What are you then?'

'Nothing. Myself.'

'You won't get a warrant, as yourself. For a Christian it is a mere formality; for Saracens and Jews there are quotas, I believe.'

'I am not going to state a false allegiance for the sake of a form,' said Palinor. 'You must write none, and we shall see.'

The prefect finished writing. 'This will take some time,' he said.

'You will find me with the fishermen who rescued me,' said Palinor, 'I shall spend the time learning to mend nets.'

'You will spend the time in the lock-up here,' said the prefect. 'I'm not having you roaming loose.'

The stranger blenched slightly. 'That is not reasonable,' he said. 'I have committed no crime, and you have no reason to suppose that I will. It would be an outrage to deprive me of liberty.'

'A man of no religion might do anything,' said the prefect. 'What is to restrain him? But while you are in my province you won't get the chance.'

He clicked his fingers, and his servants hustled Palinor away.

Jaime → J'aime

3

The youth stood for some time just inside the cathedral door. It took a little while for the darkness within, after the glare of the great sunlit square outside, to resolve itself; for the arrays of pillars, the branching vault, the heavy elaboration of the altar, the tombs, the paintings, the lamps, the incense burners and racks of candles to become clear to the widening pupils of those who entered. But the youth stood longer than that, quietly, just to one side of the door, staring. Those who walked past him, going in or out, gave him barely a glance: a country boy in wretched clothes, and botched sandals, seeming afraid – overawed, certainly. Eventually he began to move, padding softly down one of the aisles, looking.

The cathedral had been built by men of austere vision. It was of plain grey stone, roofed by a soaring vault of simple and beautiful form. A sort of polyphony of shape – the arched openings between nave and aisles, and the arched windows which muted and tinted the light of the day before admitting it – struck the onlooker like Lenten music. Nevertheless, a later age had decorated it. Behind every altar, in every chapel in the aisles, in frenetic emphasis behind the high altar, in orgies of jewelled enrichment were columns of coloured marble, riotously foliate capitals, carved angels, painted canvasses of piously gesturing saints. One might have thought the same building had been occupied in successive centuries by adherents of two different religions.

The youth seemed simply overpowered, uncomprehending. He spent many minutes standing in front of a picture of a man kneeling in an amphitheatre, in military attire, with his head about to be severed by an executioner. The executioner's sword was raised high. Behind it, and behind a bloodthirsty crowd, was a statue of a wolf, with two children crouched underneath its belly, reaching for its dugs with chubby hands. The boy stood frowning and staring, biting his thumb. But whatever story the picture told, it was not one that anyone had ever told him, and at last he moved on. Eventually he found a side chapel with a picture he recognized: St Jeronimo in the wilderness, shabbily clothed, kneeling, holding a book, and with a lion and a wolf lying at his feet. The church in his village was dedicated to St Jeronimo, and boasted a simple picture of the saint. The youth knelt down, bowed his head, and prayed.

Not for long; soon he crossed over to the opposite aisle and found what he was looking for: one of those little cupboards with curtained doors, in which confessions are made, and a line of penitents, kneeling on a bench, waiting. He joined them. When his turn came, he entered the little cubicle, knelt down, leaned his face to the grill behind which the priest sat unseen, and said, 'Help me, Father!'

'You must say, "Bless me Father, for I have sinned",' said the priest.

'I have not come to confess. Please, help me,' said the youth.

'If you do not wish to confess, get out!' said the priest. 'How dare you? How dare you abuse the sacrament?'

'Is there no mercy then? I implore you to help me!'

'If it is not with your sins, I cannot help you. You must go to the appropriate authorities.'

'There is a man at every gate who refuses me entry,' said the youth. 'And she will die.' But he had accepted that the priest would not help him; flat despair dulled his voice, like the note of a cracked bell. The priest sighed, stood up, stepped out of his booth, reached into the penitents' booth, and pulled the youth to his feet. There were no other penitents waiting – no further tales of lust and greed and cruelty to be told that afternoon.

'People die every day, and there is nothing to be done about it,' he said to the youth, taking in his poverty, his helpless demeanour.

'But she will die *unbaptized*,' the boy cried.

Severo, cardinal prince of Grandinsula, on the death of his elder brother having come to unite in one person both worldly and spiritual authority, had little use for pomp or luxury, or any of the appurtenances of power. Compared to the power itself, any benefit he might draw from it in personal comfort, or in gorgeous ceremony, seemed to him almost comically vulgar and trivial. He had a palace in the cool of the mountains, where plentiful springs of fresh water flowed unfailingly, but he had never lived there for more than a few days in the hottest weather. He lived with his secretariat in rooms above the cloisters behind the cathedral, and held court in the princes' palace occasionally, to decide civic appeals. When he received a foreign deputation in the palace, especially a barbaric one from a distant country, he sometimes put on his cardinal's scarlet, and had the royal crown of Grandinsula – he had never worn it – carried in front of him, but he lived from day to day in a simple black soutane, like one of his village priests.

His room was a whitewashed, barrel-vaulted cell, containing a narrow bed, a desk, a shelf of books, a small and roughcut cupboard to receive his clothes, and a prie-dieu, unadorned and with no cushion for the knees. Above the bed, opposite the prie-dieu, where he could contemplate it day and night, was a painting of the Harrowing of Hell. Every cell in the cloister had a painting; Severo had chosen this one for the subject, though the cell also had a window facing the sea, which admitted cool air and a view of the bay, and a door giving on to a balcony above the garden, where it was pleasant to walk. The awe in which his subjects held him was greatly increased by the impression that he lived austerely and plainly; in fact he had provided himself unstintingly with all that he needed.

His plainness deceived the boy. Having told his tale three times already to an ascending sequence of important dignitaries, the third being the canon residentiary of the cathedral clergy, in a splendidly furnished office, the boy was sulky, and disinclined to tell it all over a fourth time to this humble person found writing in a simple cell.

'If you're sending me for mare's milk,' he said, miserably, 'forget it. Let me go home.'

The priest who had brought him, horrified at his lack of respect, forced the boy to his knees, threatening terrible punishments if he did not at once kneel to and obey his cardinal and his prince, and at once repeat his story, as he had been told. The boy knelt, but was reduced to terrified silence.

'Where are you from?' asked Severo.

'Sant Jeronimo, Holiness,' said the boy.

'A long way. Have you walked to Ciudad?' The boy nodded. 'Has anyone fed you?'

'No, Holiness.'

'You must be very hungry,' said Severo. To his priest he said, 'What are you all thinking of? Give him a meal.'

'Thank his Holiness at once, and come to the kitchen with me,' said the priest.

36

'No,' said Severo. 'Why do you speak roughly to him? Can't you see that you scare him? Bring food here; we will eat in the garden. Bring a plentiful platter of plain food – no delicacies, just what he's used to. Let me see . . . a quartern loaf of dark bread, and some cheese and olives, an orange, and a flagon of water. Quickly.'

The priest withdrew. 'What is your name?' asked Severo, contemplating the boy. Someone washed and mended his clothes, worn though they were. His wrists jutted out of the sleeves of his outgrown shirt.

'Jaime.'

'Then come with me, Jaime. We will sit in the evening sun outside and talk, while we wait for them to bring supper. First tell me this – do they still pasture the sheep in the high sierra above Sant Jeronimo?'

'That is where we found her,' said the boy, eagerly, launching again into his story.

When the servant brought the bread and relishes, the telling had reached the point where the *nevados* carried the snow-girl away down the mountain. Severo had listened with a grave expression. He stopped Jaime talking while he ate – ate hungrily, rapidly at first, and then slowly, spinning it out. In a while the boy offered the bread and olives. 'Aren't you going to have any, Holiness?'

Gravely Severo took a hunk of bread, broke it in two, and gave half back to Jaime. Nobody he had ever broken bread with, such was his vow, would be less than a brother to him, or would know want while he had substance. The youth did not know that; he shared the food with his exalted companion out of the courtesy of peasants, who on the island never ate in the presence of one who was not eating. Severo took olives to eat with the bread and sat down beside the widow's son on the bench.

'To continue . . .' he said.

'It was a month, nearly, before my brother came for me. He had a new wife – did I tell you? – and I think he was sorry to leave her. When he came I was free to return to Sant Jeronimo, to my mother. I asked about the snow-girl as soon as I got home, and they said she was with Juan. They did not seem interested, Holiness. I set out to find Juan. I had a hard time; he was moving around – one town, then another town, always for market day. You know, Holiness, there is a leather market on Monday and then a fish market at Porto . . .'

'Yes, I know,' said Severo gently. 'Where did you find her?'

'It was stupid. I followed him all round the island – always a day late – and then caught up with him at home. Everywhere I went, people were grumbling about him. He had charged them to look at her, but they thought they had been cheated.'

'Why?'

'They paid to look at a wolf-child, but they thought they had seen an animal. When I caught up with him, I saw her again and I was not surprised. He had not washed her, or covered her. He is keeping her in the little cage they made to bring her down the mountain. She is starving. She refuses food. Holiness, she will eat only raw meat, and he will not give her any because he says it makes her savage. She has bitten him, more than once, and he no longer lets her out of the cage. So she is filthy. I do not think he can take her round the markets again, Holiness, because people are enraged at being, as they think, cheated, but he would not sell her to me for anything I could pay him. My mother would have pawned her rosary, but it was not enough. I implored him to give her raw meat, but he would not. All I could do was give her a little milk to drink, and come to find help . . .'

The boy's voice shook.

'Would not the priest at Sant Jeronimo help you?' enquired Severo. 'Does he know about this?'

'He knows. He did nothing. I thought if I came to Ciudad . . .'

'And here you found all doors closed to you except that of the confessional? I suppose I am not surprised. My officials are beleaguered; they have too many requests, no doubt. But I am surprised at the priest at Sant Jeronimo. Are you telling me the truth, Jaime?'

'Yes, I am, Holiness, but . . .'

'But?'

'But Holiness, you have not seen her. She is – she is *terrible*. Everyone turns away, but I do not blame them. If I could stop thinking of her, I would. Holiness, when you see her, blackness . . . it is blackness in your heart. You are cast down, you cannot bear it. It is the worst thing you could ever know . . .' He recovered himself a little, and said, 'He said it would be blasphemy to baptize such a thing.'

Severo paced up and down the garden for a while. Then he clapped his hands, and when a servant appeared he asked for Brother Rafal. Rafal came, wearing a simple monk's habit, a young man, only a little older than Jaime.

Severo said, 'Rafal, this is my brother, Jaime.' Jaime looked up in amazement. 'I want you find him a cell for the night, and a suit of good clothes and stout shoes. In the morning you are to go with Jaime to the intramontana, and there you are to find a certain child, and bring it here. I will give you letters of authority and a purse. You are to be rapid and discreet. There may not be much time; the child seems to be dying, and the less attention we attract from the vulgarity the better. Do you accept this charge?'

'Yes, Holiness.'

'Good. Go with Rafal now, Jaime. I need to pray.' When Jaime stood up, but stayed rooted to the spot, as if confused, he added, 'You have done right, Jaime. You won't regret it.' Then, falling into Latin, a tongue very close to that of his island but different enough for him to suppose that Jaime would not understand him, he said to Rafal, 'The boy is urgent to baptize the child you are seeking, but do not do so. He will not think to do it himself; he seems not to realize that is permitted. And I would first like to see what made the priest of Sant Jeronimo refuse his duty.'

4

Palinor had been incarcerated for months in the dungeons of the provincial citadel before a clerk in Ciudad, working doggedly through a pile of requests for warrants, liberties and placets, came upon an unusual one. He was a very junior clerk, still in the subdiaconate, and of lowly rank. He raised his head and said to Laurenx, his overseer, who worked alongside him at the long table covered with vellums, papers, inkwells and seals where he sat day after day, 'What do we do with atheists?'

'Put them to death, I think,' said Laurenx, without looking up.

'We have a protocol for that?' the clerk said, appalled. 'Do I have to . . .'

'You've really got an atheist?' Laurenx asked, putting down his pen. 'What does he want to do?'

'Travel to Ciudad,' said the clerk, looking at the paper as though it were poisoned.

'Well, don't look so green,' said Laurenx. 'We don't have to burn him ourselves. Just refer to higher authority. Take the paper to the Consistory Office.'

'Yes,' the clerk said, getting slowly and reluctantly off his stool. 'But what will happen to the man, Laurenx?'

'I'm sure we burn atheists,' Laurenx said. 'If they don't recant, that is. I expect he gets a chance to recant. Just refer it upwards and forget about it, friend. It isn't our responsibility.'

*   *   *

41

The order from the Consistory Office baffled the prefect. 'Transfer the alleged atheist at once, under escort, to Ciudad,' it said. It did not say why. It was an unusual order, and the prefect could not discern from the paper surrounding the line in a crabbed official hand, whether the prisoner was to be sent under escort because he was, after all, a person of importance, or because he was a dangerous criminal. Naturally, it was to be hoped that it was because he was dangerously criminal; if he were really of importance, then the prefect might be in difficulties for having locked him up. It was in any case hard to decide whether the escort should be of a kind to honour or to disgrace the escorted. No guidance. The prefect looked all over both sides of the paper in case anyone had thought to scrawl him a note. Then he sent his servant to the dungeon tower at the lower end of the citadel to discover if the atheist was still alive. There were no arrangements for feeding prisoners; their families, or sometimes their parish priests, from charity, looked after them. The prefect was vexed with himself for not having considered that if the atheist's story was true he had neither resource. And clearly it would be embarrassing if the man had died while in his keeping, whether he was wanted as a personage, or as a criminal.

Palinor was alive. Months in the dark had cast a sickly pallor on his skin, and he was as filthy as prisoners usually were, but he was not starving; Lazaro's mother, out of a blend of hope and charity, had fed him every day. The prefect stood just inside his windows and watched Palinor, released into the sunlit space within the citadel walls, where wild fig and cactus and rosemary grew in an impromptu garden, blink at the light and take uncertain steps along the path. The prefect decided that 'at once' could be thought to mean in three days' time – a little space in which the man, if permitted exercise, would recover

42

the ability to walk steadily. He watched with irritation as the ragged creature below him picked a sprig of rosemary, crushed it, and raising it delicately to his nostrils breathed its aroma like some effete aristocrat or silly girl. A ruse had occurred to him; if he escorted Palinor to Ciudad himself, he would surely be in the clear. Either as honouring or as securing the prisoner, he might be thought unduly diligent, but could not be seriously in the wrong, either way.

On the third evening he summoned the prisoner and said, 'You are sent for to Ciudad. We will ride there in the morning.' He watched closely to see if any trace of guilt or alarm crossed the man's face. Palinor said only, 'Could you make arrangements for me to wash, in that case?' Suppressing an impulse of rage at the man's insolence, the prefect said that he could. Later he wondered why he found the man insolent, and realized that it was simply that the prisoner was not cowed. His unease increased.

In the morning the horses were brought to the gate-house tower. A bush of broom like a fanning fountain of yellow flower leaned over the road and carpeted the ground beneath the horses' hooves with fallen petals. The prefect came last, and found his soldiers mounted and the prisoner, hands bound behind his back, seated on horseback, wearing a clean shirt and patched rustic trousers like a working man. He was clean again, his beard and hair glossed by the early light. He had a good seat, upright and steady in the saddle, so that the sight of his hands tied seemed ridiculous, and the prefect ordered them to be unbound. A shouted order, and the string of horses clattered away through the town.

Good housewives were awake, early as it was, and sweeping their frontages. A farmer with a donkey-load of fresh greens for the market was setting up stall in the square. From the church tower a bell spoke the hour. Early as it was, Lazaro's mother had got up to take her

43

leave of Palinor, waving as he rode past in clothes that had belonged to her dead brother, and calling to him, 'Don't forget us in the great city!'

Beyond the square the houses were poorer and the street dusty; then they were riding into open country. The road was lined with roughly piled stone walls, and it twisted about and climbed into wooded hills. The cool of the night lingered in the shade of the pines, and below the road, sparkling between the trees, was the sea. They could hear it, sighing and fidgeting against the shore below. Then the road rounded the headland, plunged inland and descended towards the heat of the plain. Palinor rode beside the prefect, looking around him.

The plain was thickly carpeted with a deep pile of flourishing green wheat, spread out below the trees of thousands of orchards. Fig and almond trees were planted everywhere, with here and there a grove of oranges, a grove of apricots, or a vineyard. Once they passed a peasant ploughing with a donkey hitched to a hand-plough, cutting a furrow of startling blood-red earth. Hills of modest height but dramatic outline, with fretted and broken crests, rose in the distances, the grey rock overtopping the mantles of green-blue woodland which clothed them. On all the crests of the gentle undulations of the plain stood little towns; the golds and greys, ochres and terracottas of their stone and their roof tiles tinting them with the colours of the ground from which they rose. In each one the largest and the highest building was a venerable church. They trotted in a moving cloud of white dust raised from the road by the horses' beating hooves, and soon were coated in dust themselves, so that they looked like millers.

The road led from town to town – or perhaps they were only villages – into narrow streets, twisting through them into a central square, with the church on one side of it, and sometimes trees for shade, out into narrow streets again, and on towards the next little place. Twice they stopped to rest the horses and let them drink – there were basins in the village squares. The second time the prefect dismounted, and dipping the chained cup into the water basin, drank deeply. Then he filled the cup again and handed it up to Palinor. Gracefully, his prisoner leaned down from the saddle to bring his lips within the scope of the extended chain holding the cup. His horse jittered sideways, not liking the pull of the leaning rider, and Palinor soothed it, speaking foreign words to it and caressing its neck as though he owned it.

As they rode further, a great range of mountains moved into sight in the west, some thirty miles distant, but even at so great a distance impressive. They were so sudden and so soaring that they looked as though they were painted on a curtain, hanging vertical at the margins of the plain. What seemed at first to be a band of bright cloud standing over them, revealed itself as the road edged nearer to them to be a region of sunlit snow. Much nearer the road an equally sudden height reared up abruptly from the plain, topped with a tower and bells.

'Why is there a church so far from any town?' Palinor asked the prefect.

'That is Monte Mauro. It is a sanctuary. The famous hermit Learned Mauro lived and died there, long ago. Now there is a monastery. It is a place of pilgrimage.'

'There are pilgrims?'

'Every feast day. And there are many sanctuaries. This is an island of saints and hermits.'

'What is the secular government here?'

'We have none. Our cardinal is our prince.'

'But you – you are not a cleric?'

'I am in minor orders. I shall not rise beyond the rank of prefect. But there are four prefectures; I might one day get a richer one.' Suddenly the prefect bit his lip, and fell silent. He realized that he was talking to the man like an equal. Yet there was a need to talk. The hardships of the long ride were shared; while they rode there was heat, dust, thirst in common, and that was all.

By and by Palinor asked, 'What are all these windmills for? They cannot be needed to grind wheat?' They were approaching Ciudad, and little towers topped by a ring of sails like the petals of a sunflower were scattered everywhere, spinning in the evening air.

'They raise water. By late summer the plain is parched. The Saracens taught the peasants how to do that, I believe.'

'Can I stop long enough to look closely at one?' Palinor asked.

'If you wish. What do you want to see?'

'How the drive is transmitted.' The prefect did not answer; he did not understand. But he ordered a halt while Palinor inspected a windmill, and the cistern full of green water that its arrangements of buckets and chain had filled from the depths of the earth.

'Isn't the water brackish?' Palinor asked, returning to the prefect's side.

'No; the wells are sweet and fresh.'

'There is something to be said for the Saracens then.'

'If you are a Saracen,' said the prefect, 'you have only to say so. There is a Saracen quarter in Ciudad. As long as you obeyed the curfew and kept within the city walls you would be at liberty. The Saracens can even worship – there is a permitted mosque – as long as they do not proselytize. There is some trade with Egypt; Saracens can come and go . . .'

'But I am not a Saracen,' said Palinor.

'A pity,' said the prefect. They crested a little rise in the undulating road, and Ciudad came into view, ringed by golden walls, with stout square bastions, a fine castle topping a hill within the walls, and beyond a great sweep of golden sand curving round a wide bay. A little forest of ships' masts marked the port, and the long roof of a buttressed cathedral, prominently in view when the city was first seen from the road, dropped out of sight behind walls and buildings as they drew nearer.

'What is to be done with me?' asked Palinor, softly.

At this first tiny sign of the abject mind of a prisoner, the prefect's heart began to harden again. But he spoke truly when he said, 'I don't know. I advise you to dissemble.'

'I thought God had proscribed lying,' said Palinor.

'But you do not believe in God, you say.'

'You do,' said Palinor. 'And lying would demean me.' They entered the city gates at a smart trot, and turned towards the cathedral.

'I fell in,' said Palinor, to the panel of the Consistory Court. He no longer laughed at it. His months in the citadel dungeon had given him time to realize his predicament and perceive the difficulty of reversing what he had thought of at first as temporary misfortune. The conversation was in Latin, in which he was fluent; the churchmen had conceded that to interrogate him in their own tongue, of which he knew only a few words, would be oppressive.

'So, to recapitulate,' said Fra Felip, who was in charge of the session, 'you say that you did not intend to trade, to parley or to survey the island. You say that you had no intention of coming here at all. You vehemently deny being an agent sent to subvert the faith of true Christians . . .'

'I had no plan for any dealings here of any kind,' said Palinor, 'because I had no intention of coming here at all. My arrival was an accident.'

'You fell in.'

47

'And then I swam ashore.'

'You say you are a person of importance in your own country?' The questioner was the oldest of the three men facing Palinor. He had thin features, withered like leaves in winter into a pattern of some beauty, which they might not have possessed in full flush. Behind the three men on the bench, behind the narrow table at which they sat, was a triple stained glass window narrating the mysteries of the faith in glowing colours suffused by transmitted daylight. Palinor's face, though he did not know it, was blotched with a splash of carmine light cast by the wound in the side of Christ, portrayed in the central light, crucified.

'I am a king.'

'You claim to be the king of – where was it? – Aclar?'

'Not the king; one of several.'

'There can never be more than one king,' said the third adjudicator, frowning.

'I am a prince, then.'

'You are the son of a king?'

'No; I am a prince not by blood but by achievement. I am an architect and engineer. It is the gratitude of my people that has brought me the rank of prince.'

The three men exchanged glances. 'Tell us this, then,' said Fra Felip, 'how could a vessel fail to stop and rescue a person falling from it, if the person was of any importance?'

'It was night,' said Palinor. 'A calm night of the brightest stars. We were setting course by them, but although I have often done that, I had never seen such brilliance. Perhaps it was because the moon was at her slightest crescent. I went up on deck to look again. I leaned over the stern of the vessel, and I exchanged a few words with the steersman. I noticed that he was a stripling, very young, and very sleepy, so I offered to take the tiller for an hour while he slept. He curled up on the deck at my feet, pillowed his head in his arms,

48

and fell asleep at once, while I stood content, feeling through my hands how the waters pulled on the rudder and admiring the magnificence of the celestial night. The other vessels of the fleet . . .'

'There was a *fleet*?'

'Seven vessels. We were on an errand of some importance. The other vessels were all ahead, being less laden. I felt something snag the rudder – a jar, and then a loss of movement in the tiller I was holding. Something had jammed it. Most foolishly, I swung myself over the rail and climbed down to see if I could free it. But whatever it was floated free of its own accord; the rudder swung suddenly, and plucked me from my foothold. I fell in. I think the boy on the deck above me did not wake; and you would be amazed, sirs, how fast a vessel that has seemed to be moving gently in light airs pulls away from a poor unfortunate in the water! And, of course, it was moving on the wrong degree, because the rudder was free.'

'So you are saying that nobody would have known you had fallen in?'

'They must have searched for me eventually; but how could they have found me in many miles of water, and in darkness? Retracing an uncertain course, not knowing the moment when I was lost?'

'And so you swam, you say?'

'The stars were bright, sirs. And I had some memory of an obscure island lying to the west of our intended course, some distance . . . I trod water for a while, considering my plight, and then began to swim. I swam westwards by the stars while they lasted, and then away from the rising sun. Then towards the land which rose in the distance before me. Before nightfall of the second night I reached a rock, far out, and almost submerged, but it allowed me rest. When the sun rose again I left the rock and swam ashore.'

49

'You have no mark of rank. You wear common clothes,' said Fra Aguilo.

'When I fell in, I was wearing a quilted jacket embroidered in gold, and studded with pearls,' said Palinor. 'It soaked water at once, and dragged me down. I struggled out of it for my life. The full folds of my shirt and trousers likewise hindered me, and I abandoned them.'

'You were not wearing jewels, or rings?'

'I think I was wearing a ring. I do not know what became of it.'

'This story is as full of holes as mouldy cheese,' said the second inquisitor. 'How do you expect us to believe that a man of rank would attempt to repair a rudder himself, with his bare hands?'

'My eminence is as an engineer. I think it no shame to use my hands, although usually my weapon is a pen. I admit at once that it was the height of folly not to wake the boy first.'

'And taking the tiller in the first place? For a prince you have a strange disposition towards menial tasks.'

'He was drowsy, sirs. He had that long-limbed look that boys get when they spurt in height, and for a while outgrow their strength . . . I have a son at home of just such an age as he . . . In short, I was tender to his sleepiness.'

'So what would you say if we pointed out to you that any vagrant rogue might devise a story such as yours to defraud charity?'

'I would say this is a blessed island, if vagrant rogues here can converse in Latin with learned men like yourselves.'

Once more the adjudicators exchanged glances.

'Well, well,' said Fra Felip, 'in the end it is not this farrago of the man's arrival that need concern us; let us get to the point. Fellow,' he said to Palinor, 'there is written on your warrant the claim that you are an atheist. A confusion, no doubt. No doubt you are a gentile of some kind, a pagan of some kind?'

'I do not believe in God,' said Palinor.

'Sometimes people get confused, and confess that divine matters are beyond their understanding, and call themselves unbelievers,' said Fra Felip. 'We would have no quarrel with a gentile; we would attempt his instruction, but let him depart in peace, converted or unconverted. It might be possible to treat an unbeliever as an unconverted pagan. But only a servant of the devil could be an atheist. You should think carefully before you reply to this.'

'Is there an appeal?' said Palinor. 'I am a free man in my country, where in matters of conscience all are free, even the least of us. I appeal.'

'There is no appeal from us except to the cardinal prince himself.'

'To him, then.'

5

The roads out of Ciudad radiate across the plain like
the spokes of a wheel. Most of them are straight,
or fairly straight, and bear the names of their desti-
nations among the little towns. Only the road to Sant
Jeronimo and beyond in the high mountains fails in
directness, and that lies on the mighty slopes that
it gradually and painfully ascends like twine that
has fallen from a shuttle, turning and returning in
the sharpest of bends, making many miles and a
tolerable gradient up the face of the mountain. The
roads are dusty, but not neglected – breaking stones
and filling holes being given as a customary penance
to able-bodied sinners. One road leads along the foot of
the mountain some distance, and then turns abruptly
between two mighty free-standing peaks, great volcanic
plugs with sheer sides rising to flat-topped crests,
and, passing below them in a narrow and spectacular
gorge, enters an intramontane valley. The valley floor
is occupied by an ancient fig orchard, with wheat
spreading beneath the armies of trees. A torrent, violent
in spring and dry in summer, cuts a serpentine gully
full of stones alongside the road. There are no villages
here, although there are barns and byres – the whole
valley belongs to the monastery of Galilea, which
stands on an eminence at the northern, remoter end.
 Those who founded the Galilea sought solitude,
and the monastery originally occupied a group of
caves and ledges in a cliff-face. The fame of its
austere and pious founder spread; pilgrims made

the two-day journey from Ciudad; by and by the ledges were fronted with sheltering arches, the caves opened to balconies and porches with outlooks down the valley, and eventually at the foot of the cliff, beside the monastery church, a cloister and a library spread out below the vertiginous structures clinging to the cliff wall. After the first century and a half of the monastery's existence, the abbots had been able to build alongside the original church a grander and larger one, but piety and love of the founder forbade abandoning his church, and the two naves shared an aisle and opened into one another.

Remote as it was, the Galilea was a centre of learning. Every priest on Grandinsula had sat for some months daily on the benches that occupied the older church and learned theology from one or other of the famous teachers of the order. There was also an oblate school, at which any clever boy, however poor, could get an education in exchange for a promise to enter the order if God called when the time was ripe, and at which the princes of the island could taste discipline, from fearless masters. There, long ago, Severo had been beaten for mistakes in Latin grammar and had learned humility. There the great scholar Beneditx, who had shared an oblate's bench with Severo, now sat at the window of one of the highest painted caves, bent over the works of the fathers, day by day, indifferent to his fame for sanctity and learning, having long withdrawn from teaching and disputation, devoting himself single-mindedly to his great treatise on the knowledge of angels.

He had copied into his papers 'Boethius says: through Himself alone God disposes all things' when, looking up, he saw the rider, far below, on the road up the valley. It was early evening, and the amphitheatre of mountains which towered around was an over-lapping sequence of outlines in greens and blues,

the shadowy masses dissolved in light as though
translucent. The little dust cloud raised by the rider
caught the sun and showed like a trailing halo behind
him. He was riding fast and coming late, where pilgrims, walking, came early, but Beneditx had no
curiosity to spare for him. He returned to his book.

ignores reality

'To the contrary, Gregory says, "In this visible world
nothing can be disposed except through invisible
creatures."' Beneditx laid down his pen and closed
his eyes. He saw visions of angels at work in every
moment of creation. Their hands flexed the tops and
branches of the trees to raise the wind; their hands
carried each single snowflake in the myriad storms
and laid it softly down; their delicate fingers unfurled
the scrolled leaves on the fig trees and silently opened
each blossom on the almond boughs. They poured the
springing torrent where it flowed, they stirred the sea
and raised the breaking waves, they drew the curtain
of nightfall across the sky and lit the lamps of heaven,
day and night.

When reluctantly he opened his eyes again – did
angelic fingers lift his lids for him? – the rider was just
entering the gate. He wrote, 'Moreover, Origen says,
"The world needs the angels, who rule over beasts,
preside over the birth of animals, and over the growth
of bushes, plants, and other things . . ."'

His was among the highest of the ancient troglodyte
cells, reached by a veritable Jacob's ladder of stone
steps and narrow passages criss-crossing the ancient
cliff-face behind the perched curtain of walls and
arches. Below him he heard the slap of running
sandals on the stones. Someone ascending in haste.
A lay brother on an errand . . .

'But even in rational creatures an order can be
found,' he read. 'Rational souls hold the lowest place
among these, and their light is shadowy in comparison
with that of the angels . . .'

A lay brother stood at his cell door, breathless from the climb. He held a paper in his hand. Sighing, pushing aside his interrupted volume, Beneditx took it and read:

'A hard thing must be decided. Come to me. Severo.'

The news that Beneditx was preparing to depart ran like wildfire through the warren of the Galilea's cells. A thousand whispers broke the vows of silence that were supposed to possess the night. Even the little boys in the oblate dormitory learned in the light of the flickering candles that kept night-frights at bay that the great scholar was leaving them. No more could they hope that the great man, passing them in the cloister and seeing tears, would take the smudged slate from their hands and write the lesson clearly, explaining in soft words. The news cast down the lowliest scholars in the place, their hopes blighted if Beneditx was gone. Not that he taught them, nowadays. Not that they knew anything about him except that their teachers held him in awe. But as any one of the churches of the island valued its holiest relic, so the Galilea valued Beneditx. As pilgrims came to venerate holy relics, so scholars came to the Galilea, seeking out the remote valley on the distant island to find Beneditx and talk to him. The wisdom of Paris and Padua, of Monte Olivetto and Oxford flowed in the discourse that ensued; the exquisite discernment of the Galilea's great scholar travelled to the ends of the earth when the visiting learned men departed. Naturally, some of them wished to depart with Beneditx himself. But it was the work, not the glory and influence it could bring, that Beneditx desired. The abbot of the Galilea knew very well that only the books in those famed and far-off libraries could tempt his great man to leave; in a dozen scriptoria in as many countries, monks laboured to copy for him so that Beneditx would want for nothing.

It never ceased to astonish the abbot that Beneditx was humble. Not a trace of scorn disfigured his soul for any, even the stupidest student. He would sit on the bench beside any baffled novice and sweetly and eagerly expound, explain, resolve the most elementary difficulties, his face luminous with joy at his powers of clarity, as though the dullest bovine pupil had been one of the visiting mighty scholars. When once the abbot had commented on that, Beneditx had said that reason, even at the height of its powers, was like the mounting block at the monastery gate – it served to give a leg up to faith. 'Many a rider who struggles to mount, once in the saddle rides like the wind,' he had said.

And now at dawn a horse was led out for Beneditx, and the cloister was packed with grieving brothers come to take leave of him. The abbot offered his own joined hands to Beneditx as a mounting block, and Beneditx got easily into the saddle and rode away.

It was late when Beneditx reached Ciudad. A cell was prepared for him near Severo's, and the cathedral clergy ran about, bringing hot water to fill a bath for him, since he came covered with the dust of the road, finding him a clean soutane, laying a breviary open at the evening office for the day. They were in awe of him, of his fame. He chastened them by making no demands, by remembering the names of those among them whom he had once taught. He asked for Severo, and they led him to a side chapel in the cathedral, screened from the nave by a heavy decorated grille, where the sacrament was reserved. There Severo, by the flickering light of devotional lamps and stands of candles, could be seen stretched out prone, arms extended, upon the floor, keeping vigil. 'Do not disturb him,' said Beneditx. 'Whatever it is will keep until morning.'

6

It was nearly midday, however, before the friends could talk alone. There was mass to be said, communion to be given to the people, some affairs of state to be settled. At last the two men could retire to Severo's balcony, break their fast together, and talk.

'Supposing, Magister,' said Severo, 'there were a man who had been taught not that God exists and deserves worship, and demands obedience, but that this was a matter on which each man was free to decide for himself. Supposing he were a citizen of a country in which no absolute doctrine was promulgated to the people; in which a man might decide that there was indeed a God and worship him according to the manner of a Saracen or of a true Christian at his whim . . .'

'There is no such country,' said Beneditx.

'We are to suppose that there is. It is called Aclar.'

'Well, and if there be? Are we to suppose that the true faith is known to some people there and can freely be taught there?'

'As I understand it, yes. But bear with me, Beneditx. There are Christians in this country, and Saracens, and Jews, and various pagans, and those of no allegiance at all. As you might expect in such a babel, there are unbelievers. But now you are to suppose that in that country there is a man who concludes that there is no God . . .'

'He is a fool,' said Beneditx.

'Possibly.'

57

'Certainly. Is it not written, "The fool hath said in his heart there is no God"?'

'You would need to assert, not that such an opinion may be that of a fool,' said Severo, mildly, 'but that only a fool could hold such an opinion.'

'A fool, or worse. But Severo, you did not summon me away from my peaceful labours in order to chop logic with me about imaginary countries and supposed states of mind. What is afoot?'

'There is a man under this roof who calls himself an atheist. He has appealed to me. Before I see him, I need advice.'

'An atheist from Aclar?'

'So he says. And Beneditx, the question is, could an atheist conceivably be in good faith? If, clearly, as I understand from this transcript, he knows of Holy Scripture, but has rejected it.'

'A transcript?'

'Of his interrogation by the Consistory Court. But they had barely opened proceedings when he appealed over their heads to me.' Severo put the curling papers on the table between them and waited, sipping at his wine and water, while Beneditx read.

When Beneditx looked up, Severo asked, 'Is this man under an obligation to accept Holy Scripture as the word of God?'

'Every Saracen and every Jew on Grandinsula, and in many another place, has encountered Holy Scripture . . .' said Beneditx, 'but we allow that before ever they met with it, they were immersed in a contrary teaching. So that one who has been persuaded from childhood that Mohammed is the one true prophet and has superseded Christ cannot be expected to see the Gospels in the light in which they appear to the soul who approaches them free from any burden of error.'

'But,' said Severo, 'this man seems to have met the Gospel as only one among many sacred texts. How do we judge someone who has met the truth amidst a plethora of contending claims and a clamour of voices each declaring the truth of their own message and the error of every other? Someone who knows many religious systems at once in a land where authority has abdicated and nothing is taught to the people as having a prior claim on their assent? Might that be an obstacle in the path of understanding as extreme as the prior acceptance of false teaching?'

'It might indeed,' said Beneditx. 'Or perhaps, Severo, a worse one. Such a situation would be a scandal to the people, it might corrode the very idea of a single truth, a one true way; it might lead a man to suppose that any religion was as good as any other . . .'

'Do you think it might excuse a man who said there was no God?'

'It might excuse a good deal of confusion.'

'We are not talking of someone who calls God by strange names or offers him barbaric worship and alien obedience, however. We are talking of someone who goes beyond doubt and declares himself certain that there is no God. And I am asking you, Magister, whether it is true that such a one must have refused grace, must have sinned against truth. Surely, the existence of God is known to natural reason?'

'It is knowable by natural reason, Severo. But the reasoning in question is arduous, and many men have not the strength of mind for it, while the majority of men could never have the leisure and the freedom from worldly duties to undertake it.'

'There is not an obligation to reason for oneself that God exists?'

'An obligation to try is not an obligation to succeed.'

'Then I need not condemn the man?'

'Oh, yes, Brother, you must. We cannot talk as though a man might be without knowledge of God by some accident, as he might be without knowledge

59

of Latin. For knowledge of God is inborn. Innate in every human soul. So powerful, so clear that in nations far from the mercy of God men are driven to worship idols, calves of gold, sticks, stones, rivers and trees, the moon and the sun . . .'

'And a man who worships nothing . . .'

'Has darkened knowledge; refused enlightenment. Is one who has once known the truth and has reneged on it. Is a heretic.'

'But Beneditx, is it known for certain that knowledge of God is innate? Do all the doctors of the church agree on that? I cannot clearly remember the texts, the exegesis for that . . .'

'Give me a few hours, Severo,' said Beneditx, 'and I will show you something.'

Beneditx was gone some hours. His quest took him, not as Severo had supposed it would, to the cathedral library, but into the streets of Ciudad. And when he returned, shortly before sunset, he did not return alone. He was carrying a bundle of rags and accompanied by a woman. The woman was dirty and barefoot, and her clothes, which were ragged and faded and knotted together on her person, as though every lace and button had been torn from them, had once been of bright colours – scarlet and yellow and blue. She was nut-brown, with the haggard features of poverty. Beneditx strode, unhesitating, through the gates to the cloister, and the woman, uttering a faint sound of dismay, made to follow him, but the porter stopped her. In a furious tone he growled the usual prohibitions about women in a nest of clergy, and stepped in front of her, his arms outstretched to bar her way. She called frantically to Beneditx's retreating back, 'Master!'

He looked round. 'Can you cover your head?' he asked her. She found a loose stretch of torn blue muslin about her somewhere and covered her matted dark locks. 'Let her in,' said Beneditx.

'But, Magister, it is forbidden . . .'

'Nothing is forbidden to the pure in heart,' said Beneditx.

'But . . .'

'I command you.'

The porter stepped aside, and the woman scurried under the arch to join Beneditx as though it were death to be parted from him. 'Keep your eyes on the ground and follow me closely,' said Beneditx, crossing the courtyard and opening the door to the clergy's lodgings. As though every priest in the entire establishment, every deacon, every humble clerk had seen the little scene at the gate, as though the news could travel through the walls of the cells and offices, an appalled murmur followed them, doors were opened a crack, every pen in the scriptorium was stilled as they passed the door which stood open to admit the evening air and dilute the smell of ink. Someone ran for the canon residentiary, to fetch him to eject the unthinkable intruder; a little group of the bolder prebends, whispering in horrified tones, followed the woman along the corridors to Severo's cell nearly as closely as she followed Beneditx, and at the gate the porter loudly complained to a pair of prebends who had come to anathematize him.

'What is that?' he was saying. 'I have never heard that: "nothing is forbidden to the pure in heart?" That is what he told me.'

'That's antinomianism, I think,' said Prebend Pere.

'What's antinomianism?'

'A heresy. A deadly and recurring one, Brother.'

'Holy Mary protect us all,' said the porter, crossing himself.

Severo, reading the evening office, heard something –

the unusual footfalls and agitated voices. Like fluttered feathers in a pigeon loft, the barely audible sounds wafted a sense of something wrong. Then, knocking once, Beneditx entered his cell. A very unhushed angry voice was raised at once. The canon residentiary, saying, 'How dare you bring a . . . a . . . to the cardinal's private quarters!'

'She is quite safe,' said Beneditx. 'I have not brought her to yours!' And pushing the woman into Severo's cell, he slammed the door in the canon's face and slid the bolt, rattling it noisily. She leaned against the wall just within the door, trembling. Beneditx put the bundle of rags down on the table among Severo's books, whereupon it emitted a faint and bleating cry.

Severo, who till that moment had remained kneeling, with his breviary open before him, rose. Beneditx, leaning over his bundle, was unwrapping a baby. 'Come and look,' he said. The baby was very new. Its legs were drawn up to its chest, and its feet were crossed over. Severo, astonished, reached out a finger and touched the sole of one tiny wrinkled foot. The toes flexed upwards at his touch. The babe's arms waved aimlessly, now it was unwrapped, like fronds in a gentle wind, until, its hand encountering Beneditx's finger, it held tight, all five of its curled fingers together grasping one of Beneditx's to the first joint.

'I didn't know . . .' said Severo.

'That they could be so small? They are grown considerably before the parents bring them for baptism,' said Beneditx.

'A marvel, indeed,' said Severo. The babe smelt of milk and sourness.

'Look at her eyes,' Beneditx told him. 'What do you see?'

Her eyes were dark. They seemed large for so small a visage. As Severo leaned over her she kicked and almost smiled. But the swimming vagueness of her eyes did not change. They were like windows to the night sky, or the deeps of the sea. Beneditx said, 'Later, they focus on the world. Later, they see the visible universe around them. But what do you see there now?'

'Infinity,' said Severo.

'At first they see only God.'

'Yes, Beneditx. But I will show you another thing. Come with me.'

The sun had descended, and dusk had crept over Ciudad while the little scene in Severo's cell was played. Now, as the two friends stepped on to the balcony, the evening star shone like a bright candle above the lemon tree's fragrant branches, and the garden below them was a pool of shadow, in which gradually, as they stepped away from the light of Severo's open door, their eyes distinguished the fountain, the path, the bench. Severo led the way down the stair into the dark garden. With Beneditx close behind him he crossed the garden and opened the little wicket-gate at the far end. Beyond was a yard, within a high curtain wall, cluttered with gear – barrels, carts, tools, a stack of roofing tiles, and blocks of masonry waiting for the repair of some quoin of the great building. Beneditx blinked at the dim obstructions.

Severo called, 'Jaime?'

A voice answered at once from the mason's shack, 'Holiness?'

'Have you offered food tonight?'

'Not yet, Holiness. I was waiting till darkness.'

'Try now. Can we have a lantern?'

'Best not, Holiness. It is so hated . . .'

'Very well, then. Open the cage and fetch the food.'

At that moment someone high up above them in the prebends' house lit lamps, and the glow from the window cast a glancing and indirect light into the yard. The youth called Jaime departed by a door into the bowels of the building, and there was silence. Then there was a scuttling sound from behind a tilted cart. Severo put a hand on Beneditx's sleeve, as though to restrain him from movement. Something ran out from behind the cart. It ran on all fours with a lolloping movement. It lurched from side to side of the narrow yard, as though looking for a way out. Beneditx thought of a dog – a mangy dog. It squatted in the darkness by the stack of tiles and urinated. The warm stench reached him. Then it came towards him. He moved, suddenly, stepping backwards, saying, 'Severo . . .'

The beast snarled at him. It growled ferociously and bared its teeth, which showed white in the faint illumination from the window. Then suddenly it turned tail and ran, retreating to the furthest corner of the yard, where it turned about again and faced them. He could see nothing but the blue glint of its eyes, glaring at him from near the ground, as once he had seen those of a fox cornered in his father's barn, visible only by the twin mirrored glint of the lantern.

Jaime returned, bearing a trencher with three bowls.

'What have you brought?' asked Severo.

'The same, Holiness. Milk. Stewed beef and vegetables. Raw meat and bones.'

'Try.'

Jaime put down the bowls in the dust where the light of the window fell brightest. Then he stepped back into the shadows. They did not have long to wait. The beast crept forward. It sniffed at the bowl of milk, lowered its shaggy head, and drank, lapping like a dog. It sniffed at the second bowl and left it untouched. It sniffed the third bowl only for a second, before lowering its head and bolting the food, seizing the meat between its teeth, raising its head and swallowing rapidly with convulsive movements of its upper body. Then, knocking the bowl away, it took the bone in its mouth, and ran away with it out of sight.

'Bring a lantern now,' said Severo.

By its light Beneditx saw a strange sort of bald and flat-faced dog sitting under the cart, holding the bone down with its front paws and rubbing it on the ground to loosen the scraps from it. It tore at the adhering scraps with its teeth, and though it stopped feeding briefly to snarl at Jaime when he came too near it with the lantern, it had no attention to spare from its food. Beneditx saw also, in the swinging lamplight, the face of the cardinal's kennel boy, taut with some storm of feeling – fear? loathing? – and moist as with sweat or tears.

'Come away,' said Severo, pulling on his sleeve. 'Jaime will lock her in again.'

'A bitch of some kind?' asked Beneditx, mystified, standing again in the garden, in the fountain of fragrance released by the lemon tree into the night air, under a thickening plethora of stars.

Severo spoke gravely, even gently, but with a shake in his voice. 'That also, you see, Beneditx, is an unbaptized child.'

Severo's cell, when the two men re-entered it, was full of the frantic raucous sound of the babe. Its face was puckered and red, and it was emitting a hacking, desperate cry, at full lung. The woman, very agitated, was rocking and shushing it. Of course, thought Severo, ruefully, she is locked in.

'I'm sorry, Holiness, sorry, but she is so hungry . . .'

'Feed her, then,' he said.

'May I? Here?'

'Certainly. The poor thing is in urgent need, from the sound of her.'

Severo spoke calmly, but he seemed greatly taken aback when the woman, instead of bringing a beaker of milk from her bundle, sat down on the floor and, blushing deeply, uncovered her breast and put the babe to her nipple. The babe shook its head from side to side for a second and latched on hard. The crying ceased abruptly, and in the sweet silence that followed Severo could hear funny little sniffling and sucking sounds. Once, as if to punish its mother for her tardy response, the babe released the nipple and uttered a single afterthought of a cry. A tiny fountain of milk spattered its face; pinching her swelling breast between finger and thumb, the woman guided the nipple again into the urgent little mouth. The child's tiny hand lay delicately couched on the white cushion of flesh, with its marbling of blue veins, and as the two men watched, a sense of ease slowly infused the process before them. The child sucked less violently, and its lids drooped and opened again. And the mother's face, so bitten and hard-lined and worldly, took on an expression of angelic calm and joy. Then the babe fell suddenly asleep, and the woman pulled her clothes to cover herself again and sat still.

'What is your name?' Severo asked her, speaking quietly.

'Maria, Holiness.'

'The babe's name?'

'Felicia.'

'And the father's name?'

'I do not know, Holiness.'

'He left without telling you his name?'

'It was Pere, or Felip, but they both deny it.'

'Heaven help us! How will you live?'

'I am a gypsy, Holiness. We know how to live. Most of us never marry.'

'And when you come to die? What then?'

'We call for a priest. All is forgiven us.'

'You do very wrong. That is a wicked heresy.'

Beneditx said, 'Severo, I promised her if she lent me the babe no harm would come to them.'

'I have no other mind than yours,' said Severo. 'Maria, what is your heart's desire, in all the world?'

'A blue silk shawl, Holiness.'

'And for the child?'

'Enough to eat for seven years. That makes a child grow beautiful.'

, Severo nodded. 'May I hold her?' he asked. He stooped and took the babe from its mother's arms, while she got to her feet. He reached for a little flask of water that stood beside his bed. The babe in the crook of his arm burped, and its parted lips brimmed with a trickle of creamy regurgitated milk. Severo poured a drop of the water on its downy head, and said, *'Ego baptiso te Felicia, in nomine Patris, et Filii, et Spiritus Sancti, Amen.* Will three gold pistoles feed her for seven years?'

'Easily, Holiness.'

'And a fourth would buy a blue silk shawl?'

The woman nodded. Severo took a paper and wrote. He gave it to the woman. 'Bring this to the sacristy in the cathedral tomorrow, and the treasurer will pay you four gold pistoles. The child is my god-daughter; you may bring her to me for a dowry, but only if she is to be married at an altar. Do you understand?'

'Thank you, Holiness.'

'And, Maria, sometimes pray for me. Good night.'

Beneditx led Maria all the way back to the gatehouse, smiling sweetly at scowling faces till the outer gate was closed on the woman, and order was restored.

Returning to Severo's cell, he asked, 'Have you ever seen that before?'

'Never,' said Severo.

'Nor I, my friend. Or, rather, only in paintings. Paintings of the Virgin.'

'There is such a painting in Piedmont. I saw it when I travelled as a young man. It shows that little jet of milk as the child turns its head . . . I took it to be an allegory, a representation of the flow of human kindness from mother to child. It never occurred to me . . .'

'That it could be real?'

'That it could be true in the flesh. But then, I would have doubted the possibility of either an atheist or a wolf-child. Come to me in the morning and let us talk in earnest.'

7

Every window of every house in the Camino sa Eglesia was shuttered against the heat. The children were indoors, the cats had retreated from the sunlit to the shaded doorsteps to sleep, the flowers with which the citizens beautified their steps and windowsills wilted in the blazing light. Behind the houses were benches under the citrus trees, under the canopies of vines, where usually it was pleasant to sit out the siesta in a dappled shade, with glimpses of the towering mountains and little gusts of mountain air, but nobody sat in any such garden now; the broken shards of sunlight fingering through the leaves were fierce and sharp enough to burn. In the entire town of Santanya only one person was about, and that was Josefa, the daughter of Taddeo Arta, the cordwainer, and she, half-blinded with sweat from under the brim of her hat, was hoeing the lettuce plot and spreading manure from the donkey byre at the far end of the garden, out of the shade of the trees.

When she had done, she splashed her burning face with water from the pump, washed her hands, slipped off her sandals, and went as softly as she could indoors. Not softly enough; Margalida heard her, and called out at once, 'Josefa? I told you to see to the garden!'

'It is done, Margalida,' said Josefa.

'Bring me a goblet of water!' Margalida called.

Josefa returned to the pump. She filled a jug and carried it to the kitchen. She poured the water into a goblet, and went slowly and sulkily up the stairs with it. She entered the bedroom reluctantly. Margalida was lying stretched out on the bed, wearing only a thin shift, unlaced at the neck. Her hair spread lavishly over the pillows, the very pillows on which Josefa's mother had tossed feverishly only a year since. The little painted picture of Sant Catalida which had been propped as long as Josefa could remember beside her mother's bed had gone now, replaced by perfume bottles and a trinket box.

'There is a pile of sheets in need of pressing,' said Margalida, without moving, as Josefa put down the water. 'Go and do that.'

'I am going to rest,' said Josefa. 'I will iron when the heat eases, later.'

'You will go now, at once, and do just as I tell you,' said Margalida, opening her limpid eyes, and adopting a furious tone, half masked by sleepiness.

'Even a dog has a siesta,' said Josefa.

'I will tell your father!' said Margalida. But for once this threat failed to work. Josefa climbed the stairs to her room, stamping on the wooden treads so that Margalida could not fail to realize that she had gone upstairs, and not downstairs to more work.

But in the safety of her room she did not lie down. Instead, she sat in the little rocking chair that had belonged to her mother and that she had rescued just in time, when Margalida would have sold it to a passing tinker, and sat rocking herself and thinking. Her face was still burning from her exertions in the heat, but that would cool and fade faster than her bitterness at her stepmother.

Margalida did indeed complain to Taddeo when he returned at dusk. Josefa, standing at the head of the stairs, heard the voluble flow of the stepmother's voice and the low rumble, indecipherable, of her father's replies. Sighing, he sent one of her little brothers to fetch her, and attempted to sort it out. He sat in his chair at the end of the family table, and she stood facing him from the other end.

'What is this I hear?'

Josefa made no answer.

'If you have quarrelled with Margalida, you must apologize.'

'Father, am I a daughter in this house, or a servant?'

'A daughter, Josefa, of course, but . . .'

'Then why must I obey her every order, like a drudge? Why must I work through the heat of the day, while she lies at ease?'

'You are to do your share. You are to obey her, because she stands in the position of mother to you . . .'

'Father, she is barely three years older than I, and besides . . .'

'She is my wife, Josefa. You must respect her.'

'And besides, if a mother gives orders it is with kindness. What mother sends a daughter to work in the sun at midday?'

'Did she order you to work in the heat, today? What work was asked of you?'

'Hoeing and manuring the garden patch. At noon. She did not tell you that? She did not tell you that she was taking a siesta, herself?'

Taddeo frowned. 'I expect you misunderstood,' he said, and then saw with distress that his daughter's face was covered with flowing tears, although she made no sound.

'There, there,' he said. 'I will speak to Margalida. But if you two cannot get along, what is to be done?'

'You must find me a husband, Father,' said Josefa.

'Well, but that would not be easy! You are very young, and what with the expenses of the wedding and the new rope walk . . . in short I need time to amass a sufficient dowry . . .'

'If I am a little younger than Margalida, I have

71

twenty times more sense!' said Josefa. 'And you took her without a dowry!'

'That's different!' said Taddeo, angry now.

'Why? How different?'

'Because she is as beautiful as a flower, and you are ugly,' he said.

The only mirror in the house was in the parental bedroom. At that moment Margalida was clashing pans in the kitchen, pretending to be engaged with the evening meal, which Josefa had cooked and made ready before her father's return. She left him without a word and marched straight to it. She drew breath, like one plunging into cold water, and then confronted herself through the misty and flecked medium of the glass. She stared for a long time. It had never occurred to her that she was ugly, because she had been tenderly loved, and as clearly as the boys looked like their father, she looked like her mother. But she saw it now, in the light of her ruthless stare. A long and bony face stared coldly at her out of the glass, with flared nostrils and red-rimmed eyes, like a startled horse. She had cut her hair short as a sign of mourning when her mother died, and it had grown again coarse and spiky like a bush of thyme. Looking, she learned despair.

Later, lying close by his wife, but not touching, because of the heat, Taddeo asked her, 'Did you really send Josefa to work outside at noon?'

'It wasn't so hot,' said Margalida. 'You are judging by how it was on the quays, where you were, but up here there was air from the mountains. It was almost cool, in fact. In fact, I thought the air would do her good . . .'

'Couldn't you ask her to do something and leave her to choose for herself when to do it?'

'You promised me I should be mistress in the house and have all things at my disposing,' said Margalida. 'You promised. Now she defies me.'

'She asked me to find her a husband.'

'Now that's a good idea! I would be rid of her, and if it's what she wants . . .'

'It would be some time before I could find a dowry for her. Nobody will take her without a good one. And we would need to stint ourselves to find it.'

Paddling a tender finger in the hollow of her husband's cheek, Margalida said, 'The nuns at Sant Clara will take her with a small one. With very little; almost nothing . . .'

'Holy Mary!' cried Taddeo, sitting bolt upright. 'Even the cats are allowed to litter before they're spayed!'

'What a way to talk about a life of prayer, husband!' said Margalida, genuinely shocked. 'We could ask her, couldn't we?'

'We must speak softly; she will hear us,' said Taddeo. 'Won't it be too much for you, doing her work as well as your own?'

'I can make sacrifices to see the motherless girl well-placed,' said Margalida.

Taddeo lay awake for a long time.

In the morning, two conversations took place. Margalida went to visit her mother. After all, she needed to know what an older woman might think of her if she contrived to get her stepdaughter sent to Sant Clara. Margalida's mother reassured her. 'They won't have her as a novice, Margalida. Only as a servant. You have to have some schooling to be a nun. And a servant can always be fetched back again if you need her later. Don't let Taddeo overdo the dowry at the last minute. Men are so sentimental. A few goats will do.'

While Margalida was gone, Taddeo put the suggestion to Josefa.

'Is it the only alternative to staying here, Father?'

'I'm afraid so. But you may choose either possibility, as you like.'

'Take me to Sant Clara, then,' she said.

73

Like the Galilea, the nunnery of Sant Clara was remote. The road to it ascended the face of the mountains, rising from the plain a few miles further north than the road which passed through the gorge to the Galilea. It was steep and rough all the way, and Taddeo and Josefa had to stop several times to let their donkeys rest. At last it arrived at a narrow pass between bare crests, going along a rocky, narrow floor below the facing steeps. Nothing grew so high but little clumps of thorn and a pungent form of creeping thyme that scented the donkeys' steps. There was no beauty; everything was grey, rough and harsh; the pass looked as though some giant had smashed the face of the land in rage and tumbled the debris around. Josefa showed no emotion but kept her thoughts to herself; they rode in silence all the way.

When the road emerged from the narrow defile at the other end, it was already descending, and it shortly plunged into woods. Sparse woods, at first, of stunted trees, stooping beneath a wind that did not blow that day. But as they moved down the turns of the track, the woods stood upright, prospered and thickened. The sweet balm of the scented pines drifted on the air, and there were woodland flowers growing. On that further side of the mountains the land dropped steeply and abruptly into the sea, and soon the two travellers could see the water below them through the trees. Its blueness was bleached out by its sheen, and it showed like grey silk covered with tiny sequins. Gulls drifted, poised motionless on the ascending air. The road turned suddenly inland and entered a little valley, a thousand feet above the shore, a thousand feet below the crest, and Sant Clara lay in view. They were looking down on it from above and could see it in plan – a courtyard, with a cloister round it, a simple church, opening into the cloister. On one side it had

74

edged to the brink of the drop to the shore; on the other a cluster of farm buildings and a garden stood between the nunnery and a few fields, folded into the shelter of the wooded heights. On this rainy side of the mountain, everything was verdant and dewy. The nunnery was built of gold-coloured stone and roofed in brown-earth tiles. A little cupola above the church was decorated with blue and green tiles and topped with a cross of gold. Nothing had prepared Josefa to expect beauty.

The abbess of Sant Clara, Mother Humberta, had been offered many ill-favoured girls in her time. She was always torn. Torn between rage for her master, the Lord Jesus, who was offered the second best, the leavings of the feast, those whom nobody else had a use for, instead of the fairest and brightest of the flock; and, on the other hand, pity for ugly and rejected poor girls, whose prospects in the harsh world of the island were so unpromising. She was not an islander herself, having come from France with her order, and felt free to disapprove. She looked at Taddeo with cold blue unflinching eyes that comprehended only too well.

'She asked to come, Mother,' he said.

The abbess turned her eyes on Josefa. Big face, big hands. Had the look on the girl's face been docile, the abbess would have accepted her at once as a lay sister – a farm servant was needed. But she was met with an expression of such grief and rage on the child's face as astonished her. 'Did you?' she asked.

'Yes, Mother.'

'You wish to be a nun?'

'The world is hateful to me, Mother.'

'That's a possible starting point on the journey, certainly,' said the abbess, looking balefully at Taddeo, 'though not the best.'

'The best is not for me, Mother,' said Josefa, surprisingly. 'I will gladly take any way possible.'

'There's a humility,' thought the abbess, looking at her with interest. 'Can you read and write, child?' she asked. Taddeo said, 'No, Mother,' and Josefa said, 'Yes, Mother,' in one breath.

'My mother taught me,' said Josefa, looking scornfully at her father.

The abbess got up, slowly – she was an old woman now and walked on two sticks – and moved painfully to a secretaire placed on a side table. She brought a sheet of paper and a pen. 'Show me,' she said to Josefa. 'Sit there and write something.'

While Josefa bent over her task, the abbess said to Taddeo, 'We require a dowry.'

'I cannot afford much, Mother,' said Taddeo. 'A few goats . . .'

'How many is a few?' the abbess enquired.

Taddeo meant to say five, but cringing under the remorseless gaze of the old woman's cold blue eyes he said, 'Ten.'

'We don't need goats,' she said. 'We need donkeys. And a donkey cart; we could do with a donkey cart.'

'I haven't any . . .'

'Then sell those ten goats in the market at Sant Jeronimo, and buy a donkey and a donkey cart. Off you go now; you can leave your daughter here, and return with the dowry later.'

Josefa finished writing and put down her pen. The abbess watched. Taddeo shifted from one foot to another. He said, 'Goodbye, then, Josefa.'

'Goodbye Father,' the girl said. She did not get up from her chair.

'Show me that,' said the abbess, pointing at the paper on the table in front of Josefa. The girl brought her the paper. In a large, clear hand she had written, 'I believe in God the Father almighty, Creator of heaven and earth, and of all things visible and invisible; and in

Jesus Christ, his only son, Our Lord, born of the Father before all ages; God from God, light from light, true God from true God . . .'

'Kiss your father, Josefa,' the abbess said. 'It is the last time you will kiss a man as long as you live.'

8

In the cathedral precinct at Ciudad three men sat
round a table in a room that opened on to a sea of
roof tiles and a row of worn gargoyles with eroded
grotesque faces. An odour of incense filled the room,
which was above a side door into the organ loft of
the cathedral nave. On the table were a bowl of figs,
a bowl of almonds, a flask of wine and two glasses. One
would have thought the three were friends, pleasantly
talking. But the third man was Palinor.

'It makes a great deal of difference,' Beneditx said to
him, 'whether you call yourself unbeliever or atheist.
An unbeliever, one who is simply uncertain whether
there be a God or no, is in principle convincible;
one more day's experience, one better argument encountered, may overpower his doubt and bring him
down on the side of belief. If my friend were an
unbeliever, I would both argue with him and pray
for him, and though he were to continue long in his
state of doubt, I would remember, in hope, that to doubt
something is to admit its possibility.'

'I am not in principle convincible,' said Palinor. 'I
do not doubt.'

'You do not recognize yourself in my definition of an
unbeliever? Then let us try the definition of an atheist.
There might be two kinds. An atheist might be one
who is against God; who knowing his existence has
willingly enlisted in the service of the devil and acts
to thwart whatever seems to him to be God's will . . .'

'That sounds to me more like a form of madness than

78

the position in a disputation of a reasonable man,' said Palinor.

'I have known it,' said Severo. 'It was long ago, and I was newly in office here. And it did not occur to me at the time that the man was mad, though perhaps it should have. He had murdered a child, and he raged and cursed God, and uttered dreadful blasphemies all the way to the gallows.'

Severo spoke softly, concealing his consternation at Palinor. What had he expected the atheist to be like? Not like this, certainly. Brought to a private chamber to pursue his appeal, finding Severo seated with Beneditx, instead of standing, rigid with apprehension, just inside the door, he had advanced immediately to the table and confidently awaited the invitation to sit down. Severo noticed that there was no third plate on the table with a twinge of inappropriate embarrassment, as though Palinor had been an invited guest.

'I am not a murderer,' said Palinor. 'And I do not see how I could blaspheme, exactly, though I can curse mildly in my native tongue. As for being against God, that would simply be a negative state of belief, I think. Offer me your other kind of atheist.'

Severo, while carefully peeling a fig, was closely observing the man. He addressed himself courteously to Beneditx, but with some just discernible difference of manner he made clear that he knew where worldly authority lay.

'The other kind of atheist would be one who has convinced himself by false reasoning that there is no God.'

'That would come nearer,' said Palinor. 'What is the difference in the treatment you accord these different kinds?'

Beneditx was appalled. It had not occurred to him that the stranger, offered the familiar distinction

79

B
Surprised

between unbeliever and atheist, could possibly answer
as atheist. Nobody in Beneditx's long experience of disputation had ever done so before. He caught Severo's
eye.

'Tell us about Aclar,' said Severo, interrupting.

'Gladly,' Palinor said. 'What do you want to know?'

'How is it governed?'

'It has a council, chosen by lot from the adult
citizenry.'

'You told the Consistory Court that there were many
religions in Aclar, and all were permitted. Does that
not lead to faction and disorder? To insubordination
among the commonalty?'

'Occasionally. But I think . . . of course, I have not
been at liberty to wander freely in Grandinsula and
observe your ways here, but I think religion is much
less important among us. We hold it to be a private
matter.'

'So how, in Aclar, is an atheist dealt with?'

'Not dealt with at all, unless he breaks the law. As
far as I know, atheists are no more likely to be thieves
or drunkards than believers are.'

'Surely an atheist, moved neither by hope of heaven
nor fear of hell, would feel free to defy laws and run
amok?'

'No doubt for a believer, desire to please God is a
strong motive,' said Palinor. 'But a rational man may
have sufficient reasons in this world to concede the
necessity for laws and the benefits of obeying them. I
think for most people in Aclar, a desire to stand well
in the eyes of the neighbours is reason enough.'

'So an atheist is allowed to proselytize and over-
throw the belief of others?'

'If he wishes. I don't think it happens much. In
private conversation, perhaps. I am by now more than
a little curious to know what happens to atheists of
each kind on Grandinsula.'

80

'We burn them,' said Beneditx.

Palinor flinched visibly. 'I suggest that it would be less trouble to let me leave. Since I came here only by accident.'

'There is no such thing as an accident,' said Severo.

'Are you saying that nothing is ever lost? That jars are never broken without malice? That neither friend nor stranger is ever met by chance upon the road? That I must deliberately have thrown myself into the sea?'

'You are seeing accident in terms of human purposes,' said Beneditx. 'But we mean that there are no accidents in the mind of God. Before all ages and until the end of time he purposes all things. Nothing befalls outside his providence, and all that is, is as he wills it. What seems chance to us serves him. You fell into the sea and are delivered into our charge for a reason, friend. The most likely reason is that we should enlighten your darkness, and convince you that there exists your God and your Redeemer.'

'I should have swum the other way,' said Palinor.

High Mass intervened to postpone further conversation. But Severo could only with difficulty bend his thoughts to attend to his duty. Weaving and doubling like a hare pursued by hunters, overleaping obstacles . . . swiftly, from every point to which he directed them, his thoughts returned to Palinor. Many years since, during the reign of Severo's father, Severo had been sent on a foreign mission. First to Rome, of course, and then to the Low Countries. If, during the yearning plaintive notes of the Kyrie, he kept seeing in his mind's eye the narrow, bronze-brown hook-nosed visage of the atheist, the dark beard and tender mouth, the fingernails paler than the skin of the broad hands, the calm and alert demeanour of the man, well, it was an ordinary thing to find the concern of the hour before the service lingering and impinging on prayer. But why, when the great choir from the gallery began full-voiced upon the Gloria, should Severo be wandering along a waterside, on a land so lush, so fully watered that the grass seemed burning green, so flat that the magnificent sweep of the sky above seemed curved, like an overturned dish, since it could not otherwise touch the horizons of the vast level land, flat as a marble floor and veined with brimming courses of standing waters? If they flowed, it was not visible to the eyes. Great brown-sailed barges moved solemnly through the fields; and though he had been walking away from the city for several hours, it lay behind him in full view: churches, windmills, walls, the distance visible only in its diminished size, the time needed to retrace his steps inestimable. It should have been dark, he remembered, but the light lingered, and lingered in a prolonged soft and declining radiance; the sun set behind him, and yet the darkness did not come. When he re-entered the city, there were children playing along the street, along the banks of the canal, under the dusky trees, below the windows just now being lit by indoor candles, and there was light enough to follow the trajectory of their soaring ball.

Uninvited, his mind returned to him the feeling he had then experienced. Not pleasure – something far sharper and more challenging – joy, rather. And not in the least any wish that anything about this remote and astonishing land might be shared by his own island, for it was the difference in and for itself that so struck him. How the loss of familiarity in everything had woken him up and sharpened his senses! It had been like taking off one's outer garments in a cold wind and being immersed in the sting of chill air over the entire surface of one's skin. How intensely he had lived his few weeks in the northern summer! How vividly, how acutely sensible had the qualities of the island

82

appeared to him, seen in contrast for the first few weeks after his return! Dulled again only too soon – the world not known because too well known. But while it had lasted how vivid had been his joy in strangeness!

He had been shown a curious thing, while he stayed in Utrecht. They were hanging a new peal of bells in the Ouderkerk; the old ones, dismounted, were slung from beams in the bell-tower, waiting for the rigging of ropes and pulleys to lower them safely to the square. The clerk of the works took him to the top of the tower to see the new peal, and showed him how if you struck the new tenor bell smartly with a piece of wood and then quenched the chime at once with the damper, you heard the old one, unmoving, still as death, giving voice, very faintly, a just discernible deep resonance on the quiet air. 'Touch it,' the clerk had said. Severo had reached out and touched the dull bronze of the dusty bell and felt it tingle at his fingertips.

By the time the service moved to its magnificent climax, while the choir sang the Sanctus, Severo had realized the meaning of his rebellious and drifting thoughts. Talking to the atheist had offered to his intellect, what the Low Country had offered to his senses – the exhilaration of strangeness. He was hungry for more; he wanted to walk in that chill and unsheltered country. Something in his soul was ringing with an answering resonance to a note struck by Palinor. He was tingling with gladness at what should have appalled him – that such a thing as an atheist could exist. He knew no name for such a feeling. He would not have called it love. *like Joseta → Amara*

'Well?' Severo asked Beneditx. 'What do you think? He is a conundrum, isn't he? Counsel me.'

'A difficulty, certainly. What puzzles you about him?'

'Now you have seen him, do you still say he cannot be in good faith?'

'I did not need to see him to know that. However plausible he is, the truth is that he was born like everyone else with knowledge of God. One has to ask what he has done with it.'

'It does not come with baptism?'

'No. Baptism confers grace, and dispels sin. We are talking now of neither grace nor sin, but knowledge.'

'But, Beneditx, on the face of it, the intellect depends on the senses for the origin of knowledge, and knowledge gathered from sensible things cannot lead the human intellect to the point of seeing the divine substance . . . A babe hasn't the means . . .'

'You speak of evening knowledge – knowledge of things as they are and have been in the visible world. I speak of morning knowledge – knowledge of things as they were created, things as they are meant to be. The knowledge of angels is of both these kinds at once, but in mankind there is a difference. Inborn knowledge of God is morning knowledge.'

'So you would say that even that poor creature locked up in the yard there, knows of God?'

'Yes. Even such a thing as that.'

'She seems to know only what a wolf knows.'

'But knowledge of God is the precise difference between a human being and an animal.'

'So in the mountains, in the dark cave, in the bitter snows, with no tenderness but that of a wolf for a whelp and not a word spoken to her, you say that child knew God?'

'If she could speak and answer questioning, she would tell you that she did. That she knew of an immanence all around her, sustaining all things, though she knew it nameless.'

'Could she be taught to speak, I wonder?' Severo was

thinking aloud, but Beneditx at once said, his face lit with eagerness, 'It would have to be in seclusion; her teachers would have to vow to make no mention of God and to refrain from teaching religion. Then when she spoke it would prove beyond doubt what has often been in dispute. Nobody has been able to make trial of this before; it would involve a deliberate cruelty to a human child. But this child having been raised apart from all society by accident . . .'

'There is no such thing as an accident, Brother,' said Severo gently. 'Not even falling in the sea.'

'An accident as far as human purpose is concerned. The cruelty is that of the wild beast which stole the child. But out of it good may come; we may find proof absolute that every soul knows God. Who is to say whether perhaps in the providence of God this is the reason why he allowed such a thing to happen to the child? And I have no doubt that the proof would force you to do what I see that you are reluctant to do, and condemn the atheist.'

Severo considered his friend's words. It seemed to him that Beneditx's mind had not wholly caught up with his body – that he was still engrossed in his books and had not recovered the knack of attending to the material world. That would be why Palinor seemed to him less of a conundrum than he seemed to Severo, why Beneditx could encompass him so easily in a statement of principle.

'Beneditx, are you not struck by his courage?' Severo asked. 'When it would be so easy simply to lie, and evince opinions which would lead us to free him? When you come to think of it, a man who believes in God might expect punishment for lying about his inner state of mind; God knows the secrets of all hearts. But one who does not believe in God should feel free to lie with impunity and say anything we want to hear.'

He told the adjudicators that such a lie would demean him. Are you not impressed?'

'Like you, I cannot see why he should be honest. And it does him credit, I admit.'

'And Beneditx, should we not be able to convince him by argument?'

Beneditx said, 'It is difficult to proceed against the errors of one single individual. Firstly, because the remarks of individual sacrilegious men are not so well known to us that we may use what they say as the basis for proceeding to a refutation of their errors. The fathers of the church refuted the errors of the gentiles when they had lived amongst gentiles and knew well what positions such men were inclined to take. Whereas we know nothing of Aclar.'

'He is willing enough to tell us about it. What you need to know about the beliefs of Aclar in order to refute them can be obtained from him by question.'

'Well. But further, Severo, remember that this man does not agree with us in accepting the authority of any scripture by which he might be convinced of his error. Against Jews we can argue by means of the Old Testament, and against heretics by means of the New, but against this man . . .'

'We must therefore have recourse to natural reason, to which all men are forced to give their assent. Did you not teach, Beneditx, that although some truths about God exceed all the ability of human reason, others, like the fact of his existence, can be reached by it?'

'Yes. All the doctors hold that the existence of God lies within the scope of proof.'

'Then this is what I shall do,' said Severo. The power that he held was like a sword, seldom taken from the wall, but always wielded in earnest. He had considered carefully, he had listened to the scholarly advice of his mentor and friend. But decision fell to him, and now he had decided. 'I will see if the wolf-child can be taught to speak and discover to us if she knows of God without instruction. And I will detain the atheist to await the outcome. But it will take some time and may not be possible at all. Therefore, meanwhile, you will argue with Palinor and by the light of reason prove God to him. He has a soul worth saving. Save him for me, Beneditx.'

In some ways, it seemed to Severo, Jaime resembled the great and learned Beneditx. Both saw with the eye of faith. One saw innate knowledge of God, and the other saw a human soul in a creature degraded to the likeness of a wolf. Jaime had saved the snow-child twice – once from death at the moment of capture, and again from death by starvation in unkind hands. No-one could doubt his faith, or his charity. But the third virtue also was needed for life in this world, and perhaps the third virtue, hope, was the most fragile. It was baptism Jaime had sought for the child; and since Beneditx seemed to think that baptism did not affect the question of knowledge one way or the other, Severo could see no reason to disappoint him. The child was already a crushing burden on the young man's green, untempered, and uneducated spirit.

Towards sunset, therefore, Severo took Rafal with him and went to the mason's yard. Jaime was there, keeping his watch, sitting on a barrel and cutting a whistle from a length of wood. As she usually was at dusk, the snow-child was awake, snuffling and running in her cage, pawing at the ground with her hands as though she might have been seeking to dig herself out.

'Have you thought of a name for her?' Severo asked. 'We are going to baptize her.'

'Now, Holiness?'

'Now.'

'Holiness, I do not think we can take her to the

font in the baptistry. She will resist, howl, foul the floors . . .'

'No need, Jaime. Baptism is as valid under the open skies as under the grandest roof. Indeed, what church is roofed as splendidly as the open air by the setting sun? All we need is a little water. Can you bring her to me?'

Jaime opened the cage door cautiously and drew it shut behind him. The child backed away to the far corner, snarling, a soft and warning sound. The bared teeth caught the low rays of the sun behind Severo, showing yellowish between her rolled-back lips, and her eyes returned an alien reflected glare. Jaime was talking to her, saying, 'Come, little one . . . no harm, little one . . .' She sprang at him at the same moment as he sprang at her. She knocked him flying, and they rolled over and over in the dust. Jaime's arms were clasped round her belly, but her arms were free. They heard him cry in agony as she mauled him, clawing at his face, sinking her teeth in the thick of his arm.

'In the name of Christ . . . can we help?' cried Severo to Rafal.

Rafal picked up a balk of timber and entered the cage. Waiting for his moment, he struck the child with it. She released her grip on Jaime and turned on Rafal, snarling round his ankles, but the swinging folds of his soutane were all she got a grip on with her snapping teeth. Jaime got up and, picking up a piece of canvas, threw it over the child. 'Get some rope,' he said in a shaking voice. Severo ran to bring it, to pass it into the cage. The two men struggled together to tie the child firmly into the bundle, only her head emerging. The bundle heaved and fought in their arms. They could not hold her.

'Put her down,' said Severo. They put her on one of the blocks of stone, like Isaac on the altar.

'You are hurt, Jaime,' said Severo. 'I am sorry; I did not realize . . .'

'I will manage, Holiness. I will get bandages when the thing is done . . .'

'Her name, then?' But Jaime, blood flowing from wounds in his face, his sleeve soaking darkly, swayed on his feet and did not answer.

'A black and bitter name!' said Rafal.

'Amara, then,' said Severo. 'In Latin, "bitter",' he explained to Jaime.

And as he poured the water over the filthy forehead of the creature, looking down he saw its eyes rolling in its head, and the features twisted into an expression of blind terror, as though the devil himself were within the child, and facing the presence of God.

'I baptize you,' he said, 'Amara . . .' He would have added, 'And God have mercy on you!' but he stopped himself just in time; for was it not to be forbidden to mention God to her?

Because Jaime was bleeding, they dumped Amara back in her cage and left her tied up, and Rafal took him in haste to the infirmary. Jaime did not sleep in the yard that night, but in Severo's cell, Severo's bed, while Severo, returning late from penitential prayer, stretched out on the floor instead of waking the boy.

In the morning he sent Jaime away. 'You have done well in this, Jaime, my brother,' he said. 'You have known in your heart what wiser men should have known, and I commend you. I am making a gift to you; I am giving you gold enough to buy three fields or so. Make the most of it; I will not be sympathetic if you return to me asking for more.'

'But Holiness, what will become of her?'

'You are still troubled by that, after what she did to you last night?'

'But Holiness, she does not know what she is doing . . . and . . .'

90

'And?'

'I so pity her.'

'Listen, Jaime. On your obedience to our Holy Mother the Church; on your obedience to me, your prince and your cardinal; on your hope of heaven and fear of hell, I command you to go your way and think of her no more.'

'I will obey you if I can,' said the boy, dejectedly. 'But I don't know if I can help thinking of her. Since the moment that we found her . . .'

'You must treat such thoughts like thoughts of lust, or impulses of anger; avoid them if you can, confess them as sins if you cannot.'

'Yes, Holiness. But . . . what will you do with her?'

'Did you not hear what I commanded you? Go!'

10

The nuns of Sant Clara were thrown into extreme panic by the announcement of an unexpected visit from the cardinal. The messenger said he was already on the road and would be with them by nightfall. Armed with dusters and beeswax, the sisterhood attacked the fabric of the building, rubbing woodwork into fragrant gloss, washing floors, burnishing the silver on the chapel altar, emptying vases and cutting fresh flowers from the gardens, crushing lavender between muslins to hang in the guest-house, hoeing the weeds mercilessly in the garden in the cloister courtyard, dragging the plough and harrow into a tidy corner of the farm – one task no sooner accomplished than someone thought of another. One would have thought it probable that the cardinal in Ciudad had heard rumours of slack housekeeping at Sant Clara, and had come looking for a mote of dust to reproach them with. If he came looking for uncleanness, however, as the abbess well knew, it would be of a less literal sort. She summoned Sor Agnete to her office after the Angelus, and closed the door.

'Tell me I am right, Sister. We could not have given scandal of any kind? None of the sisterhood has committed a crime?'

'Likely to have reached the ears of the cardinal?' said Sor Agnete. 'Certainly not, Mother. By the grace of God this is an orderly and a peaceful house. The worst a sister might have done is fall asleep during late office, or forget to milk a goat.'

The abbess nodded.

'We are all well known to each other,' Sor Agnete added, 'except the new novice. And she is harmless.'

'Yes, yes. Then it is not scandal that brings him.'

'What put such a thing into your head?' said Sor Agnete. 'He is in need of a little peace and quiet, and some of Sor Coloma's pasque-bread, more likely!'

Josefa, meanwhile, was working hard, and in a daze, for the crisis had engulfed the place when she had barely learned her way around it. She had swept the yard, washed the flagstones of the kitchen floor with milk – an instruction she had accepted with astonishment, till she saw with pleasure the sheen the milk gave to the stones as they dried – helped with weeding for some hours, and then climbed down the steep path to the shore to gather a basket of mussels for the cardinal's supper. The sun beat remorselessly on the path as she climbed back with her heavy basket, striking off the rocks on either side, getting under the brim of her hat. Her novice's habit, of heavy dark broadcloth, was suffocatingly hot, and when she regained the kitchen and put her burden on the kitchen table, she was flushed scarlet and sweating freely. Sor Coloma, the cook, looked up and saw.

'My poor child, sit down at once, and let me bring you a sup of water,' she said. Josefa sat down gratefully on a stool. The glass of water Sor Coloma set in front of her was cloudy – a fresh lemon had been squeezed into it.

'We are working you as hard as ever that stepmother of yours worked you, without a doubt,' said Sor Coloma, chopping onions on a board and weeping freely.

'Oh, but it's different, Sister!' said Josefa at once.

'How is that?'

'I don't mind working where everyone works.'

'Do you think you will like it here?' Sor Coloma asked her.

'Yes. Everyone is kind to me here. It is like having my mother back, many times over.'

'Ah, well, it's just as well,' the sister said. 'You live your life out here, either way, and it's hard on us all when someone hates it. Can you open mussels?'

But just then Sor Agnete appeared in the kitchen. 'Oh, there you are,' she said to Josefa. 'Now, I've a job for you. You are to go to the top of the orange orchard, and sit under the tree. You can find a shaded spot. Take your prayer book with you; no need to be idle. From there you can see the road coming down to us. When you see someone coming, come back here in haste, and tell me.'

Off went Josefa, to spend the next hour deliciously, sitting on the damp grass in the shade of the orange tree, crushing leaves between her fingers for the oily fragrance, and looking at the soaring mountains above her and the pretty little cupola of her new home below her, against the hazy dazzle of the sea. She tried hard not to fall asleep, and almost succeeded. The clatter of horses' hooves on the stony path and the drift of voices woke her; so that the first sight of Sant Clara afforded to Severo and Rafal and their servants included a glimpse of an ungainly nun, her habit hoisted almost to her knees, running pell-mell through the orange grove and across the farmyard.

'We are announced, I think,' said Severo, laughing. 'I did not know a nun could run – If I had thought about it, I would have supposed their vows had hobbled them!'

Under the archway of the abbey gate, the abbess waited for them. She stood erect, with the aid of her sticks. Coming from the blazing sunlight of the road, Severo did not at first see her standing black-garbed in the shadows. He reined in his horse and dismounted to find her standing at his side.

94

'If I kneel to you, Holiness, I shall never get up,' she said. 'Welcome.'

'We can dispense with bodily ceremony,' he said. 'My blessing upon this holy house.'

She glanced at his companion; at the two servants and the horses. A very large basket was slung between two mares. She clapped her hands, and lay sisters came to help unburden the horses and lead them to the stables. 'Put the basket in the shade, and do not open it,' said Severo, going gratefully to the room in the guest-house that had been made ready for him with such agitation.

Later, washed and rested, he walked in the garden, overlooking the sea, and wondered exactly how to explain the trial to the abbess. There was not much time; the child would need food and water, the basket would have to be opened at dusk.

It was possible for Severo, of course, simply to command the abbess. She owed him an absolute obedience on which he could rely. But so to command someone older than himself, older in the service of God, and in a matter of such delicacy, was not his way. The thing seemed to require both tact and gentleness.

Since the woman could no longer stand or walk without pain, Severo summoned her to the garden of the guest-house, and commanded her to sit on the bench provided for him. He told her that he had come to lay an arduous task upon her and her nuns, and that the task involved teaching a most difficult and pitiful child. He told her everything he knew about the child, and she listened in silence.

Then she said, 'Permit me to say, Holiness, that the teaching of children in solitude is not the best way. In playing with other children, every child is happiest. The company of other children is the best teacher of such simple things as walking and talking. Most humbly I suggest, Holiness, that the foundling hospital at Santanya would serve better.'

'I have three reasons for not accepting that advice,' said Severo. 'First I am concerned to protect the child from the curiosity of the people. It is not fitting that she should be a subject of vulgar gawping. Santanya is too much visited. Nothing discreet could go forward there for long. The seclusion here . . .'

'Yes,' she said.

'Then, the savagery she learned from the wolf, her foster-mother, would make her very dangerous to other children. She can inflict deep wounds – she has done so. To lay such risks on those who have devoted themselves to lives of self-sacrifice is one thing; to ask it of abandoned orphans with none to speak for them . . .'

'We will accept the risk,' she said, serenely, 'and offer our wounds to our Lord Jesus in mitigation of the sins of the world.'

'My last reason is the overriding one. You must prepare yourself to find it harsh. I want to be sure – absolutely – that those who have taught the child will have done so without ever mentioning to her, in any way, the fact of God. I shall require an oath from everyone in your community that they will never reveal their knowledge to the child, but keep it from her wholly and entirely secret. This I could not ask of half the population of Santanya. I need the dedication and self-discipline to be found here, at Sant Clara.'

The abbess was silent for a long while. Then she said, 'Holiness, may I ask you why you require such a thing?'

'I want to discover from the child whether the knowledge of God is innate.'

Again she was silent. 'I should seek the answer to such a question, if I needed it, in the teaching of the Church, Holiness,' she said at last.

96

'The teaching is uncertain. We know that the knowledge of God can be attained by reason. We know that it is found in revelation. But we cannot find clearly stated whether it is given to every soul, even to those without revelation and those who have not undertaken the attempt to reason it out.' She made no answer.

'Clearly, children usually learn of God as they learn of many things, from their parents and teachers, the people all around them. But if the wolf-child, when she can be questioned, knows God, it cannot be from such sources. Provided your community can do as I ask, it will be proof absolute of innate knowledge.' To himself he added, *'And if she does not it will prove that there is no such thing.'*

'You will be obeyed, Holiness,' she said. Such resignation in her tone!

'You dislike the command?' he asked. 'Why? Because it is hard?'

'Because it is unkind,' she said.

He blinked. It was more than twenty years since anyone had rebuked him, and he was rocked by a little spiralling impulse of rage, of which he was instantly ashamed.

'It is not my idle curiosity I seek to satisfy,' he said, mastering himself. 'Souls perhaps, a life certainly, depend on it.'

'Have I not said you will be obeyed, Holiness?' she said in a tone of mild amazement.

He went on, 'The sufferings of the child must have a meaning in the providence of God. It seems to us possible that God's purpose in her is to offer us a proof of what otherwise cannot be known. If so, it is God's work I ask of you.'

She turned to him a visage clearly minted with an expression of benign puzzlement. She was at an age at which the soul's character is deeply stamped on to the face. Her eyes were cloudy, full of a soft suspended

97

mist, and he realized with relief that she would see only veiled the horror he had brought her.

'It is enough that you ask it, Holiness, in order for it to be God's work for us,' she said. 'Where is the child now?'

'In a basket, in your gatehouse,' he said.

'Holy Mother of Mercy!' she said, struggling to her feet. 'All this time . . .'

Severo braced himself for what was to come.

First his servants carried the basket – stinking now – to the hermitage. The hermitage was a squat square tower of two storeys, occupying the last level corner of the little valley of Sant Clara, atop the cliff-face descent to the shore. It was older by far than the nunnery, having been a watch-tower once, or perhaps a beacon tower. Because it stood alone it was used as a penitentiary – the upper room contained a bed of wooden boards and a crucifix, and nothing else. The lower room was a byre and lambing shed, with an earth floor covered in straw. Here the basket was opened. The creature scuttled out at once, and with a loping seesaw gait made for the darkest corner, and crouched there, back turned to the abbess and Severo, and Rafal, who had opened the basket.

'That is a girl?' said the abbess softly. 'I cannot see clearly . . .'

'Amara!' called Severo. The creature covered its ears, wrapping its arms round its lowered head. Severo gestured to Rafal, who approached her where she crouched. She ran away, and her legs gave under her, so that she collapsed in the straw. Rafal went outside to the well and brought a pan of water. 'She needs food at once,' he said. 'Raw meat. She only eats raw meat.'

Even the noisy lapping of the child at the water dish did not cover the sound of dismay that the abbess uttered. 'Holiness, have you forgotten that we keep perpetual Lent here?'

He had.

'We do not eat meat,' she reminded him, 'and we have all vowed solemnly never to touch it. How can the child be fed?'

'We must think of something,' said Severo, distraught. He was tired and hungry himself, and battling with irritation at the gritty difficulties of the day. All very well for Beneditx to suggest experiments – he didn't have to arrange them. Severo's angel, however, was dutiful that evening. The immediate problem was solved by Rafal, without permission asked or given; he simply stole a hen from the farmyard, thrust it into the lambing shed where Amara was locked for the night, and closed the door on both creatures.

Meanwhile, Severo sat enthroned in the vaulted chapter house, facing the rows of nuns and novices. Twelve women, young and old, and four girls at the back in the postulants' bench. He told them the story of the child; he laid the task on them; he forbade them to mention God to the child, and he told them why he forbade it. He made them one by one approach him, and swear on the abbey's great and ancient Testament that they would do as he commanded. Then he raised the question of preparing meat. He offered to absolve one of the sisterhood from sin in breaking her vow . . .

Blushing scarlet, and shaking in her shoes at her temerity in rising to her feet and speaking to a cardinal, Josefa stood and told him that she had not yet taken any vow and was free to do any service, however menial and despised. Severo, thanking God for her, swore her into her novitiate on the spot, editing the Sant Clara vow to permit her to feed the snow-child for as long as necessary. The abbess, fumbling, half-sighted, fixed her novice's wimple of coarse linen, and the cardinal himself put the bridal ring on her finger. It was to

99

Christ that he wedded her, but it seemed to Josefa that it was to the snow-child.

When he rode away at daybreak, into the dark shade of the mountains cast by the morning sun, the ugly and passionate face of the new novice stayed in his mind for the first several miles. Where had she come from, he wondered, so – a propos? But then, after all, he did not believe in accidents.

11

'My yoke is easy and my burden light,' the Saviour had said. The Blessed Alicssande, who had founded the order of the nuns at Sant Clara, had written a rule for her holy women that was gentle and simple. They were to work for their sustenance, and never be at any charge on the laity, or on the coffers of the Church. They were forbidden extreme penance or harsh discomfort. They were to withdraw entirely from the world, and their discipline was prayer – an endless holy office, at the canonical hours. They were to love each other, and study books of devotion. The Blessed Alicssande had detected a taint of spiritual pride in the more difficult disciplines ordained in rival houses. She specifically enjoined her daughters to take joy in cleanliness and domestic order; to eat simple food, but be sure it was well cooked and wholesome; to have everything they needed for simple comfort, and everything serviceable and plain. Nothing was to be painted in more than one colour, or be one twitch more elaborate than it needed to be, but everything needful was to be at hand. The sisters served God by living a life of prayer. That was all. That was enough.

Josefa's cell was painted white. It had a window giving on the prospect of the sea. It had a wooden table, painted ochre, and a dark blue bowl and ewer for her daily washing. The door was painted pale blue, the simple chair light green. No aim at beauty having been intended, the accidental result was beauty, a childlike simplicity and sufficiency in which every need was supplied by a modest object – a model for the modest sanctity the sisters of Sant Clara were to achieve. Of course they were the bishop's to command, but nothing like this task had ever before been demanded of them.

They set about it with a will. Severo's party had barely moved out of sight round the first turn of the track when a little bevy of nuns made their way to the hermitage. In the lead was Sor Coloma, and with her Sor Agnete and Sor Blancha and several others, with Josefa bringing up the rear. They opened the lambing-shed door and found the chaos of blood and feathers left by the death of the stolen hen. The snow-child fled to the furthest corner of the room and crouched there, facing them and snarling. The nuns quailed at the sight, but unflinching they advanced on her. When Sor Coloma tried to hold the creature it snarled, a low rumbling warning growl, and then struck out with its nails, leaving a line of parallel scratches down the nun's arm, with the droplets of blood starting up along it. Bravely, Sor Coloma tried again. This time her hand was bitten severely enough to wring a cry from her, and the creature dashed away to a far corner of the room. Minutes later Sor Agnete was also bleeding, and the child crouched, glaring at them, in the first corner. The three women retreated and conferred together. Sor Blancha, who kept the abbey's flocks, picked up a panel of wattle that was leaning against a wall – the wattles were used to make pens at lambing time – and the others copied her. A wall of wattles advanced upon the child. Cornered, she cowered, seeming terrified. At the last minute she turned her back, and crouched facing the wall.

Peering over their wattle shields the nuns stared at the blueish, naked back, and huge grey head of a monster.

'What are we to do with her?' said Sor Coloma, sucking the gash on her right hand.

'We must cut her nails,' said Sor Agnete.

'We shall need a draught of poppy water,' said Sor Blancha. 'I will fetch some.'

Reaching gingerly round the end of the wattle-walls, they placed a dish of poppy water near the creature. But the water was sniffed at and refused.

'Patience,' said Sor Blancha. 'Sooner or later thirst will overcome refusal.' As she spoke, the creature slunk across to the water dish, and sniffed at it again.

'It is thirsty,' said Sor Agnete, 'poor thing.'

But the child did not drink. Having smelt the water, it retired to its corner and turned its back again. No amount of calling, soft talking and tapping the dish, splashing with a spoon to make the water plash, or anything else the sisters could think of made it take the least notice.

'We must wait,' said Sor Blancha. 'And watch for the moment. We will take turns.'

It was a hot day. But the ground-floor room in the watchtower, with its thick walls and straw-covered floor, was not as hot as the world outside. The sun struck through a broken slat in the ancient wooden shutters across the seawards window, but in too narrow a ray to load the air with warmth. Nevertheless, even in a cool chamber, sooner or later the child would be forced to drink.

It did not happen quickly. All day the snow-child seemed drowsy, spending most of the time curled in the straw, raising her head now and then to glare at her keeper. Josefa came at dusk to take a watch, while the nuns all attended vespers and the common meal was eaten. By then the child seemed more wakeful. She ran round the walls of the room, pawing at the straw, lingering under the windows, sniffing at the outside air. Once she took a running jump at a window, leaping from the ground and hitting the shutter with some force before falling back. At last she abandoned

103

this seeming search for a means of escape, and began a restless, unceasing circuit of the place at a lolloping run, swerving at each turn to avoid Josefa and returning to the bowl of water, sniffing at it, and leaving it untouched.

At moonrise she began to howl, a blood-curdling sound, resounding in the bare cell-like chamber, and after some time answered faintly by some free nocturnal creature on the mountainside above the nunnery. Now it was Josefa's turn to cower, horrified, in a corner. Through the unglazed windows and broken shutters the ferocious sound reached the peaceful cells of the sisterhood, striking fear and appal into their God-fearing hearts. Sor Coloma came running with a lantern to make sure Josefa was safe, but when she was halfway across the garth between the cloister and the watch-tower the sound stopped as suddenly as it had begun. Finding Josefa unharmed, though trembling, Sor Coloma returned to her duties, but she left the lamp with Josefa.

Josefa retreated halfway up the stair to the upper floor, barring the way below her with a wattle, though she had concluded that the child would not initiate attack, but reserved her ferocity for those whom she took to be attacking her. Josefa hung the lamp on a hook above the stair, and sat down quietly. She could not see clearly what the child was doing – the throw of the lantern was not wide – only hear the dry scuttle of her hands and feet running on the floor, and glimpse now and then a twinned glint of the lantern in her passing eyes.

Towards the end of Josefa's watch it began to rain, that fierce and sudden downpour with which the mountains were kept green on the western slopes. The sound of it on the tower roof above her and the noisy gushing of the spouts which drained the roof through the battlemented parapet stirred the restless creature below her to frenzy. Josefa heard suddenly a lapping sound. She unhooked the lantern and held it up, leaning over the rail of the stair, and saw the child lapping at a puddle of water that was forming in the hollow of the threshold, fouled as it was by the filth of the floor. Shuddering, but seeing her chance, Josefa pushed her wattle barricade aside, and moving as swiftly as her heavy garments allowed her, she seized the dish of poppy water, and poured it into the puddle. The child went on drinking.

When Sor Agnete came at dawn, she found the snow-creature lying asleep in the straw, and Josefa sleeping where she sat on the stair. The bright incursion of morning light through the open door woke Josefa, but the snow-child remained asleep, making, they saw as they stood over her together, little twitching movements and tiny sounds, like a dog that dreams at its master's fireside. They picked her up and carried her to the infirmary.

Drawn by pity, horror, and curiosity in equal measure, the nuns of the little community gathered in the infirmary, and watched Sor Blancha, the best of them for knowledge of animals, inspect the creature. The bluish appearance of its skin was only a deeply ingrained filth, and the distorted huge head it seemed to possess was the matted and encrusted mass of verminous hair, which overhung the face. Now that the child was drugged and the face was not screwed into an animal grimace, the human features could be seen to be normal: what was not normal was the child's posture. They had laid her on her back, and her knees were drawn up to her chest in a foetal position. The knees thus presented for attention were capped with a thick layer of cracked skin – heavy callouses, caused, Sor Blancha supposed, pointing them out to her audience, by wear on the knees caused by running on them. The child's elbows, when inspected, were similarly calloused. Rolling up her sleeves, Sor Blancha attempted to straighten the child's crooked legs. Although the child was relaxed in sleep, the legs would not pull straight; they locked in a still crooked position, and the child stirred and whimpered, so that it was evident that the pull caused pain. Sor Blancha shook her head, and moved to inspect the child's feet. The toes were all bent upwards, and would not pull down in line with the soles. The toenails had grown to an immense length, and were folded back under the feet in the likeness of claws. Sor Blancha next inspected the child's hands. The fingernails were similarly extended, and curved back towards the palms of the roughened and thickened hands, making a set of dangerous weapons, for they were thick and sharp. Gently Sor Blancha held and moved the child's thumbs and fingers. They moved freely now, while she was slack with sleep.

'There is nothing wrong with this creature,' said Sor Blancha, 'other than what is caused by running on all fours. But it will take some time to correct that, I think.' She picked the child up by the armpits, and the dangling legs maintained their crook. 'A bath of hot water,' she ordered, 'and a razor. And a sharp paring knife. Before she wakes, we will disarm her.'

The novices – there were three besides Josefa – ran to fetch water and fill the bath. Immersion in water woke the child to struggle and howl, but doped as she was with poppy water she was easily overcome and scrubbed clean by the combined efforts of a dozen pairs of hands. It took Josefa's strong grip round her wrists to hold her hands while Sor Blancha, grunting with effort and concentration, pared off the monstrous nails. Then they shaved her head, getting flea-bitten all over their hands as they worked. At last they rubbed her dry in clean towels, and contemplated the results of their labour.

Lying still and denuded, the child was very small. Every bone of the emaciated body showed through the skin, which was covered all over with a myriad scars and scratches in every stage of healing and rawness. Her ears, which seemed large, stood at an odd angle to her head, and her jaw – she was working it in her sleep – seemed to move sideways further than it should.

'How old is this child, do you think?' asked Sor Agnete.

'Nine?' asked Sor Eulalie. 'Nine, and starving.'

'Not so old,' said Sor Blancha. 'Seven, at most. And badly malnourished.'

They put a clean shift on her, giving her suddenly the look of a normal waif, an orphan of the poor, obliterating the animal appearance, the nakedness which had effectively concealed her from them. Seeing her clad and human, Josefa began to weep silently for the sufferings of the poor monster. None of the sisters asked her why. In that moment they all looked tenderly and hopefully on the task of training and teaching. It was only a girl, after all.

Quite suddenly the child's eyes sprang open, and she leapt from the table on which they had laid her, and dashed to the darkest corner of the room. She clawed at her shift with her now harmless fingers, and then gripped the cloth in her teeth, and tore at it frantically. Head lowered, she tried to back out of it, and then catching it between treading foot and gnashing teeth, she tore herself free of it. The moment she was naked again she fouled herself, and then, growling at the detested company, she began prowling along the line of the wall, pacing it backwards and forwards, and eyeing the door as though to escape confinement.

Josefa watched her attentively. She noticed that the child kept picking up its hands and looking at them, missing the claws, as though seeking to observe what had happened to her. That, Josefa thought, showed

107

more perception than an animal might have. She also noticed, when she brought a bucket and rags to clean up the floor, that the child's ordure did not smell sickeningly human, but had the innocent stench of a byre or a sty.

'I have seen a wolf's den,' said Sor Blancha. 'When I was a child, I went with my brothers when they tracked a wolf that was stealing our sheep. We killed it, and then saw its cubs at the back of the cave. It was clean, in the cave. Absolutely clean.'

'What do you mean, Sister?' asked the abbess. The child had been in the nunnery for a week, and the sisters were in confabulation about her, sitting round the table in order of rank.

'There was filth from the carcasses it had been eating, all outside the cave, at the entrance,' said Sor Blancha, 'but within not a scrap, not a bone nor a morsel lying around. And the cubs' dung had all been removed – the mother wolf had cleaned it up. It smelt like a well-kept kennel. Quite clean.'

'But what are you telling us, Sister?'

'They say this child was reared by a wolf. Well, if so, it must have learned some cleanliness in that regard. We should give it the means to be clean, and see what happens.'

'A litter tray, do you mean?'

'And see what happens. Standing upright and wearing clothes and learning words will all be very difficult; but using dug earth . . .'

'Josefa,' said Sor Agnete, making Josefa jump out of her skin – she expected to be disregarded, not called upon to speak, being the newest and the least of the company – 'you have spent most time with the child. What do you think?' Then, when Josefa coloured and stammered, she added, 'Give us the benefit of any observations you have made.'

'She is unhappy,' said Josefa.

'Unhappy?' said Sor Agnete in amazement. 'That isn't what I meant to ask at all . . .'

The abbess laid a gentle hand on Sor Agnete's sleeve. 'Tell us what you meant, Josefa,' she said.

'Not unhappy as one of us might be,' said Josefa. 'Not in the mind. But in the body, like a raging thirst. She hates us; she hates confinement; she longs to run free. I think we have no hold on her; only meat. She is hungry all the time, and if we were cruel enough, she would perhaps do things for meat.'

'If we were cruel?'

'If we withheld food, unless she did things.'

'I don't know how much scope we have for that,' said Sor Blancha. 'If she doesn't give in and get food, she may starve in our keeping. She is nearly starving now.'

'Have we any other way to try?' asked the abbess.

Nobody knew of one.

'Then we will try the litter tray, and we will try withholding food unless she is wearing a shift. One thing is certain – we cannot present a stark naked female to be questioned by a cardinal. She must wear clothes.'

'Mother,' said Josefa, greatly daring.

'Yes, child?'

'I think we should talk to her more. Whoever is with her, should. Talk. About anything except . . .'

'What is the point of talking to a thing that understands not a single syllable?' asked Sor Juana.

'That is how babes are loved,' said Josefa. 'A mother sings and talks ceaselessly to a babe from its first hours. She has no thought of waiting for it to understand her.'

'Did we undertake to love the creature?' said the abbess. 'Perhaps we did. Perhaps when we agreed to teach her, we agreed to that. Well, God will help us. If it is for his greater glory that we should succeed, he will show us the way. Talk to her, then.'

12

Everyone knew, of course, that Lazaro and Miguel had been promised gold by the swimmer. And of course nobody, not even Lazaro and Miguel, expected them to get it. Not, that is, until the swimmer had managed to get himself home again. All the while that Palinor had spent in the prefect's lock-up in the citadel, the idea of the promised reward had been clearly in suspense; Esperanca, Lazaro's mother, visiting and feeding the prisoner, had been the butt of extensive if not unkind laughter. Setting a sprat to catch a mackerel was what she was about – everyone could see that. But poor Esperanca could barely afford the sprats. The fish Palinor had eaten in prison had been easy, they had been taken straight from Lazaro's catch. The loaf a day had been far harder to find, and although Miguel's wife had done her best to help, she had children to feed and very little to spare. Esperanca had offered to make shirts for the baker's children in exchange for Palinor's loaves. The children were numerous, and she could not afford lamp oil to work after nightfall, so she had sat at her neighbours' hearths, in the light of their lamps, for many evenings, while they teased her, and demanded to know what the gold, when it came, would be spent on.

'Lamp oil of my own, first,' she would say, smiling.

'Why, but you won't be sewing when you're rich, will you?' the householder would say. 'You'll be wearing other people's needlework and lording it over us.'

'I would never forget a kindness, even if I was as rich as the three kings,' said Esperanca.

'Come, tell us what you would buy if you had five gold solidi,' her neighbour's husband asked her. It was a good game; everyone wanted to share it.

'A change of clothes for Lazaro, so he wouldn't have to stand mother-naked while I scrub fish-scales off his trousers,' she said, the darting needle held in suspense while she closed her eyes and dreamed. 'And the same for me. Honey-plums for Miguel's children – and for yours, of course, neighbour . . . a pane of glass for the window that faces north . . . I don't know. What does one do with money?'

'Money can breed money,' said the neighbour wisely. 'A new boat for Lazaro, and he would prosper.'

But Esperanca thought if he didn't need to fish every day Lazaro would lie in the shade lazily mending nets. As she sewed, she plotted and planned. She had washed the clothes Palinor had been given by the townsfolk in the excitement of his first arrival, more than once collecting them from the prison and returning them at evening. But they were stained and filthy from the dirt of the lock-up. When his warrant to travel came through, she knew he would need something decent. She had opened her dowry chest and cast a shrewd eye on her brother's things. He had drowned a quarter-century ago, and she had never let her husband have them, but now she had thought she might be able to let them out a bit for Palinor.

When Palinor had ridden out of the town escorted by the prefect himself, the news had given both Miguel and Lazaro and their families a time of glory – Esperanca especially, since she had been the one who had kept Palinor alive all those months. They thought at first that the moment he reached Ciudad a rider would come galloping back with the purses of

111

gold and rubies; but time went by and by and no such thing occurred.

Sor Blancha was right about the cleanliness of wolves. The moment she was provided with a tray of loose earth, the child defecated only there, and covered her turds at once, scratching loose earth over them. It became plain to Sor Blancha and to Josefa that she disliked urinating on the floor – she did not use the earth box for that – and that she scratched and whined at the door before wetting herself. They put a belt around her, and looped a rope through the belt, so that they could open the door and let her out at such times. She would resort to the nettles to pee in, seeming insensitive to the weals the stings raised on her buttocks and sides.

Over the wearing of a shift however, a long and terrible battle was fought day after day. She resisted it as though it were death. Day after day, as evening approached, two or three of the sisters would arrive to help Josefa. They would overpower the child and force her, rigid with fright and hatred, into the coarse linen shifts that old Sor Berenice cobbled up for her day after day. When the shift was on, Josefa would at once produce the dish of raw meat – the abbess had secured a supply of carcasses from the shepherds on the nearest pastures – and the child was so frantic with hunger that she would run, down on her hands and knees, shift and all, and eat. She put her face down to the bowl and bolted the food, throwing up her head and swallowing with convulsive movements of her upper body. When the dish was empty, she would tear off her garment and then curl naked in the straw and sleep, though the least movement towards her, however much asleep she seemed, would rouse her to a wakeful, baleful stare, and a rumbling growl.

112

Sor Berenice devised a shift of heavy canvas, buckled with leather straps. Though it took the child several hours to extricate herself from that, she managed it by morning. Every morning when Josefa crossed the garth and opened the door of the wolf-child's pen, the child was naked in her straw. Josefa thought she was thinner than ever, but dared not break the link between food and clothing by giving her any morsel to eat in the day. Fretting about the child's stunted and starving appearance, Josefa tried mixing other things with the meat – some vegetable roots, some scraps of bread – but with an uncanny skill the child separated the meat and ate only that, leaving the mild and wholesome savours in the bowl.

Josefa was as good as her word about talking; she droned on hour after hour, calling the child by her name, Amara; telling her all about Margalida, and how she was sure her father by now regretted letting his daughter go; and about the little ups and downs of the nuns' kitchen and kitchen garden; and then telling her the goblin tales and magic stories she remembered her mother telling, long ago. She kept well clear of the lives of the saints, in case God got into them while she was unawares. She had convinced herself, before the end of the summer, that the daily struggle over the putting on of the shift had become less desperate and that Amara was listening to her flow of talk – not, she had to admit, as a child might listen, but as a dog might.

The change of season at Sant Clara brought drifts of mist, floating in from the sea and engulfing the wooded heights and crags of the mountains. The nunnery was not dependent on the world beyond the mountain passes, and a sort of relief, a certainty of peace descended on them with the mist that isolated them for days together. The days were without distance and the nights without stars at such times, and dusk crept on by such small stages that the canonical hours went by guesswork.

In such a mist, and when they least expected it, the abbey had visitors. They were announced by the sound of baying dogs and the clatter of horses' hooves on the stony path – an uproar of dogs and horses, neighing and clattering at the gates, the tinkle of harness and the sound of men's voices. A hunting party, lost in the mountain forests, coming by accident upon the path to Sant Clara, hungry and damp and cold, were asking for shelter. The abbess went down to them, with Sor Agnete at her side.

'I am Guillem Nagarri, Mother,' said the hunt leader. 'I and my friends are severely lost; we have been on the open mountain for two days. In Christian charity, can you shelter us till the mist lifts off?'

The abbess stared at him. With a more piercing gaze, Sor Agnete stared too. She saw a young man in the prime of youth, gorgeously dressed, though all his clothes were wet. A silver hunting horn hung from his buckler, and his horse was a fine mount, with chased and gilded harness. A merchant's son, perhaps. He had a coarse and florid complexion to an eye used to gazing only on the faces of clerics, or women, but an expression of brainless benignity. Around him his hounds swarmed restlessly, swaying their great heads. Behind him his companions stood, gloomy and blue-lipped with cold.

'This is a nunnery,' said the abbess. 'We cannot admit you here.'

'We are desperate with cold and damp,' said Guillem, 'and very tired. A farm outhouse would do. A barn; any roof.'

The two nuns conferred together. 'We have a guest-house with its own garth,' the abbess said. 'You may stay there; we will send firewood for you to have some warmth. Your dogs and horses you can put in the upper barn. But going between house and barn you must take the long way round; you must not set foot in the cloister. None of you. Not for one minute, not on any pretext. But if you give me that assurance you may stay.'

'My word of honour, lady,' said Guillem, pulling off his sodden hat and bowing gravely. 'And my thanks.'

'You are welcome, on those conditions,' the abbess said. 'Bread and herbs will be all we have to sup you on.'

'We have killed a boar,' said Guillem. 'If you can give us a cauldron of water, we will boil ourselves a stew on that promised fire.'

Sor Coloma grumbled at lending her iron stewpot, but sent it in the end with a bundle of leeks and a head of garlic, and a handful of salt. The scent of wood smoke and boiling broth from the guesthouse chimney diffused in the mist and reached the forbidden regions where the nuns moved in their cloister, wakeful and keeping the hours of service long after the huntsmen had eaten and fallen asleep.

The huntsmen had been forbidden the cloister. But the cloister was not entirely enclosed. It surrounded its garden on all four sides on the upper storey, but on the ground level the fourth, the seaward side consisted only of pillars, with no ground-floor cells, so that the cool air of the sea might enter and refresh the garden and the colonnades. Esteban, the kennel boy, who had slept with the hounds and horses in the barn, woke early and, since the dogs were restless, he let them out and began sleepily to look for the saddle-bag of meat and oilcake to feed them with. He heard them, a little distance off, begin the raucous baying that meant they had picked up a scent and were summoning the hunt to follow them. The horses began whinnying, jerking their heads up to the limit of their halters, and kicking at the donkey stalls where they were tied. Cursing,

115

Esteban ran outside. The dogs were running round the pillars of the colonnade, in and out of the cloister garth, howling. He saw the flutter of white wimples and dark garments in doorways as frightened nuns opened their doors and slammed them shut again, as startled faces leaned out of upper windows.

Esteban ran into the forbidden garden and, clapping and shouting and blowing on his little hand horn, chased the dogs out through the avenue of columns. A little cluster of affronted sisters ran after him, likewise chasing him. He was too late to head the dogs off towards the barn again; they were in full cry going towards the watch-tower. When they reached it they ran around, noses to the moist earth, circling the building and weaving along invisible trails, honking their soft baffled sounds. What had they latched on to? Reaching the tower, Esteban opened the door, hearing too late the cry of prohibition from the nuns behind him.

He had expected the dogs to run in and fetch out a fox or a rat or some such; he had not expected something to run out – passing him in a single bound and mingling at once with the pack. He ran with his dogs, blowing the feeding call on his horn, which brought them to heel, running along behind him, their brown and white backs undulating, their eager panting and the chink of their collar-brasses filling the morning with dog music, flowing back towards the barn. He could not see where the unexpected thing had gone, but he heard the cries of the nuns behind him.

There was a fenced yard in front of the barn, and Esteban opened the gate to it and hustled the pack in. He glimpsed a hairless sort of dog among them, and cursed. It would get torn to pieces, whatever it was. He ran to the side door of the barn to fetch the meat from his bag – not till they were fed would the dogs calm down once they got the wind up like this. The nuns were far too close; they were leaning over the fences, their unfamiliar high-pitched voices exciting the pack to frenzy.

'Get back!' he called, still running. 'Stand clear! Away, back away! They are ferocious when they are feeding!' And he tossed the feed into the pen. By now some few of the huntsmen, Guillem among them, had woken to the uproar and come up to see what was afoot. Only after he had thrown the meat into the pen did Esteban get a clear enough glimpse of the hairless creature to see what it was. He thought to see the child mauled to death.

The dogs were fighting over scraps, but it ran fearlessly among them, going on all fours. The king of the pack growled; the child crouched. Running round it the king dog sniffed its anus, and then returned to the fighting over shares in the meat. The child bolted a share, unopposed. Then, taking a bone in her teeth, retreated to a corner and settled down, calmly holding the bone under her arms as if they were paws and rubbing it on the ground to loosen the scraps of flesh.

'Get her out of there!' a young nun cried to him, tugging at his sleeve.

Esteban vaulted over the fence and, striking to left and right with his stick, attempted to quell the hounds and beat a path through to the child. The dogs defended her; he might as well have been trying to separate one of them from the rest. At last he reached the child and picked her up. He held her high, out of reach of the dogs jumping round him, and waded back towards the gate to the pen. He intended to pass the child bodily over the fence to the outstretched hands of the waiting nuns, but as he held her out she ducked her head and suddenly bit him hard and deep. He dropped her, and she fell outside the fence. Instantly, she bounded away into the

117

scrubby herbage beyond the barn, headed across the path into the forest, and was lost to sight.

'I am sorry, lady,' said Guillem. He was in front of the abbess, on his knees. 'It was a mishap; no harm was meant . . .'

'Follow her and bring her back,' said the abbess.

'My men are mounted and ready to ride. The hounds have been given her rags for a scent. We will do what we can,' he said. Something told him not to ask questions of this stern and formidable woman. It was clear he had wronged her.

'Most solemnly I adjure you,' she said, 'if you find her, not to swear or pray in her hearing, or mention God to her in any way.'

'Mention God?' he repeated stupidly, staring at her.

'Swear not to.'

'I swear, if you like,' he said, getting to his feet. Esteban was holding his horse's bridle for him, waiting in the gate. The hunting horns were blaring, and the hounds were running free, surging up the steeps, leading the huntsmen upwards, deeper into the mist. Guillem left the nunnery at a gallop. The abbess was as mad as a mushroom eater, he thought, as his mount picked her way delicately over the detritus of needles and branches on the dark forest floor. Were all her nuns likewise deranged?

13

'This is madness,' said Palinor.

'The Apostle Paul said it was better to marry than burn,' said Severo. 'Regard the project in the light of a courtship; embrace it as you would a bride.'

To his consternation, tears sprang suddenly to Palinor's eyes. 'I have a wife at home,' he said. 'And a son whom I long to see again.'

'I am sorry,' said Severo. 'I spoke only by way of analogy. I did not mean to make lewd suggestions to a chaste husband. You will be my guest; you shall have all you need. All that I require of you is that you should give Beneditx a fair hearing.'

'I am always ready to listen to reason,' said Palinor.

'Rooms are ready for you in the Saracen's House,' said Severo. 'And you will need a servant. I shall send Rafal to find you one.'

The Saracen's House was about two hours' ride from Ciudad, in the foothills of the mountains. The house was at the head of a pleasant valley, full of tumbling streamlets from the great spring of fresh water which rose just below the house. It was cool there in summer, and the long-ago Saracen had made the kind of garden of which Saracens are inordinately fond – a courtyard garden with a basin of water in the middle. There was a farm, and several flourishing workshops in the cellars and the outbuildings. The house belonged to Severo, having been confiscated from its owner many years ago during an outbreak of fervour by the island Inquisition.

All the property of heretics was forfeit. Severo never used it, its luxury being too much for him, though his predecessors in office had almost lived there. But it was a happy thought to send Palinor there, safely out of Ciudad. Keeping him in the cathedral cloister, which meant keeping the famous Beneditx there also, would cause tongues to wag, questions to be asked. Like many rulers, Severo strongly preferred secrecy, which he would have called discretion. Beneditx would rather have returned to the Galilea, taking Palinor with him, but Severo was afraid – or so he said – of the uproar that might erupt there if he put an atheist among the theological students. The estate servants at Alquiera, where the Saracen's House was, were all peasants, given to accepting without curiosity the doings of their betters. Besides, the Galilea was two long days' hard ride away, and Severo could not go there without attracting comment. If Palinor were at the Saracen's House, he could be visited and talked to; Severo could keep a close eye on the progress of his conversion.

When Beneditx protested that he needed his books at hand to undertake the argument, Severo sent him home to the Galilea for a few days to fetch them.

'A manservant, or a maidservant, Holiness?' enquired the indispensable Rafal.

'It is of no consequence,' said Severo. 'Whichever is cheaper.'

Rafal found a pair of striplings, boy and girl, standing hand in hand at the hiring block and offering the girl's work at half price if they could work together. They were brother and sister, Joffre and Dolca, they said, and being orphans, having only each other in the world, they were loath to be parted. Rafal struck a bargain with them for a year and sent them to Alquiera to await Palinor.

*   *   *

120

The Saracen's House was a welcome refuge to Palinor, a great relief from the prison cells and dark rooms in which he had been confined for so long. It was built on the foundations of a great solid bastion, riddled with cellars and workshops, above which the apartments of the house were reared up high. The sound of water murmured all around it, his windows opened on to the tops of trees, and he could lean on his balcony over the drop and look at the white fury of a fierce little torrent at the foot of the wall. Whoever built the house had some idea of comfort and grace; the rooms were airy and light, the walls painted in unaffected patterns of flower and leaf; there were furnishings and linens on the beds. Palinor's rooms opened on to a first-floor colonnade, which overlooked the courtyard on one side and the garden on the other.

In this pleasant place he was free to wander, or to remain within. Both the close confinement he had endured and the lack of privacy were suddenly relieved. He had books – Severo had sent him Orosius's *History Against the Pagans,* the Scriptures, several volumes of St Augustine, and a work of astronomy. He had clothes – Severo had sent him new-made shirts, doublets, hose, and a cloak of fine wool. Dolca brought hot water in the morning and washed his clothes for him; Joffre rode or walked with him when he took exercise. Palinor had no doubt of being still imprisoned; but he regained his health here, eating, walking and riding with zest. He awaited Beneditx with the kind of interest a chess player takes in the prospect of a worthy opponent.

14

Guillem had been gone seven days, seven days of misery at Sant Clara. Every sister was deep in remorse, though blameless. The abbess was mortified beyond bearing by the thought of having to tell the cardinal that they had failed in their duty, and in such a way as that! With hindsight it was easy to see that she should have hardened her heart against the hunt; healthy and well fed – grossly well fed – young men would not have come to any terrible harm from another night in the open, had she had the sense to turn them away.

Josefa wept, appearing red-eyed in the chapel, choking on her tears, unable to sing the office, unable to sleep. She was consumed with fear for what might become of the snow-child.

'She fended for herself before,' said Sor Agnete, gently, trying to console Josefa, trying to quell the unworthy thought that tears are ugly on ugly faces.

'But we disarmed her – we cut her claws,' said Josefa.

'We should face the fact that this may be a blessing in disguise,' said Sor Agnete.

'What do you mean, Sister? How, a blessing?' asked Sor Blancha. It was the recreation hour, and the nuns were sitting quietly in the cloister garden, their little projects of lace-making and embroidery on their knees.

'We are making so little progress,' said Sor Agnete. 'In so bitter a struggle with her . . .'

'Be patient,' said Sor Blancha. 'How many years did the child spend with the wolf? She has spent a much smaller time with us as yet.'

'I fear she may always be fit only for the wild,' said Sor Agnete. 'Suppose in the end we prevail upon her to wear clothes; then we must begin to bully and coerce her to eat like a Christian instead of like a dog; then . . .'

'Patience. One thing at a time,' said Sor Blancha. 'She has the use of her hands – it is only that in everything she learned from the wolf she is wolf-like. She runs, she eats as a wolf taught her, but by and by she will learn from us things the wolf did not know. In the end, maybe, she will use her hands to eat.'

'If ever we see her again,' said Sor Juana. 'But Josefa may be right, weeping her eyes out over there. I'll warrant you can't see to sew, Josefa. Perhaps the child will be unable to survive the wilderness without nails for claws. If she goes to her Maker, he will better know what to do with her than we do.'

Sor Agnete was contemplating Josefa thoughtfully. It might indeed be for the best if the snow-child had gone for good. But the novice would be distraught. She must have an exceptionally tender heart.

On the eighth day the hunters returned, their horses stepping down the rocky path quite early in the morning, their dogs all strung together on the leash. They had recaptured Amara; she was tied face down over the saddle of Guillem's horse, while he came on foot, leading it by the bridle.

The hunters were black-browed and grim-faced. They were dirty and tired. They dragged the dogs into the barn where they had been billeted before and shut them in. Then they sat about despondently, while Guillem lifted the child down from his saddle, in the gate.

'Is she unharmed?' said the abbess. She had begun her painful steps towards the gatehouse at the first sounds of their return. The child was curled into a ball and rigid in Guillem's hands. Put down she stayed locked in her contracted spasm. Her teeth were grinding, and her eyes rolled in her head. Silently a flock of the sisters had arrived behind the abbess, silently looking on. Josefa ran forward, picked up the child, and carried her away, unbidden and unforbidden.

'I must speak to you alone, lady,' said Guillem.

'I cannot speak alone with a layman,' the abbess said.

'This time you must,' he said.

Sor Agnete placed a chair in the middle of the cloister garden, overlooked by every cell. Slowly the abbess made her way towards it, and painfully she sat down. Guillem stood before her, holding his hat, blinking into the sun.

'Move into the shade, my son,' she said, and he retreated under the canopy of shadow offered by the fig tree. He seemed unable to embark on his theme.

'Now you have seen the child, your heart is troubled?' she said at last. 'Be consoled; it was not human cruelty, but the kindness of wolves . . .'

'I am willing to kill it for you, Mother,' he blurted out.

She did not answer at once. Standing back at a respectful distance, he had not heard her indrawn breath.

'It will be discreet, secret,' he said. 'We will simply say that we found her, but found her dead. The blow will be swift and painless. Her sufferings will be at an end.'

'Kill her? But you speak of a human soul . . .'

'It would be kinder; God will understand.'

'It is absolutely against God's law,' she said, 'and man's law, also. You would be hanged. And rightly.'

'I can trust my companions,' he said. 'I am willing to take what risk there is.'

'Why? Why are you "willing"?'

'If it were a dog of mine, or a horse of mine, or a wolf

124

I had captured, or a thing I had hunted and brought to bay, I would have mercy on it,' he said.

'And this mercy, would it be mercy on the creature, or on the pain in your own soul inflicted by what you see? We are forbidden murder absolutely, even to relieve such horror as she arouses. Begone.'

He stood his ground. A flush of colour spread over his face. He said hoarsely, 'If you keep her, prepare to find that she is pregnant.'

'What?' cried the abbess. He did not answer. 'She is only a child,' she said. 'It is not possible.'

'I do not know about these things,' he said, hanging his head. 'But she may be old enough . . .'

'Where did you find her?' asked the abbess. 'You must tell me.'

'With the shepherds on the high pasture, many miles from here. Rough young men.'

'Go on.'

'It is not fit to speak.'

'Go on.'

'They said she had killed a lamb with her bare hands. They caught her. They had tied her over a ram's back. They were using her . . .' He spoke now in a muted whisper.

The abbess rose to her feet. 'God curse them!' she cried. 'By Holy Mary, the Divine Mother, by the blood of her son, Christ Jesus, by the Holy Catholic Church, by every saint in heaven, and every saint as yet unknown here on earth, by every prayer I have ever said, by all the merits earned by every nun at Sant Clara, past and present, I curse the men you speak of! May they be damned in the deepest pit of hell and share the sufferings of Lucifer!'

'No!' he said. 'Take it back. You cannot blame them . . .'

'Christ have mercy on me!' she said. 'What do you mean?'

'It's a sin, of course,' he said. 'And a black one. They are rough men. But they spend months at a time up on the bare mountain, far from their womenfolk. They resort to their ewes for relief. What did you think would happen if a girl started running around up there among the flocks, showing her bottom?'

The abbess swayed on her feet. She reached out blindly for the chair to support herself, and lost her balance. Seeing her faint, a dozen of her nuns came running and carried her within.

Shortly, Sor Agnete came out to Guillem, standing defiantly under the fig tree. 'She is recovering,' said Sor Agnete. 'She bids me tell you go in peace; she will pray for you.'

Guillem put his hat on, and went.

The abbey chaplain, Pare Aldonza, was very elderly. He was a humble man of modest capacities who had worked hard in a remote parish for many years, and whose position at Sant Clara had been given him to ease his last few years with some comfort and light labours. His was the care also of the scattered folk who farmed or fished in the few hamlets this side of the mountain. He was very agitated to be summoned to the abbess's bed to find her in great distress, and uncertain health.

'I have heard such a terrible thing,' she told him, 'as I can barely believe . . .'

'Oh yes,' he said, when he understood what she was asking, 'it is common, Mother. The shepherds confess it, and do penance.'

'What penance can you give for such a sin as that?' she asked. She was deeply distressed.

Pare Aldonza was nonplussed. He disliked being the bearer of harsh truths. But no nun, he knew, likes to find herself out of touch with the world, especially the dark side of it. They all flatter themselves that they have intimate knowledge of all they have renounced or sought shelter from. He decided on harshness.

'I give them three days' breaking stones and filling holes in the road, usually,' he said. 'How do you think the miles of track to Sant Clara are kept more or less in repair?'

the road up to the big church in the mountains is maintained by sinners.

15

'This may not be so difficult,' said Beneditx. The two men were sitting at ease on the colonnade outside Palinor's room, or between their rooms, rather, for on his return from the Galilea with a trunk of books Beneditx had settled himself into the rooms at the other end of the airy balcony. Joffre had set a table and chairs at the end of the space presently shaded from the sun, and Dolca had brought a jug of lemon juice and a basket of figs. Some time after she left them, her voice could be heard, mingling with the sound of tumbling water from below, where she knelt on a wet rock, washing Palinor's shirt. She sang something wild and plangent, with a sweet high voice like a woodland bird.

'There is an elegant short cut that might appeal to you,' said Beneditx, eagerly opening his notes. 'First you are to imagine God. You are to imagine, that is, a being possessed of every perfection. Can you do that?'

'I am to imagine a being perfectly good, perfectly powerful, with perfect knowledge, and so on?'

'Precisely. You are to imagine one than whom nothing more perfect can be conceived.'

Palinor leaned back in his chair, and closed his eyes. His eyelids, which were thickly fringed with dark lashes, were the colour of a purple tarnish, darker than the hue of his countenance, as though he had been made of fine bronze, differentially weathered in light and air. 'Done,' he said.

'But now,' said Beneditx, 'how could you assert that this being that you imagine does not exist? For a being in all particulars exactly like the one you have imagined, but existing, would be more perfect, and therefore would be greater than the non-existent one. But you were to imagine the most perfect being possible. To have understood the definition of God correctly is to understand that he must exist, by definition, in the same way as a man who has understood what a triangle is must know that it has three angles equal to one hundred and eighty degrees.'

Palinor laughed. 'I wish I had such power,' he said, 'as to call something into being simply by imagining it. Is this a serious proof?'

Beneditx hesitated. Should he admit at once that St Thomas did not think this proof held water? No; why should he blunt one of his own barbs? 'It was offered by St Anselm,' he said. 'I don't think he was joking.'

'Well,' said Palinor, 'suppose I imagined a perfect outcome to this escapade: a ship from Aclar, coming to rescue me. And suppose I told you that this ship must exist, because a real one is more perfect than an imaginary one, would you run down to the harbour in expectations of seeing it coming?'

'I do not believe in Aclar,' said Beneditx. 'I asked everyone at the Galilea, and nobody had ever heard of it. There is no such place.'

'What exists when I imagine your most perfect God, or a ship from Aclar,' said Palinor, 'is an idea of the thing in my mind. But an idea in my mind is not a ship in the harbour. It is madness to get confused about that. You have proved to me that I can imagine what you mean by God. But I never denied that God could be imagined; it is only too clear to me that he can be.'

'Well, this proof is notoriously contentious,' said Beneditx. 'I have always rather liked it myself, but I will not pursue it. There are other ways to come at the matter.'

'Before we leave the sophistical St Anselm,' said

Palinor, 'can I point out to you that it is a very different thing to prove something to the satisfaction of somebody who has never doubted it and to find a proof that overcomes doubt? This proof that defines God into existence – you say you like it. But it was not this that convinced you, I think. You believed already when you first heard it.'

'Yes I did,' said Beneditx. 'Everyone on Grandinsula believes in God.'

'I can agree that anyone who knows what a triangle is knows a good deal about the angles it contains,' Palinor continued. 'But that is not to know that anything in the real world is actually a triangle.'

'You should grant me, I think,' said Beneditx, 'some authority about belief, since I come from an island rich in faith, and you from a country where it is hard to find.'

Palinor smiled at him. 'I know more, perhaps, than you expect about ideas of God, since this sort of discussion is the delight of my circle of friends at home, and many of them believe in and worship God in some form or other; but it is whether these ideas correspond to anything in reality that is precisely the ground of our disagreement.'

'You wouldn't disagree if I said that there is such a thing as truth?'

'No,' said Palinor. 'I'll grant you that.'

'That is self-evident,' said Beneditx, his expression once more lit with eagerness. 'For whoever denies the existence of truth asserts that truth does not exist. How, then, could such a one deny that the proposition "Truth does not exist" is true? But if there is anything true, there must be truth. God is truth itself. All discourse, therefore, all statements in all sciences, all refutations and disproofs contain the idea of God, because they contain the idea of truth. Even the notion of falsity contains the idea of truth. The existence

130

of God is self-evident, everywhere assumed, even when men believe themselves to be talking of other things.'

'Alas, my friend,' said Palinor sweetly, 'there is a flaw in your reasoning. I would say rather, if there is anything true, there must be *truths*. A very different statement from yours.'

'Surely for a statement to be true, it must partake of the truth?'

'I would not put it that way, Beneditx, and some of our difficulty in agreeing arises from the fact that we put things differently, and how you put things makes a considerable difference to how they seem.'

'Well, tell me how you would put it,' said Beneditx.

'I would not think of truth as single, like a great ocean, but as multiple, like many rivers,' said Palinor. 'If I say to you that the bird singing on the branch there is a warbler, how would you discover the truth of my statement? The truth of a statement that names something could be confirmed in a book of names, or by asking a speaker of the language in which the name is uttered. If I tell you that my servant can swim, the truth of the statement can be discovered by throwing him in the river; if I tell you that in my country the sun sets at midnight on midsummer day you will need to travel there at the right season to confirm it, and so on. Each of these statements is true in a different way, and a different process of confirmation – or, of course, of refutation – is required for each, although the words "true" and "false" are used to describe the results of all the investigations. In the many different kinds of procedure needed to verify things, I would find evidence that truth is of many kinds: were there such a thing as "The Truth", surely one way of investigating matters would always reveal it. You say that God is truth itself – could he be said to be truths?'

'That doesn't sound right at all,' said Beneditx. 'For God is one and unchanging.'

'You see what a difference it makes when one uses a different way of speaking,' said Palinor. 'The existence of truths does not so easily lead one to say that there is one overriding truth for God to be. Of course, if you can lead me from truths to one truth, I will gladly follow you. All you will then need to do is to prove the identity of this one truth with the God of your belief.'

Like a chess player who has lost some small advantage in the opening game, Beneditx took the measure of his opponent, perceiving him formidable. Formidable, and unlike the opponents imagined in the books with which Beneditx was so familiar. There were warning words about the difficulty of dealing with men who did not accept the Scriptures in the opening words of the great *Summa Contra Gentiles* of St Thomas; Beneditx had quoted them to Severo. But Palinor was not like any kind of gentile envisaged by the saint, as far as Beneditx could see, except in the absence of shared ground on which to refute him. It was not so much that Beneditx really understood why Palinor should be so interested in the different means of checking the truth of things as to divide truth on account of them; he was not a practical man, and investigation was a word to him rather than a process. But he had seen at once that it would take some preparation and some deep consideration to embark on an attempt to prove that all truths were one. Instead, he decided to call a halt to the discussion for that day, and think further.

'I am at your disposal,' said Palinor, with ironic courtesy. 'And, Beneditx, I am very bored.' Seeing Beneditx's expression, he added hastily, 'Not in the least while we talk together, but in the long hours spent here without occupation. Would anyone mind, do you think, if I turned my attention to improving the flow of water through these gardens? Whose permission would I need?'

'Severo's, I imagine,' said Beneditx. 'I will mention

it to him when I write; but I will take it upon myself to give permission meanwhile.'

Palinor thanked him and wandered off into the gardens, exploring the various streams and walking beside them against the direction of flow, learning their origin. As though to side with Beneditx against him they diverged from a single forceful spring that filled a deep basin on top of a tall cliff, overhanging the narrowing valley of the garden, and spilled in a waterfall of considerable force and height. The waterfall hit a tumble of rocks and was deflected into multiple streamlets. Though as a dialectician Palinor could make no use of such a flow, as an engineer he found it satisfactory, and he began to make drawings and seek from the gardeners to know where he might acquire clay pipes.

16

Josefa was anxious on being summoned to speak with the abbess and Sor Agnete. 'Have I done something wrong, Mother?' she asked.

'Not at all, child,' said the abbess. 'It is just that we need to know something. When you have cleaned and tended the wolf-child, have you found blood?'

'There is often blood, Mother,' said Josefa. 'She seems not to feel pain, and cuts and scrapes herself constantly.'

'We meant monthly blood,' said Sor Agnete.

Josefa looked startled. 'She is too young,' she said.

'We thought so,' said the abbess. 'But it is hard to be sure.'

'We must be practical,' said Sor Agnete. 'Have you washed her since she was brought back to us?'

'No, Sor Agnete. I thought it best to let her rest. She loathes water, and she seemed frantic.'

'I will come and help you bathe her when you think she has recovered a little,' said Sor Agnete.

They found blood. They found injury also. But even if they had not found either, Josefa would have guessed that some outrage had befallen the child during her escape, because she seemed to be for the first time cowed, for the first time half willing to be handled, as though she had learned to divide detested humanity into friend and foe. Josefa even found her, the following evening, trying to crawl into the tatters of the ripped-off shift from the night before, pre-empting the struggle to dress her by

134

dressing herself, though she could not manage it.

Then, before any softening in the child's feelings could unfold, she fell ill. For the first time she left meat uneaten in her dish. Flies buzzed on the darkened meat, and crawled on the child's face. The fuzz of soft dark curls that had regrown on her head was stuck to her scalp with sweat. The sisters carried her from the watchtower which had so long been her home, and put her in the infirmary. Sor Blancha made up some drink to bring her fever down, but she would not take it, and soon sores erupted all over her body. A row of blisters marked the edge of her lips, and she tossed and whimpered night and day, rubbing the sores till they oozed foul matter and bled. Josefa sat at her bedside, gently rubbing an ointment prepared by Sor Blancha into the ever increasing and spreading sores. Those on the child's knees and elbows and on the knuckles of the first joints in her fingers broke through the callouses of thick skin that her manner of running had made, and she could not bear any covering except the lightest and smoothest sheet. She seemed not to feel the cold, but Sor Blancha was afraid to leave her uncovered when she was feverish, even though the infirmary was the only room in the convent kept warm at that time of year, so the best sheets were laid over her, and carried away stained. At length the child had no more strength even to cast off the sheet, or lift her head to drink, and Sor Blancha feared she was dying.

The abbess sent a message to Severo, telling him of the child's danger, but not of her escape, for the two things were not necessarily connected, and she saw no need. Severo sent a doctor, choosing for the task a famous man from among the *conversos*, – Jews who had submitted to Christianity thirty years before to escape an outbreak of fervour in the Inquisition. Such a man was not supposed to practise medicine, but the sick have no scruples, only need of help, and the *conversos* were widely believed to have a better fund of knowledge and skill than Christian doctors, who too easily prescribed submission to the will of God. Severo told him nothing about his patient, only to ride to Sant Clara and save the child if he could.

The doctor was called Melchor Fortessa, and he was old enough to find the journey to Sant Clara a great matter. Nevertheless, a convert always lived in the island on sufferance, and could not afford to refuse a request from Severo, nor be dilatory in performing it. Melchor managed the long ride over the mountains, and on arrival stayed in the guest-house only long enough to wash off the dust of the road before asking to see his patient.

A curious sight met him when he entered the infirmary. A young nun, coarse-featured and with large hands, was leaning over the bed. An expression of intense concentration and tenderness suffused her features, and she was in the act of applying an unguent. The patient, who was covered with terrible weeping sores, was lying in a strange position, very twisted, and was very wasted. He rolled up his sleeves and examined her, lifting her sunken eyelids, and attempting to straighten her limbs. Josefa and Sor Eulalie watched him.

'This is a very severe spasm,' he said. 'How long has she been like this?'

'She was bent before she was ill, sir,' said Josefa. Her eyes were fixed on the doctor's face. He was very old, with long wispy white hair and a flowing beard. His complexion was sallow and heavily wrinkled. But it seemed to Josefa that he was kindly, and she was burning with a painful despairing hope that he might bring help.

'What has caused this rigidity, I wonder?' he said, running his long blunt fingers along the thin bones of the child's legs. 'Was it from birth?'

136

'We do not know,' said Sor Eulalie. 'But she was like that when she was consigned to our care.'

'Was she also starving?' he asked. 'How does it come about in a house of charity that I am called to a patient and find her starving?'

'We have great difficulty feeding her, sir,' said Josefa. 'She refuses all sustenance except raw meat. We have tried feeding her with everything we can think of, without success.'

'Odd,' he said. 'I must ask you to retire while I examine her intimately.' Once he was alone in the whitewashed, barrel-vaulted room, smelling of herbs and the sour odour of sickness, he picked up and smelt the jar of unguent and, bending over the child, again tried to draw out the crooked legs. Whimpering, she opened her eyes, and at the sight of him seemed terrified. He frowned. Everything about this case was curious.

Later he presented himself in front of the abbess. Sor Agnete, the abbess's eyes and her second opinion, was there as always.

'I confess I am baffled,' he said. 'I can offer some advice, but I am not sure of its efficacy, because I have never seen a case like this before. Can you tell me more about her?'

'Only that she came to us in the state in which you see her. The cardinal has appointed himself her protector, and consigned her to us. We have done all that we can; Sor Blancha has made up herbal medicine . . .'

'Can I speak to Sor Blancha?' he asked.

Sor Blancha was summoned, and reported on exactly what was in her concoctions.

'Good,' said Melchor. 'You have done well. But the source of the trouble is not the site of the trouble. You are treating a disorder of the skin, but it is not because the skin is disordered that she suffers these blemishes,

137

but because she is malnourished. A way must be found to feed her properly, or she will die very quickly.'

'We have tried everything except the most extreme force to persuade her,' said Sor Blancha, 'Nothing works.'

'You will try milk sweetened with honey,' he said, 'very little honey. Then very gradually you will add meal to the milk until it is a thin gruel.'

'We will try, sir, but I doubt of our success.'

'I am going to give you something else to add to the milk,' said Melchor. 'It is a powerful elixir. Once you have insinuated a few drops of it she will be frantic for more of it, and I think she will drink.'

'And afterwards?' said Sor Blancha. 'When the elixir is all gone? What then?'

Melchor reflected that the sister he was talking to had some experience of the world – she knew enough to fear to follow his advice. 'Then she will be difficult for some days. There is a risk attached to giving elixirs. We must take this risk, because if she will not eat better food, she will die. Now let me advise you about the spasm. If she is not released from it, she will never walk, nor even sit normally for the rest of her life. Who nurses her?'

'Several of us,' said Sor Agnete. 'But mostly Sor Blancha, and our novice Josefa.'

Melchor looked at Sor Blancha's arthritic hands and said he would train the novice. Then he told Sor Blancha that she should coat her hands in hot wax several times a week and leave it to cool on her hands if she would delay the progress of the stiffness and pain in the finger joints. Then for the second time in a month the abbess was confronted by a layman demanding to speak to her alone. She had her chair put in the cloister garden once again, and let him have his audience.

'It is hard for a doctor, lady, to advise on a case about which the truth is withheld from him,' he said.

'The child was rescued from extreme neglect,' she said, 'and it is our duty to gentle her and teach her if we can.'

'You have had the care of her for some months?'

'Yes.'

'She has recently been violently assaulted,' he said.

'She escaped. She was brought back to us in the condition in which you find her.'

'Was she walking and talking when she escaped?'

'No. She could do neither.'

'A child of that age?'

The abbess saw her chance. 'Of what age do you estimate her to be?' she asked.

'Somewhere between eleven and thirteen,' he said.

'Surely not . . . She is not large enough . . .' Collecting herself, she said unhappily, 'The men who recaptured her taught me to fear that she might be pregnant. I had thought she was too young.'

'It is not likely in one so ill-grown and mal-nourished,' he said. 'Nature usually protects the most grossly unfortunate.'

'I would have said it was God who protects,' she reproved him.

'Neither God nor nature has been sufficiently vigilant here,' he said. 'I have never seen so damaged a child. But now we will rely on the diligence of your good novice, and we will have some improvement, I think. How much will depend on what native intelligence the girl has. She may be able to respond. We must hope so.'

It had seemed to Josefa that the child would surely die. It had seemed to Josefa to be the most terrible thing that could happen. The child was in many ways appalling, repellent. Looking after it was a chain of disgusting and unpleasant tasks, a dispiriting drudgery, which had fallen on her shoulders while her sisters serenely lived their calm and uplifting days. It is a burden to be hated; it is a burden to reach out towards a creature who always flinches, to speak to a creature who never answers, to use kindness that is repaid unvaryingly by snarls, bites and scratches, to keep company with a creature who is wretched, and constantly pining to flee away. Pity is soon beaten into the ground by such trials, even a rampant pity like Josefa's. But the child needed her with a simple and absolute need, the need for food. While it would eat only meat, and only Josefa could prepare it, it needed her as a babe needs a mother's breast. While it would eat only meat, the whole sisterhood needed Josefa, in order to keep their promise to the cardinal, and although she was modest, she saw the importance that she was given.

A strange emotion flows between the helpless and the helper. It binds like rods of iron. Josefa thought of nothing but Amara, day and night, and was hard put to it to pray, except for Amara. If she was at holy office or commanded on some other task for an hour, she was full of fear and a fierce physical need to return, like a woman who has put down a baby at the corner of the harvest field and who runs on her errand and runs back again all the way. Josefa had looked after her brothers, and they had needed her in a way, but they could walk, they could ask for what they wanted. That had been different. Now only she could truly understand the child's diseased behaviour, because she had watched for longest, she had thought about her hardest. The other sisters, she could feel in her bones, though no such words were spoken, had given up, had concluded that the child was a hopeless case. The more dejected they became, the more they turned their attention to other things, the more passionately Josefa drove herself. She would never give up. She would never desert her charge. The child would live, the child would walk, the child would speak, or she, Josefa, would die in the attempt to save her.

'We shall have a broken spirit there, if she fails,' said Sor Lucia to Sor Blancha, watching Josefa carrying water from the stove to the infirmary. But Josefa would not even think about failing. She would have called her feeling – a heady brew of fascination and revulsion – a struggle to devote herself to her duty; she might have called it hope, perhaps. She would not have called it love.

At least, after Melchor's visit, they had instructions, could follow his instructions to the letter. Sor Blancha gave the child sips of milk, laced with three drops of the elixir he had left for her and sweetened with honey. While she was still feverish, they gave her water also. And Josefa's special task, massaging the child's legs and arms, was begun at once. Seven times a day he had prescribed, and Josefa marked the times by the canonical hours. While her sisters knelt and prayed and sang the ancient music with which God had been praised from time immemorial, Josefa dipped her hands in lamp oil and rubbed Amara's limbs. First she straightened a leg as far as it would go, and then gently pummelling with her fingertips, she worked on the muscle to loosen it further. As she worked she talked and sang softly. First one leg, then the other, then the arms, then the hands, working the thumb across the palm, touching its tip to the tip of the little finger, making each finger move independently of the others.

Whatever the elixir was, the child became frantic for it. Eagerly she would drink the milk in which it was given to her, even consenting to suck it from the rim of the dish in the likeness of human drinking when she was too weak to raise herself on all fours and lap at it, as she had always done before. In her eagerness she would reach out her hands for the dish and draw it towards her mouth, so that she was holding it in

141

human fashion and raising it to her lips. It seemed she could never have enough of it, and though she spat and whimpered at first when a little meal was added to the milk, she still drank it, and licked round the dish when she had finished it. Greatly daring, Josefa made a mash of vegetables, cooked so soft they were almost liquid, and added to that three drops from Melchor's bottle, and Amara ate it.

At some time in the month after Melchor's visit – it would have been impossible to put a finger on the exact moment – the child turned a corner. Her fever abated, and a pale ring of healed skin spread slowly round the sores and grew inwards, very delicate and tender at first, but clearly healing. A day came when Josefa returned to the infirmary from the kitchen and found that Amara had climbed out of bed and was moving slowly round the floor. She ran to Josefa at once, reaching for the dish she was bringing. Josefa, on impulse held it high, out of reach. The child pulled herself up, dragging on the bedstead with one hand and reaching out with the other. She was half standing before Josefa let her have the dish. The moment she had it in her hand she tipped it, and spilled it, and went down at once upon the floor to lap it up, but Josefa had seen the way forward. She had seen also that the child's legs were crooked at less acute an angle than before. She massaged Amara with renewed energy, born of hope, and she began to talk to her about the outside world, about walking in the woods, or by the shore, or buying fish and bread from the markets.

By teasing her with the dish, the dish of ever thicker and more nourishing gruel, or with the meat she was still allowed each second day, it was possible by and by to make the child stand briefly on her hind legs to reach it. Later, Josefa's walking backwards in front of her, holding it out, would make her take two or three staggering steps, half upright. Very slowly the crook in her legs was unlocking, and she was able partly to straighten up if she urgently wanted to. She had become accustomed to the people she saw every day, though she still ran away and hid in corners from anyone else. She seemed to be reconciled to clothing some of the time, and would even try to struggle into her shift when she was hungry, holding it clumsily in her unpractised hands. Days passed all the same at Sant Clara, except for the slow swing of the seasons, and the time all this was taking did not worry anybody; they knew no reason why it should matter if it took half a lifetime to achieve.

Then months of tending the child suddenly overcame Josefa, and she herself fell ill.

Amara is like condensed evolution

17

On reflection, Beneditx felt some relief at the failure
of his a priori proof. If the a priori proof were really
unanswerable, then it would be difficult to see how to
defend anyone who had ever heard it from the charge
of apostasy from the truth. Beneditx, who was a man
of the utmost gentleness, revolted from the idea that
by putting an indefeasible proposition to his opponent
he had entrapped him into condemnation. Seen in
that light, it might appear that he was engaged in
a lethal trick, played upon a helpless fellow man.
But St Thomas had rejected the ontological proof,
very fortunately. Beneditx knew his books. He knew
also the peril in which Palinor stood. The Church
was not likely to persecute an adherent of a strange
religion, merely for having been born in the wrong
country, having learned a false creed, being ignorant
of the truth. Such a person could be in good faith;
and in good faith or not, did not affront the pious
true believer unless he proselytized. But a person who
had once received the truth, who had been a member
of the Holy Catholic Church, fell for ever under her
jurisdiction. For someone who has known the word
of God to reject it, then pursue false gods, there is
no defence. The sin of rejecting the truth once it is
known is so terrible that those who commit it must be
hunted down, forced to admit their guilt, and punished
by death. Beneditx had never doubted this.
   The contumacious and rebellious folk who brought
this down upon themselves were usually Christian

144

heretics – Cathars, Donatists, Pelagians, or the nameless confused who were seized of some garbled version, some misunderstood doctrine, and refused to be corrected and chastened by their Holy Mother, the Church. Beneditx, who had seen every possible confusion arising among his students at the Galilea, who had seen how swiftly a thinking man needs guidance, and who knew very well how little teaching the common people had from their parish priests, felt as much sympathy for error and hatred of inquisition as any man could.

The problem was that Palinor could not avail himself of the argument that any Saracen or exotic foreigner could use – that he was of another allegiance, and outside the scope of the Church. Not, that is, if what he was denying was not some particular part of the teaching of the Church, but something known to all men, either by innate illumination, or by the light of natural reason. It simply was not open to him to deny God. It was a most impudent and terrible blasphemy, worse than any heresy about the nature of Christ, or the foreknowledge of God, or free will or any such thing. And what excuse could be imagined for such an error in such a man? Not for him the exculpation of the stupid, that he had been misled, mistaught.

But of course, if Beneditx could convert him by force of reason, the question of what he ought always and from birth to have known would have only a historical interest, being overtaken by a present enlightenment. Beneditx could not believe that the pleasant and intelligent man who confronted him could really be unconvincible – Beneditx was a man who had faith in reason. He set about preparing to expound the proofs St Thomas did think valid; there were five of them, when one, surely, should be enough. And having prepared himself, he went cheerfully to his next encounter with Palinor.

In a green and shady garden walk, with a brooklet

channelled to run beside it, making a pleasant sound beside their steps, the two men walked slowly. 'Firstly, nothing in nature moves, unless it be moved by something else,' Beneditx opened. 'As a rod that is brandished is moved by a man who holds it. But this mover must itself be moved by some other thing, and that other thing by yet another . . . This cannot go on endlessly, receding to infinity, because then there would be no first mover, and consequently no other mover. Therefore it is necessary to arrive at a first mover, put in motion by no other, and this everyone understands to be God.'

'I am to answer this?' asked Palinor.

'Wait; I will lay three stout foundations of belief before you, and you will see if you are not convinced by them.'

'I am in your hands, my friend,' said Palinor. He spoke gravely, but with an undertow of affection, amusement almost. He was experiencing the pleasure a cultivated adult feels in the presence of a marvellous child, whose perception is acute, and innocent. Besides, nobody could mistake the eagerness Beneditx evinced in his efforts to persuade him, or fail to see how well-meaning, how would-be benign, was the attempt. Obviously Palinor could see more clearly than Beneditx how hard a thing was being embarked upon; but as in the case of the romantic ambitions of a child, it was kinder not to be too crushing.

'So, secondly,' Beneditx continued, 'in the sensible world around us, we find that there are chains of causation. One thing causes another thing, and in its turn is the effect of some previous cause. Nothing can be its own cause, for to do so it would have to be prior to itself, which is impossible. But it is not possible for the chain of causes to recede to infinity, because then there would be no first cause, and therefore no effects, since to remove the cause is to remove the effect. The presence to our senses, therefore, of causes and effects compels us to put forward an uncaused cause, a first efficient cause, to which everyone gives the name of God.

'Thirdly, we find in nature things that could either exist or not exist, since they are generated and then corrupted, they are born and then die. It is impossible for these always to exist, for that which can one day cease to exist must at some time not have existed. Therefore, if everything could cease to exist, then at one time there could have been nothing in existence. If this were true, then even now there would be nothing in existence, because that which does not exist comes into being by something already existing. Therefore, if at one time nothing was in existence, it would be impossible for anything to come into existence, and thus even now nothing would exist, which is absurd. Therefore, not all beings are merely possible, but there must exist something the existence of which is necessary. But a necessary thing has its necessity caused by something else; and we cannot go to infinity in a chain of necessary things, as we saw in relation to movers and to causes, so we cannot but postulate the existence of some being having of itself its own necessity and not receiving it from another, but rather causing in others their necessity. This all men speak of as God.'

There was a silence while Palinor contemplated this. They reached the end of the garden walk, where it opened upon a prospect down the valley, a widening and gently sloping outlook on orange orchards and the silvery green colour of the olive trees beyond, lightening and darkening in the breeze of morning like wind on lake-water.

'These arguments amount to the same,' said Palinor. 'Everything that moves is moved by something else; therefore there is something which moves everything that moves. Every effect is brought about by a cause; therefore there is some cause which has brought about every effect. Or, to continue, every road goes somewhere, therefore there is somewhere to which every road goes; every river has a source, therefore there is some spring which is the source of every river; every son has a mother, therefore there is someone who is mother to every son; every tool serves a purpose, therefore there is a purpose which is served by every tool . . . Need I go on?'

'Wait,' said Beneditx. 'You speak like a man who, seeing that a twig springs from a branch and that many twigs spring from many branches, denies the existence of a trunk to the tree. Follow the multiplicity back and back, and you will find the single trunk.'

'Follow it further and you will find the dividing multiplicity of roots. And stand back, you will find the tree one of thousands in the forest. The trouble here, Beneditx, is that you assert that things in the world around us are impossible, and require an explanation, and you offer God as the explanation. But the world around us is not, to me, in doubt, nor does it stand in need of explanation. It seems to me that what exists before our eyes and to our touch and taste and smell is possible; and what is possible is not impossible. Whereas I do not see a need for God.'

'You will,' said Beneditx, in sudden passion. 'I will bring you the proofs from degree and design – you will see!'

18

Without Josefa the child became recalcitrant again. She would not wear her shifts, she would not attempt to go upright, she sulked and snarled, and resumed the habit of skulking in corners. Sor Blancha tried to coax her back to her best behaviour, but truth to tell the sister resented every moment of it, because she was anxious about Josefa and wanted to nurse and coddle *her*. It was probably just fatigue that had led Josefa to tumble suddenly in a dead faint in chapel, but her lassitude had lasted now for days. The sisters took turns to sit with her, clucked over her, brought her little gifts of flowers, cherished her, and tried to evoke a wan smile on her face.

Meanwhile, the snow-child fretted and prowled, going again on all fours and trying to the limit the patience of whichever nun was guarding her. At first Sor Blancha took no notice of the funny snuffling and coughing sounds the child made while she sat with her. She had brought a task of grinding herbs, and sitting on a stool in the corner of the room to which the child had been consigned, and holding the pestle between her knees, she worked the mortar round and round, taking no notice. The child came closer. She was shaking her head violently, like a person who sneezes. 'Ssfa! Ssfa!' She crept close to Sor Blancha, and pulled at her hems. Then she lolloped to the door, and scratched at it, coughing away, 'Ssfa! Ssfa!' and whimpering.

Sor Blancha looked up. She tried to find some compassion for the poor wretch, so baffled and incapable, and now lacking her most familiar attendant. What was it she wanted, scraping the door and crying like that?

'Josefa will be back . . .' she began to say.

'Ssfa! Ssfa!' the child uttered.

Then, with her spine tingling, and her scalp prickling, Sor Blancha realized what she was hearing. She put down her mortar of herbs, and taking her skirt in her hand, and flinging open the door, she seized the child with her free hand, and ran with her, calling her sisters, calling the abbess. Like fluttered doves in a coop, the nuns came running at her call, flocking to the courtyard. The child loped around them, looking up into the ring of faces and whimpering. 'Ssfa!' she said. 'Ssfa!'

'Listen!' said Sor Blancha. 'Oh, listen to that!'

'Praise be!' said Sor Agnete, 'She is trying to say "Josefa". She is speaking to us at last!'

'It must work,' said the abbess. 'She must find that it works. Take her to Josefa at once!'

When the door to Josefa's cell was opened, the child stopped short, as though she could smell sickness. Then she loped in and brushed her face against Josefa's limply dangling hand, and said again the 'Ssfa, Ssfa,' sound. Then she bounded up onto the bed and curled herself at Josefa's feet. Josefa opened her eyes, and said to Sor Blancha, hanging over her anxiously, 'Is it Amara? Can she stay?'

The nuns retired to the chapel to give thanks to God, for they were forbidden to let the child hear them. But this simple limping pair of syllables having opened a vista of hope to them, they battered the ears of the Almighty day and night for weeks that he might let his servant the wolf-child find tongue and bear witness to his glory.

From that moment, instead of just chattering to the child, the sisters began to teach her. They began the great game of pointing and naming, greeting mumbles and broken sounds with pleasure, and rewarding anything remotely like the desired word with smiles, and praise, and promises of meat. Josefa got up and applied herself so eagerly to this task that she had to be ordered to take her hours of sleep. But her eagerness was matched by everyone else's. That instinct to foster, to cherish and teach, that flow of tenderness towards the helpless which was dammed up in the nuns by their childlessness, suddenly found an object and a purpose – a purpose moreover which was blessed by sacred obedience.

Like any child, Amara played one sister off against another, ran away and hid when Josefa looked for her to massage her legs, refused to eat at mealtimes, and then begged pitifully for food an hour later, discovered quickly where the soft hearts and swiftly relenting natures were to be found. 'She doesn't lack native wit, thank heaven,' said Sor Agnete, talking to the abbess.

'Why should she?' the abbess asked. 'She could hardly have survived in the mountains without what you are calling native wit. And she must have survived there for some time.'

'It is just that it had occurred to me to wonder . . . The strangeness of such a child might be the result of her having been abandoned to the wolves. Or she might have been abandoned to the wolves because there was something wrong with her.'

'Keep that thought to yourself,' said the abbess.

Through the mild winter and the brief spring and into the heat of summer, Amara went on learning easily. She knew several dozen words, and added several more each day. She knew 'meat' and 'milk' and 'water' and 'out'; she knew 'bed' and 'blanket'; she could call 'Yossefa!' and 'Blancha!'; she could name chickens and cows, and olives and oranges, she even began to sing, a sort of tuneless humming, joining Josefa's voice when Josefa sang to her. And at last Amara's legs would straighten, and she could stand upright. She had changed so little for so long and was now changing so fast that Josefa was dazzled. Standing upright, she came to Josefa's shoulders – she no longer looked very small, very young; it was possible to believe that she might be thirteen or fourteen. She did look pitifully thin – a whiplash, narrow figure, her shift hanging loose on her, a tumble of dark hair surrounding a narrow face. She hung her head slightly, and looked on the world from under a tilting brow, with eyes that seemed never to catch the light. Seeing her moving carefully across the cloister, a stranger might not have noticed anything odd; not unless he saw her eat.

At home in Taddeo Arta's house, Josefa had had the care of her two brothers. When she remembered them, she was troubled. Not about them; she trusted her father to look after his sons. Nor even from missing their company, they had been rough and lordly with her, troublesome and rebellious. No; rather it was the difference her recollection cast between her growing brothers and the wolf-child's growth. Those brothers had never sat still for an instant, knew not an idle moment, tumbled, climbed, fought and ran every moment of the waking day, made treasures out of toys, stones, olive pits, cried 'Mine!' and came to blows or tears over possession of them, nosed into every box, crook and cranny of the house, their inexhaustible curiosity leaving trails of cracked crocks, lost pins, spilled bottles, overset baskets wherever they went. They came weeping to Josefa to be comforted for the tiniest scratch; if she asked them for something or commanded them in something – 'Give me that' – or 'Come here' – they obeyed or argued at once. Their chatter was full of yesterday and tomorrow: yesterday Father had taken them to the rope-walk with him, tomorrow they would visit Aunt Ana, and ride her donkey.

Amara needed to exercise, and ran in the orchard for an hour each morning. But once indoors she simply sat down and stayed, for hours at a time. Her stillness was not thoughtfulness, nor boredom, it seemed to Josefa, but simply that of one who needed no occupation. She had been given things: her own bed, in a cell next to Josefa's; a little duck carved in wood by one of the gardeners, a string of beads made from a broken rosary. She left things lying as indifferently as the stones in the path, she showed no attachment to anything, and could not be taught the word 'mine'. Josefa could show her things, like the inside of her little workbox or the farm sheds where tackle and harness and plough were stored, but she never looked into anything herself, or opened any lid or door. She seemed to feel no pain, and sought no sympathy, and if Josefa had not watched carefully, Amara's feet and hands would have been covered with unwashed and unregarded cuts and grazes and nettle-stings.

Josefa could talk to Amara, and Amara responded, but never herself started any conversation, except to ask for food. She would answer questions – 'What is this, Amara?' – but never asked any. Strangest of all, Josefa thought, anxiously watching her companion, was the absence of recollection in Amara's world. Anything she named in her husky, limping voice was in front of her eyes; she never named something seen yesterday, or understood a promise for tomorrow. The only thing she ever asked for when it was not present was meat. Perhaps her world was without time, for another odd thing was how sometimes she would take no notice at all of a request or a question for so long that Josefa would have assumed it not heard or not understood. Then suddenly Amara would answer, naming the orange held out to her half an hour earlier,

153

or going to stand by the door many minutes after Josefa asked if she would like to walk.

The sisters were ill-placed to perceive how strange Amara's preference for solitude was, how unlike a child it was to like to sit vacantly for hours, unmoving and alone. But Josefa knew. And only Josefa knew another thing. Though Amara did not resist her massage, and liked to be with Josefa, would have slept every night, if she had been allowed, curled up at the foot of Josefa's bed, yet she disliked being touched, and could not endure being held; if Josefa put her arms round Amara, she jerked into a violent rigor, trembling, with her face constricted, and her lips drawn back over clenched and grinding teeth.

can't love

19

Severo sat with a pile of vellums on the desk in front of him. *'Severo, miseratione divina episcopus Grandillensis. Salutem in domine sempiternam . . .'* Below the formal upper lines the documents dealt with the business of the diocese. A priest ordered to put aside a mistress. A merchant ordered to pay a tithe or contribute to a church roof; a quarrel over boundaries – two parishes had been fighting and appealing to Severo for the whole of his tenure on a disputed jurisdiction over a single farm of three fields. Severo signed and sighed. The room was chokingly hot; there had been no rain for weeks, and the dust of the city coated the leaves of the trees in the little garth below his window.

'Severo miseratione divina etc. etc . . .' Secular documents abbreviated his sacred preamble. Someone wanted to build a house on land belonging to a church and offered a sum which the priest considered insufficient; someone wanted a licence to carve images of the Virgin and sell them in the markets; someone wanted a warrant to travel to the northern coast and someone else wanted an order permitting him to drive a flock of geese through the streets of a town, in order to get them to Ciudad; the townspeople wanted to cull his birds for their own tables as the price of passage, alleging that the foulness the birds left in their streets entitled them to some such compensation. Severo signed and sighed.

At last the documents were all dealt with. Severo stretched, rose, walked to his balcony, and breathed the vapid air. Then he had a sudden welcome thought. It was months since he had sent Beneditx off to convert Palinor, and he had heard no news of them since the initial report from his mentor. The mental picture of the two men walking and talking together in the cool air that flowed down from the mountainside, in the green shades of the garden there, was irresistible. After all, he had intended to place them where he could visit, could oversee them. When Rafal came to collect the signed papers and take them to the cathedral office, he said, 'Get some horses saddled up, Rafal; we are going to the country!'

It was an hour's ride across the burning plain before the road entered the grateful shade of pine trees and began to ascend, and the two men were covered with the grey-brown dust thrown round them in a cloud by their horses' hooves when they reached that point. The mountains which towered up behind the valley of Alquiera were shimmering in the harsh light. When the road turned sharply and began to run alongside the torrent that debouched from the Alquiera valley they stopped, and Rafal descended to the stream bank and filled his leather bottle with cool water. They drank and splashed their faces, leaving themselves muddied with wet dust but thankful for the relief. Then they rode on.

Severo had known the Saracen's House at Alquiera since his boyhood. It was full of memories for him, memories of play, of escapades. There he had been beaten by his father, for the only time in his life, because he had risked the life of his older brother by leading him in climbing a nearly sheer rock face that ascended to the hanging lake. Like almost any passionately justified punishment it had been un-fair, for Gaspar had in fact been leading him, and Severo's resentment had clouded a whole summer day. The resentment had lasted only as long as the

156

weals, and Gaspar had brought cool water from the fountain to soothe them for him; but lifelong had been the knowledge that if a risk was taken it was Gaspar who mattered. Gaspar was first in succession and would be prince, under the remote suzerainty of the mainland monarchs; he, Severo, was for a Church not short of priests.

Gaspar died in his bed, his reckless climbing and swimming having done him no harm but port fever having taken him in the last year of Severo's studies, when Severo's only ambition was to be good enough to teach theology at the Galilea under Beneditx. The Church had bishoped him once he was prince, and the cardinal's hat had followed, for there was usually a cardinal from this pious island. Severo felt unworthy, and was ashamed of the appetite for governing which gradually unfolded in his secret heart as he exercised power, power that should have been his brother's. Gaspar, of course, had not grown older, and appeared to Severo's memory in the guise of a smiling stripling boy, always restless, always crying 'Let's . . . !' and proposing a game, a journey, a challenge, a race.

Severo was thinking of Gaspar as he rode, when they turned the corner and the Saracen's House came into view. It was a tall house, and rose above the treetops of its surrounding wooded vale. Severo exclaimed with astonishment, for in front of the house, soaring above the treetops and sparkling in the light, was a column of water rising as high as the ridge tiles before turning over and descending in a spreading feathery plume. A drifting mist from the fountain caught the sun and shimmered with a faint rainbow. 'But . . . whatever . . .' Severo drew in his reins, and stared.

'The atheist asked you if he might improve the waters . . . Don't you remember, Holiness?'

'Improve them? But how did he accomplish *that*? How good it sounds!' For the soft roar of falling water

157

reached them from half a mile away. Eagerly Severo
spurred his horse for the last turn of the road.

The servants were put about by his sudden arrival.
The steward asked anxiously which of the two,
Beneditx or Palinor, should be displaced to make
room for Severo. 'Neither,' said Severo firmly.

'But, Holiness, there are no other suitable rooms.'

'I will sleep under the colonnade between the two,'
said Severo. 'Put a straw pallet on the pavement for
me.'

The steward demurred, and while Severo was insist-
ing Palinor came round the corner of the house. A
foreman was with him, carrying a set-square, and they
were deep in talk. Seeing Severo, he broke off, came
forward and slightly inclined his head in greeting.

'Is that your doing?' asked Severo, pointing to the
dancing tower of toppling water.

'I had help from your servants,' said Palinor. 'Do you
like it?'

'It's wonderful!' said Severo. 'When I have washed,
you must tell me how it is contrived.'

'It will clean you faster than a ewerful from the
kitchens,' said Palinor, 'if you don't mind the cold.
Will you swim? I'll ask Dolca to bring towels for us.'

Severo walked round the house with him. There on
the terrace below the colonnade was an ample basin,
hastily built of piled stones, where only a little pool
for the seeping spring had stood before. The great
fountain rose from this basin and fell back into it
noisily. Overcome with desire to be cool, Severo cast
off his clothes.

Hearing laughter as he walked, reciting his office,
in the shade of the garden walk, and supposing the
servants to be fooling around, Beneditx was amazed to
be confronted by a naked cardinal and a naked atheist
capering in and out of the curtains of roaring water,
running through the force of the falls, stumbling, and

submerging and swimming. Rafal, as hot as his master, hesitated on the brink, and then shed his intolerable black soutane and plunged in. More chaste, more careful Beneditx, unable to resist Severo's welcoming call and beckoning hand, merely took off his monk's gown and sat smiling on the rim of the basin, where the splashing water wet him through and ran deliciously on his skin under his soaking shift. By and by his prince and cardinal approached and pulled him in, ducking him under in a baptism of laughter.

Later, as dusk deepened into the velvet summer darkness, they sat on the colonnade. Palinor's beautiful servants set tables, brought simple food and wine in bottles dewy with cold from a basket held under running water which Palinor had contrived. The four men sat round the table, peaceful and content – or so it seemed to Severo. Dolca lit a lamp. Leaning against the wall at the far end of the colonnade, the boy servant played softly on a lute. Far off, somewhere in the unseen woods on the dark further slopes of the valley, a nightingale sang. Nearby, the fountain intoned on an unvarying note.

'Where are we, then, Beneditx?' asked Severo, leaning back in his chair and setting down his empty glass. He had not resumed any of his symbolic garments, but sat at ease in a clean plain shirt and wooden sandals. Only the gold and cornelian ring on his finger, catching the lamplight, signalled him great.

'We are with the proof from degree, I think you said,' said Palinor.

'Expound,' said Severo.

'There is a gradation to be found in things,' said Beneditx. 'All around us there are things, some more and some less good; some more and some less true, noble, beautiful. But "more" and "less" are predicated of things according as they resemble in their different ways something which is "most", as a thing is said to be

159

hotter which more nearly resembles "hottest"; "cooler" which more nearly resembles that which is coolest; so that there is something which is truest, something best, something noblest, and consequently something which most intensely *is*, something which is uttermost being, for the truer things are the more truly they exist. The most complete thing of any kind is the cause of all in that kind, as fire, which is the most complete form of heat, is the cause by which any hot thing is made hot. Therefore there must be something which is to all beings the cause of their being, their goodness, and every other perfection, and this we call God.'

The melody on Joffre's lute made a sweet descent to a conclusion as Beneditx finished.

'There!' said Severo. 'Got you, Palinor, my friend!'

'Not at all,' said Palinor, reaching over and refilling Severo's glass. 'All these proofs of Beneditx's work the same way. They all project backwards – or perhaps I mean upwards, or even onwards, or outwards. From hot and hotter to hottest. And they all simplify, reducing the complexity of the world while trying to use reality as a platform.'

'You must explain to an innocent mind,' said Severo, happily. He smiled at Beneditx across the table. How many years had it been – twenty? thirty? – since last he sat like this, body at ease and mind locked in argument? Long ago he had spent time on summer evenings sharing wine and talk and music with his friends. Beneditx then had been dark-haired, not grey; his face had not worn the lines of bitten-in thoughtfulness, but his expression had always been grave. 'Is fire then not the cause of heat?' Severo demanded of Palinor.

Palinor reached out and took his hand. 'Feel,' he said. He drew Severo's plump hand with the great ring of office against the wine bottle, and then held it between his own. 'Our hands are warmer than the bottle,' he said. 'Is fire the cause of human warmth?

What fire? When? And I will show you another thing . . .' With a raised hand he summoned Joffre. The boy laid down his lute, and came and leaned over his master for instruction. Then he went running. They heard his steps on the stair to the courtyard. Then the boy returned, holding two pieces of wood from the kindling pile outside the kitchen doors. Palinor nodded, and he returned to his playing.

'Feel,' said Palinor, placing one of the sticks in Severo's hand, the other in Beneditx's. Then he took the sticks again and began to rub them hard together, gradually increasing the speed. Then silently he handed the sticks one to Beneditx, the other to Severo. Severo took his with a firm grip and dropped it hastily – it was very hot.

'Fire is the outcome of this process, but not the cause of the heat, as you have seen,' said Palinor.

'There must be latent fire within the wood,' said Beneditx.

'If you merely mean that wood can be made to burn, yes,' said Palinor. 'But the point I am making needs your attention, Beneditx. Simply because we can find one thing that is hotter than another does not mean that there must be something hottest – let alone that that hottest thing is the cause of heat in everything else. I deny that any *more* implies a *most*; all that is required to make sense of a statement that something is hotter is any two things which differ in respect of their warmth. There is no need to go in for one of those projections of yours in which everything is supposed to spiral off into infinity and the ultimate extremes imaginable are called God.'

'You have not taken the force of the argument,' said Beneditx. 'Hot, hotter, hottest is just an analogy with the true line of thought. It is good, better, best that leads to God. From the goodness in things we can deduce the ultimate good, as from warmth we know fire . . . and

161

God is the ultimate good, the cause of all beatitude, the source of the happiness that engulfs us now, for example.'

'But, my friend, the goodness in the world we know is not one – it is never an absolute quality, but always *for* something. A good table is a bad chair. The very things that make it a good table – its height and level top – are the very same things that make it a bad chair – too high and without a backrest. A good axe is a bad hammer . . . so on and on. To get to God on a scale of goodness you would need goodness to be a single scale.'

'Even this is not the true crux,' said Beneditx. 'The thought is that as fire causes heat in material things, so the intensity of God's existence, of his being, causes everything that is in being to be.'

'But where in nature are there degrees of being?' asked Palinor. 'For once, I am the one to claim the existence of absolutes. Things exist, or they don't exist. No half measures here! And God does not exist!'

Beneditx flinched visibly at such a spoken blasphemy. They both turned to Severo and saw that he was falling asleep, nodding gently in his chair, overcome by the long day's work and the hot ride to Alquiera. Such a comment on their cogency had them both instantly laughing, and when he snapped awake and tried to cover his lapse, they laughed more merrily still and ordered Rafal to put his master to bed.

The doors to the colonnade closed behind them, Rafal blew out the lamp, and Severo, wakeful for a little longer now, lay down on the pallets made ready for him and let Rafal cover him with blankets. The cool air of the evening flowed over his face, he could see the stars askance between the columns, and the lulling sounds of the fountain and nightingale kept company in the darkness. Beneditx was a nightingale,

Severo thought, exquisitely expounding the truths of his faith; Palinor was a force of cold clear water.

'And I?' Severo wondered. 'What am I?' He thought he might lay claim to being the little candle-lamp that had cast a warm light on both their faces; but the lamp was extinguished now, and he fell asleep.

20

For a long while after her disastrous escape, Amara
had been watched every minute and kept closely
confined; as she became more tractable, the nuns
began finding tasks for her. She was clumsy, and
easily distracted. She couldn't chop carrots without
cutting her fingers, but she could knead bread. She
could card wool, though she would do it only when
bribed with meat; she couldn't spin. She was best,
really, feeding the hens and cleaning the donkey stalls
– a good helper as long as someone was with her at the
task, though she was as likely to eat a hen as feed it
if left alone in the chicken coop – and as time went
by she was allowed the liberty of the barns and yards
and garden plots, though never for a moment let out of
sight. She was beginning to string words together now:
'Me now hungry . . .', 'Go out . . .', 'Me not like . . .' She
seemed to have lost the urge to escape, and kept
close to Josefa, but she had not lost her hatred of
locked doors and closed rooms. When, on a day of
oppressive heat, Josefa found her lying in the shade,
panting like a dog and sweating slightly, she went to
find Sor Agnete and asked permission to take her
down to the shore, where they would gather mussels.

The upper reaches of the path were as hot as
anywhere in the nunnery, but Amara followed eagerly,
looking around her. Josefa pulled flowers and named
them for her as they went.

Lower down, the cool influence of the shining sea
reached them, and at last the path delivered them to

a crescent of stony strand, a sliver of beach at the foot
of cliff towers, on which the waves broke grandly,
proportioned to the distance they had come rather than
to the scale of the little beach. Laughing, Josefa broke
into a run. Amara stooped at once to go four-footed,
bounding along and quickly overtaking Josefa. She too
laughed – a funny barking laugh – and the two of
them began to play with the dancing water, running
forward after the backwash and scrambling back up
the strand in front of the breaking waves. Three or
four misjudgements, and they were both wet – Amara
all over, and to the skin, Josefa halfway up her skirts,
heavy-hemmed with the drag of her soaking habit.

At the end of the beach Josefa put down her baskets
and produced her knife. She stooped and began work,
hacking at the mussels to cut them loose. Willingly
enough at first, Amara gathered them into the baskets,
though she wandered away long before both were
filled. Josefa straightened from time to time to ease
her back, and looked for Amara, who had returned
to playing catch with the waves. Flies buzzed on the
drying seaweed that grew across the mussel beds.
The baskets were full enough. And it was hot! Even
in the breeze the beach was hot, the water enticing.
Josefa looked around. Nobody from the abbey could see
them; their eyelines went far overhead, straight out to
sea. There was not a boat on the horizon, not a gull in
the sky.

Josefa began to undress herself and drape her heavy
garments on a rock. When she reached her undershift,
she hesitated, and then cast that also and ran naked
to the water's edge. The shock of the cold stopped
her knee-deep, but a great wave broke over her and
wet her to her chin, whereupon she waded three
more heavy paces and swam, skin glowing, delectable
coolness caressing her.

She did not hear Amara whimpering on the beach

behind her, and looked round only when her companion, head thrown back, emitted a loud animal howling. Amara was down on all fours, pacing frantically at the water's edge, pawing the waves and backing away again. Full of remorse at her panic, Josefa swam in. Amara stood up and tried to walk into the tumbling water, calling, 'Yossefa! Yossefa!'

'It's all right; look, see – I am safe – it's fun . . .' said Josefa, 'Try it – won't you?' and she reached for Amara's hand and led her a step or two in. Amara seemed uncertain; but a large wave pulled her over, and at once she was swimming, afloat, paddling like a dog, head held high. They swam round each other in circles, and then Josefa waded ashore and lay on the warm stones to dry off. In a little while Amara came too, lay down beside her and began to lick the backs of her hands, seeming to relish the taste of salt. She paused now and then to scan her companion, with her odd sideways darting glance, and then suddenly put an arm over Josefa's waist, and began to lick at her naked breast, the tongue curling round the stiff contracted nipple. Burning with shame and awareness, Josefa pushed her off, rolled over, moved hastily to reach her clothes. Unperturbed, Amara resumed licking salt from her own arms. Looking down as she drew her undershift over her head, Josefa saw that one of her nipples was still tight with cold, the other slack and soft. She remembered that even where no boat, no gull, no nun could see her, God could see.

The thought of God came to her like a memory, like a thought from long ago or far away. Though she was supposed to be one of the sisterhood, though the whole life of Sant Clara revolved around prayer and made no sense without it, though every prayer named God repeatedly, yet Josefa, spending her days with Amara and forbidden to name God, had ceased to think of him. His presence, which had once followed her everywhere, an unseen element in every moment of life, as necessary, as palpable as the air she breathed, had retreated now and belonged only to the chapel hours when she was on her knees, deliberately praying. She named him then without fervour, without paying much attention. And she did not miss him much. The days did not seem empty without thought of God. Even now, when the recollection of his all-seeing eye had struck her with shame like Eve in the garden, it had quickly occurred to her that it was not as bad to be seen naked by her God as it would have been to have been caught out in her immodesty by Sor Agnete.

She forgave herself and forgot all about it as they ascended the path. Josefa was carrying both the heavy baskets, and Amara bounded ahead, walking again only as the windows of the cloister came in view. Her shift had dried out long before then; Josefa's habit was still damp, drying slowly, and leaving a salty watermark halfway up the skirt.

In the depths of the night Beneditx struggled with panic and anger. The anger reminded him of his mother, a poor hard-working woman who had kept body and soul together by plying her needle round the lonely farms. His father had been a fisherman who was lost one day without reason, his boat sinking far out in a flat calm. Left to support her son, Beneditx's mother led a wandering life. In return for food and shelter for them both, she would stay for a week or more, mending linen and making clothes. It was a hard existence; but Beneditx remembered her angry only at two things in life − blunt needles and poor thread that snapped as she worked. Untimely death, poor harvests, sickness, poverty − about all these the people of the island were fatalists; bad tools provoked them to rage. As, now, Beneditx's failed arguments, his blunted points and broken threads left him angry.

167

Of course he was angry with Palinor. And he knew the name of his own sin – the sin of pride. Since the day his mother found him writing, scratching with a stick, copying the inscription over the church door at Santanya in the dust of the little square, Beneditx had always excelled. His mother had taken him at once to the Galilea and presented him to the oblate master, saying simply that she could not cope with a child who could write. He had always known that being the cleverest man on Grandinsula was not the same as being the cleverest in the world – that somewhere there was a man who could match him in argument; in that sense he was well prepared for Palinor.

But since he had never before experienced it, he was unprepared for the sharp pain of defeat in argument – for the *indignity* of it – and repentant in retrospect, he accused himself of insufficient tenderness towards all those he had defeated or instructed in debate. And that the triumphant adversary should be not a wiser doctor, but a disbeliever! How could God, whom he had served so long, so diligently, have allowed this to happen? Why had God given him blunt tools? In a spasm of self-disgust, Beneditx knew shame for not having seen the flaws in the argument. For not seeing, now, the correct answer to Palinor's objections. That there was an answer – somewhere on the board a winning move – he did not doubt. Or, rather, suppressing panic, he told himself he did not doubt it, and rising, he went early to pray, to ask for help.

Severo went to sleep happy and woke happy. The whitewashed simple vaulted roof of the colonnade above him was suffused with the tender primrose hue of the dawn, the nightingale had fled, and in its place the birds of morning were singing. He had slept on the pavement of the open colonnade, just here, when he and Gaspar were boys, and every summer night in memory had been as warm and scented as this one, every dawn as dewy with promise. Last night he had contrived to leave his dignity behind him, and he had no intention of resuming it with his mantle this morning. Last night he had not been alone but talking freely among his companions, and that sense of the flow of talk, unconstrained by the choking bonds of respect, was as delicious to his soul as the flowing waters of Palinor's fountain had been to his skin.

He sat up. Rafal, beside him, where long ago Gaspar had slept, did not stir. What sort of life was his? Severo wondered. He knew nothing about him. That for another time; now he rose quietly and went to look for Beneditx.

Beneditx was in the chapel across the courtyard, saying his office. Severo joined him, knelt, and opened his psalter. 'May God be merciful to us and bless us; may he smile graciously on us and show us his mercy,' he read, silently. 'Make known thy will, O God, wide as earth; make known among all nations thy saving power. Honour to thee, O God, from all the nations, alleluia, alleluia. Teach them to fear thee, those nations that have never looked to find thee: let them learn to acknowledge thee the only God, and acclaim thy wonders . . .'

Only when Beneditx rose, did Severo close the book and follow him. The two men bowed deeply to the altar and left the chapel, walking into the brightening light of morning. 'Severo – Holiness,' said Beneditx, 'relieve me of the task you laid upon me; I cannot accomplish it.'

Severo did not answer at once but turned into a quiet leafy alley. Beneditx followed him. 'If you cannot, who can?' he asked. And then, 'Would you have me leave him in the darkness of his error?' And then, 'Why then did God send him to us?'

When Beneditx was still silent, he asked, 'Has he thrown down all your proofs, Magister?'

'I have one left; the best one. But . . .'

'Well, then . . .'

'But I have become afraid of him, Holiness.'

'Oh, Beneditx!' said Severo, putting his arm round his friend's shoulder as they walked. 'Remember: "The Lord is my light and my salvation; whom then shall I fear? The Lord is the strength of my life; of whom then shall I be afraid?"'

'Do you think I have not prayed?' said Beneditx. 'But I will wrestle with him again if you command it.'

'I ask it,' said Severo. 'Do not refuse me. But let us find breakfast, and be ready for the last best argument! Things always look brighter in the morning,' he added, cheerfully.

'St Augustine thought that,' said Beneditx dolefully. 'Morning knowledge being different from evening knowledge.'

'Remind me,' said Severo.

'That knowledge is called morning knowledge by which an angel knows the things that are to be created; things as they ought to be – knowledge, for example, of the nature of a straight line; evening knowledge is that by which things are known in their own nature, such as knowing that no line in the world is really straight. There is a problem over the knowledge of angels.'

With a little surge of affection, Severo indulged him. 'Explain the problem,' he said.

'In angels, is there any difference between morning and evening knowledge?' Beneditx said. 'There are shadows in the morning and in the evening. In an angelic intellect, however, there are no shadows, for angels are very bright mirrors. It is that which I was working on when you summoned me.' Beneditx's tones lightened as he spoke of angels. The familiar delight, the familiar joy in exposition was audible in his voice as clearly as Severo remembered it of old.

'My poor friend,' said Severo, smiling. 'I must let you get back to those angels as soon as possible. But now, this morning . . .'

'A bout with Palinor,' said Beneditx. 'Will you stay to hear this?'

'I wouldn't miss it for anything! Come; aren't you hungry? Bring me to some bread and olives.'

'Consider the governance of the world,' said Beneditx. The table had been cleared, and he sat with Severo and Palinor in conference. 'We see that things which lack intelligence, such as natural bodies like stones, winds, flames, streams, act for some purpose, which in fact is evident from their acting always, or nearly always, in the same way so as to produce the best result. Hence it is plain that not by chance but by design they achieve their purpose. Whatever lacks intelligence cannot fulfil some purpose unless it be directed by some being endowed with intelligence and knowledge, as the arrow is shot by the archer. Therefore, some intelligent being exists by whom all natural things are ordained towards a definite purpose, and this being we call God.'

'It is true that the world is full of pattern,' said Palinor. 'Fascinating, recurring pattern. This is a great mystery or perhaps, more probably, it is many mysteries. Perhaps some part of the reason for recurrence might be that someone unseen, unknown, has planned what occurs – has designed an aspect of the world and given it purpose as the archer gives a target to his arrow. Perhaps. But only partly.'

'Why do you say only partly, my friend?' asked Severo.

'I have a natural reason and a moral reason,' Palinor answered. 'The natural reason is that I observe how explanations recede. For example, if you ask a bell-founder, as I once asked, why he makes the rim of the bell curve outwards in just such a way, he replies that he does so in order to obtain a particular note from the bell. Now ask him why bell metal gives forth a certain note when it is shaped in just that way, and see what he says. "It just does," more than likely.'

'In the propensities of bell metal for our use, we may observe the magnanimous and marvellous designer of the world, who made creation fit for our purposes,' said Beneditx.

'But in saying that, you are imagining God entertaining a human kind of purpose – fabricating metals and secreting them in rocks for reasons which we can guess at, as we can guess why the bell-founder makes bells. Whereas I would say it makes sense to ask "Why?" only of another human being, whose answer we can understand. Look at my fountain over there. Why does the water rise to a great height and then fall back to earth? I have no idea why; but I know exactly at what height it will falter and fall – it will do that when it reaches the height of the surface of the lake from which it is fed. I do not need to know why to make a fountain, only that it does what it does.'

'You said a moment ago, I think,' said Beneditx, 'that explanations recede. But they cannot recede to infinity'.

'Well, but suppose there is a designer behind the universe,' said Palinor. 'How can he be what you would call God? Look at the chaos, the disorder, the preference one would have to admit that things have for falling into confusion. Look how hard it is to keep a roof on a house, to keep weeds from choking crops. More incriminating by far than even this anarchy, this endless rupture of order: consider the pain, the fear, the hardship and suffering in the world, and how it is inflicted on the innocent, on the

172

lamb in the wolf's maw, on the babe, on the harmless worm under the spade. Is the great designer then a botcher and incompetent? Is his power limited, so that it would make sense to say he did the best he could? Does he not care about our sufferings? If we project from the nature of his works to the nature of the divinity, would we not find him indifferent or cruel? Are you sure you would not be better to think, as I do, that the suffering in the world "just is" and does not represent any intended plan at all?'

'God would not permit evil if he could not bring out of it some greater countervailing good,' said Beneditx.

'A good beyond our understanding, no doubt!' said Palinor, dryly.

'I thought you would say this!' said Beneditx. 'And I have thought of a demonstration for you. But we must ride some distance to see it. Are you willing? Can you come with us, Severo?' Beneditx had stood up and set back his chair.

'How far is it?' Severo asked. 'I have not time to ride with you to the Galilea; that would keep me from duty in Ciudad too long.'

'Two hours, perhaps. Just this side of Sant Clara.'

'I go with you then. Rafal, saddle horses!'

It was a pleasant ride. The path ascended through a narrow pass above the hanging lake behind the Saracen's House and over a bare col through a valley of rocks and rosemary, where eagles hung overhead in rising airs. Descending somewhat on the seaward side, the narrow track wound through the fragrant woods above the glittering plain of the sea, glimpsed far below. They rode through bright air, crisp and cool, and into soft mists and out again, as the breath of the mountains disputed with the breath of the sea. They were always high; the path dipped and rose

173

but did not descend. Its narrowness spaced them out in single file, so each rider was alone and saw the splendour of the prospects in silence.

At last a great crag before them jutted out to sea, making a steep headland, and cresting it was a little domed church with a golden cross at the apex. As the path turned towards the church, Palinor, looking back, saw that a tiny settlement of houses clung to the steeps nearby, which had been terraced with appalling labour and now were shining with olive trees, bleeding between the stones with the blaze of poppies.

The riders reached the church door and dismounted. Rafal bundled the reins and tied them to a ring on the shaded wall of the church. An old woman had begun to hobble towards them from the nearest house with a basket of candles, and they waited.

'This is Sant Vicente,' said Beneditx.

Ducking in a stiff genuflection, bowing her head, the old woman gave them candles – dark brown with the detritus of unfiltered wax, smelling of honey and hive, and tacky on their warm palms. Beneditx thanked her with a handful of dineros, and they entered.

At first their eyes were unable to penetrate the gloom. Then gradually to their widening pupils a golden glow emerged and shadowy figures against the gold. In the half dome above the altar of the little church facing them was a great scene done in mosaic. Christ sat enthroned in majesty; on his right the Virgin knelt, haloed; behind her came flocking a great crowd of the just, attended by angels, whose beckoning and guiding hands urged them forwards and upwards; on the other side the damned were driven downwards by angelic spears and received by a seething mass of devils with prongs and torches, and callipers and whips.

'The judgement is finely done,' said Beneditx, bowing his head to the altar. 'But it is this that I have brought you to look at,' and he led them through an

174

arch into another, parallel nave, with angled light
descending from high windows – the church was two
churches side by side. On the south wall of this earlier
nave, heaven had begun. A mosaic showed a garden
under a sky of pure gold. Emerald trees bearing flowers
and fruit at once were underspread by a meadow
thick with flowers. White-clad virgins with flowing
hair danced in a ring, hands linked, sandalled feet
arched in delicate steps. A grave-faced angel played for
them on a tambour. A little way off, a group of saints
sat talking on the grass. Their faces were animated,
and birds with coloured feathers sat on the branches
near them, their heads cocked to attention, listening.
Another angel, smiling, poured a bright stream of
wine into a cup held by a bearded saint, while a
little angel child with downy wings came running
with a dish of cakes. The whole scene was sparkling
and glinting with light. The smallest movement of the
onlooker's head caused the highlights to move, caused
the scene to shimmer, as though it had been done on a
sheet of silk moving in the light.

'Have you ever seen a scene brighter than this one?'
asked Beneditx. 'Or anything lighter than that perfect
golden sky?' Nobody claimed him wrong. 'But look
closely now; stand near. Do you see that even to make
such a scene of brightness as this, the master artificer
needed tessarae of dark glass as well as of bright glass?
Look at the petal of this lovely lily, here where I point.
See, the pieces below it are nearly black and rough in
surface. An ugly fragment, you would think if I showed
it to you on the palm of my hand. But without it, the lily
could not be portrayed as clearly, standing as though we
could reach to heaven and pick it, for standing things
cast shadows. Look now at the sparkling sky. See how it
is made of fragments tipped this way and that, some of
which receive the light, while others are averted from
it; if every golden square alike is illuminated, the result

will be flat, it will not scintillate with points of light. Thus dullness is in the service of light here; dark pieces are in the service of the whole, just as light pieces are. Now, if we can see how the human craftsman needed dark tesserae, can we not see how God might need the blackness we find in the world, how to the mind of God it might serve a wholeness of transcendent beauty, whereas we, thinking of a tiny fragment of creation by itself, find it ugly, and childishly demand that it should not be part of the picture?'

When Beneditx had spoken, Severo returned to the main part of the church and knelt in prayer. Rafal followed him. Palinor did not answer, but remained for a long time contemplating the mosaic. It had put a quietness even on him. Then he went out into the actual sunlight, and sat down under a wind-bent pine, looking at the receding panoramas of headland offered by the precipitous shore. Partly obscured by an intervening jut of cliff and woodland he could see a little strand, some way further north; and, diminished by distance, he saw two figures on it – he thought at first a woman and a dog, but when he looked again, two women. They came towards him along the water's edge, and moved out of sight behind the nearer promontory. There must be something there – some other church, some other settlement, on the extreme margin of the island. Dwelling in remote and beautiful places would make them primitive mystics, he supposed, even without the influence of mosaic.

Emerging from the church, the others joined him.

'Will you make any answer to Beneditx?' Severo asked him.

'He offered a vision, not an argument. He has thoughts of great beauty, and I honour him for them, as I honour the maker of the image of heaven we have just seen.'

'But . . . ?'

176

'No buts. I am coming to love Beneditx. I see how it is that he has reconciled the evil in the world with a faith in a beneficent and all powerful God, as I see what kind of heaven the maker of the picture desires there to be. But to see such a vision and to share it myself are as different as seeing the image of heaven and entering it, sitting on the grass among the blessed. I would like to, but cannot.'

'Hold hard to that thought that you would like to,' said Severo, mouting his horse.

'No glass is dark enough,' said Palinor, 'to stand for the suffering of a tortured and dying child.' He spoke softly. Severo, over the chink of his bridle and the ring of his horse's hooves, did not hear him. Rafal, holding a horse for him, perhaps did.

angry because theory diverts responsibility

177

21

Strangers were rare at Sant Clara, and unwelcome.
Sometimes a holy woman or a poor afflicted peasant
wished to pray there. Now and then a cell was found
for a visitor in need of a little peace, a little gentleness,
or some of Sor Blancha's concoctions were applied
to a sufferer, who was allowed to stay for a while.
Sant Clara could comfort, if not heal. But the nuns'
purpose was not to practise charity but to pray for
the sufferings of the world. And they were far enough
away from the world, on a road that went nowhere
else, to be untroubled by visitors. So the appearance
of a little group of strangers, gathered at the gate and
murmuring, was something new and disturbing.

When they had been standing around for some hours,
Sor Agnete, with Sor Eulalie at her side, went out to
them and asked what they wanted. They wanted to see
the wolf-child. Sor Agnete scolded them volubly for
fools and the victims of tricksters. There was no
such thing as a wolf-child; and certainly no child at
Sant Clara was anything of the sort. Shamefaced, the
fellows hung their heads, and shuffled away into the
woods, but they were back again the next morning –
either those, or others, who could say? Guillem had
no doubt kept his word, but someone among his
hunters had been less discreet, and the story had got
out. Each day the strangers were dismissed by Sor
Agnete; each day there were more of them, and they
grew bolder. They even hammered on the gates. They
prowled around the hermit tower and trespassed on

the root-gardens. The two old menservants that the abbess kept for menial tasks about the farm and as night watchmen were bullied and frightened, until the abbess sent them under cover of darkness to ride a pair of donkeys over the mountain and get a message to Severo, asking for help.

Before the help came, the crowd grew bolder and broke in. Their ring-leader was a huge man with coarse features, carrying a heavy staff. He confronted the abbess, coming towards him across the cloister gardens with her sticks, unabashed.

'You just let us see the wolf-child, and we'll go,' he said. 'But we won't go without seeing her. And don't go telling us no stories about how you haven't got her, because we know that you have, see?'

'The curse of God is on intruders here,' said the abbess.

'Oh dear!' the lout said. 'We'll have to confess what we done before we die, then, won't we? Now are you going to show us this monster, or are we going to break in everywhere looking for her? How do you want it?'

'Fetch Amara,' said the abbess.

There was an expectant hush on the mob. They stood in the garden, waiting. At last two figures appeared, walking under the arches and stepping into the garden, just behind the abbess: a young nun in novice's habit and a girl in a coarse white shift, dark curls on her uncovered head, sandals on her feet.

'We are here, Mother,' said Josefa. Her voice trembled. She faced the hungry staring faces, the sticks and staffs.

'It's a trick!' someone said.

'I saw a wolf-child once, and it looked more like an animal than a child,' said someone else. The crowd pressed forward a step or two.

'Saints in heaven help us,' said the abbess, 'What are we going to do?'

179

Josefa, holding Amara's hand, felt her tremble. And then Amara howled. She tipped back her head and emitted the blood-curdling animal sound that she used to make on her first few nights at Sant Clara. She dropped on to all fours and howled again.

'Watch out! She bites!' called Josefa. The crowd fell back towards the gate.

'You are in danger of punishment; I have sent for the cardinal's soldiery,' said the abbess.

Just at that moment, a distant drum could be heard from the turn of the path, beating a little flourish of the kind that men march to. The intruders bolted, rushing out through the abbey gate and dispersing among the trees in full flight.

Amara got to her feet and laughed. Her barking mirth filled the cloister. 'Me scare them!' she said and burst into laughter again. No soldiers appeared, and the drum beat remained unexplained. But the crowd of gapers had disappeared, leaving one solitary outrider – a young man who lingered, standing well back in the shade of the trees by the edge of the ground in front of the gate, and who was still there when night fell.

Severo set a guard on the Sant Clara road, on the far side of the pass, and no more mobs appeared at the abbey gates. Only now and then there was a solitary lurker, a young man who never came near enough to be challenged.

Josefa's long labours were bearing fruit at last. Amara could dress herself, as long as it was only in the simplest garments; she could buckle her own sandals – made specially for her in the convent workshop, for her toes still turned upwards from long years of running on bent feet. She could sit in a chair; she could sit up at table to eat, and hold a spoon for gruel, though it was grasped in a stiff fist rather than held between fingers, and after one or two mouthfuls she could no longer restrain herself and would lower her face to the dish and bolt the contents.

Most important of all, she was learning to talk rapidly now, her chatter taking on meaning, her words building gradually into fragments of sense. When she was with the sisters, playing in the garden while they spent their hour of recreation walking, or sitting sewing, she charmed them easily, with the innocent selfishness of a child, demanding attention, wheedling for bits of lace or ribbon or coloured threads, running after Sor Lucia or Sor Blancha for a drink of milk or a morsel of honey-plum.

Suddenly, one morning of heavy stillness, threatening heat, Amara said, 'Mussels. Fetch. Go to the sea?'

Josefa, who was putting on an apron in the kitchen, readying herself to knead dough for bread, stopped, her heart pounding. 'Oh, did you hear that?' she asked Sor Blancha.

'The answer is no, dear. Too much work to do,' said Sor Blancha.

Josefa seized Sor Blancha's floury hands. 'But she has spoken of something she remembers, don't you see? Something not before her eyes!' Josefa's joy was infectious, and the news spread from nun to nun round the cloisters, and reached Mother Humberta before terce.

Sor Agnete was as glad as anyone – almost as glad as Josefa – at such a step forward for Amara. But as the child slowly achieved a facade of ordinary humanity, her strangeness became more striking than ever, or so it seemed to Sor Agnete. Seeing her doing as a wolf does had been pitiful; seeing a pleasant-looking young woman suddenly bolting her food, shuddering as she swallowed, or hearing a human voice move from sentences, however childish, to that inhuman howling chilled one to the bone. Sometimes her face took on suddenly a wolfish expression – her jaw worked, and her eyes darted around. Strangest of all

181

– it was beginning to strike Sor Agnete – was her appetite for solitude. What child can be left sitting still and in silence for many hours? What child needs neither company nor playthings?

Carefully at first, Sor Agnete began to send Josefa on errands, let her attend office, have the child left more to her own devices. Whenever she was not under pressure to speak, she sat vacantly, feeling it seemed no boredom, but content to be alone, silent and unoccupied, from one meal to the next. Sor Agnete had seen such behaviour once before in her life, as she told the abbess. It had been that of a boy who had survived, alone of his village, a terrible avalanche. Rescuers had drawn him to the surface from under the crushed body of his father. He had been unable to speak for many months.

Asking Josefa produced the simple statement, 'She is unhappy. She doesn't like it here,' which Sor Agnete thought, with a twinge of irritation, she could see for herself.

There are people who have a horror of heights, who are paralysed with fear on looking over a cliff-top, even though they stand secure. It is an oddity of human behaviour that such people are irresistibly drawn towards the brink – can barely help themselves. In just this way the contemplation of the terrible emptiness of Amara's life, the vast unbroken silence of her soul, the aching void where in her human body human feelings should have been, drew the thoughts of the abbess. Only the knowledge of God was a thing great enough to fill such a chasm; and she had vowed not to convey it.

Josefa was cutting nettles at the top of the root-garden by the edge of the wood. She was using a billhook. Her skirts were looped up, her hands gloved, and her sleeves tied at the wrists to keep her from being stung. Amara followed behind her, picking up the fallen swathes of nettles and loading them into donkey panniers to be taken to the heap. She seemed not to notice the stings on her reddened hands. The donkey stood impassive till she urged him on a few paces. At the far corner of the field, a young man stepped suddenly from under the trees and confronted them.

'Don't be frightened,' he said. 'I need only to speak with you.' He was facing Josefa but looking over her shoulder at Amara. Two scars ran across his face from the corner of his eye to his nose, the lower one crossing his upper lip, the upper one ploughing a furrow that kinked the bridge of his nose. But he did not have the face of a fighter.

'Go away,' said Josefa.

'Please . . . I need . . .' Following the line of his stare, Josefa saw that Amara was standing very still and staring hard in return. 'I am thirsty,' he said. 'Have you a sip of water?'

Josefa moved back to the donkey and pulled the water-bottle from the saddle-bag behind the pannier. She offered it without comment. When he handed it back, she saw that his arm – his sleeves were rolled up to the elbow – was also marked with lines of white healed scarring.

Amara said, suddenly, in her husky low voice, 'Hurt. Face hurt. What made hurt?'

'You did,' he said.

By the time the riders returned to the Saracen's House, it was noon, and the heat of the day was oppressive. Palinor swam in his fountain; Severo and Beneditx retired to rest in Beneditx's room. 'How long can you stay?' Beneditx asked.

'Till the heat abates a little. I must ride back this evening.'

'I shall miss you,' said Beneditx. 'I shall miss your moral support . . .'

Severo regarded his friend gravely. Beneditx's anxiety was heartfelt, he saw. 'My skills are not of this kind,' Beneditx told him. 'We have always known the truth, Severo, we two, like everyone around us. We have used argument to defend it, to throw up strong walls around our treasure house. That is a fine bulwark against most kinds of attack, but it does not serve against one who does not attack but merely says that all our gold is dust.'

Severo was silent for a while, reflecting. Beneditx's great reputation for learning and subtlety was for drawing out the meaning of holy truth, refining it into pure gold, gently correcting and uplifting the understanding of those too much inclined to take Holy Writ in crude senses or treat the Church's teaching as a simple cudgel. Those whom he taught had learned to see depths below depths and heights above heights in God's word, had learned to use tenderness in disputation, had learned that cleverness imposed a heavy duty of humility. No beatitude said, 'Blessed are the clever, for they shall correctly understand the truth.' Beneditx had taught him to think rather, 'The clever are humble, for they have understood how little they understand.' It was he, Severo, who had sent Beneditx, armed with thoughts of purest gold, into battle against the tempered steel of the atheist's alien mind. It was up to him now to offer reinforcements.

'It is always easier to knock things down than to construct them,' he said. 'Perhaps this procedure is wrong. Offering proofs for him to pick holes in, I mean. Perhaps it would be better to invite him to make statements of his own position, and then you can have the opportunity to demolish him.'

'I have not tried that, admittedly,' said Beneditx. 'I was so sure our proofs were good. I do not even know what he would claim to believe.'

184

'You must ask him. Surely such an odious and extreme position as his cannot be impregnable.'

'I will try.'

'I would be deeply grieved if we should fail,' said Severo, rising to take his leave.

Although he had seen Beneditx's troubled eyes and anxious brow, he was not himself concerned. He was no more afraid of the demolition of the proofs of the existence of God than he would have been afraid of the collapse of a proof that the sun would rise the following morning.

22

The clatter of the hooves of the departing horses woke
Palinor from the light sleep he had been taking in the
afternoon heat. He looked out of his window and saw
Severo riding away through the garden approaches. It
caused him no concern. Then he looked down and saw
Dolca kneeling on a rock, washing some clothes of his in
the torrent at the foot of the wall. She leaned forward,
immersing the soaking cloth, and straightened, lifting
it, working smoothly, her own clothes wet and clinging
to her in the mist-like rainfall cast by the fountain over
the garden. Palinor watched her for some time, and
then retreated to his bed again. He lay thinking of his
wife, imagining her walking away from him, as the
time went by, and he seemed to have ever less hope
of returning to her. She must think him dead. Perhaps
by now she had turned to that cousin of his she always
liked so much who always made her laugh.

When by and by Dolca came softly into his chamber,
on some small errand, he turned back the sheet under
which he was lying naked and said to her, 'Come here.'

She came and stood at the bedside. 'Off,' he said,
twitching her sleeve. He watched her undress, and
stand trembling. With a brief twinge of self-disgust,
he said, 'You can refuse, if you like.'

She said, 'It's just that I don't know what to do.'

'In that case, cover up again, and bring lamp oil, and
honey.'

When she returned, she put the jars down beside
the bed and stepped out of her shift. She was slender

and dark. Lilac aureoles surrounded her nipples, and a scatter of dark freckles lay around her navel. He pulled her down beside him, scooped oil into his palms, and began to rub her skin. Then he parted her legs, opened the petals of her flesh with the fingers of his left hand, and poured a golden trickle of honey from the jar. She raised her head from the pillow, looking with astonishment, and he smiled at her before lowering his head and licking the honey, following the flow of it as far as his tongue would go. When he felt her begin to move against his butting head he rose. Kneeling between her legs and oiling his dark member, he thrust hard into her. He felt her flinch, and he knew he would be giving pain, but his own need now was urgent, imperative. Only as he shot and withdrew, did he realize that they were not alone.

Joffre had come into the room. He was standing in front of the door, left ajar, thunderstruck. Palinor rolled off the girl, propped his head on one elbow, and said, 'Is this really your sister?'

Joffre said, 'No, master. She is my sweetheart. We lied, to be together.' His voice was choking.

'If she is your sweetheart, why are you not further with her? Why is there blood, here?'

The boy blushed crimson and said, 'I cannot . . . we want to . . . but she seems afraid.'

Palinor said, 'Close the door, take your clothes off and come here. I will show you something.'

Joffre obeyed. He stood beside the bed with his teeth chattering in his head. Palinor said to Dolca, 'Sweethearts or not, you can refuse this if you like.' She shook her head. 'Lie down with her,' he said to Joffre. Then, reaching over her, he took Joffre's wrist between his fingers, dipped the boy's hand in the oil jar, and laid it in place. As though the boy's fingers had been the keys of an instrument, he played them with his own. 'Like your lute,' he said to the boy, softly. And then, as she began to cry, 'Now!'

He leaned back and watched them. 'You are too quick,' he said in a while, 'There's more. I'll finish for you.' Taking her again, he lingered, moving slowly, till he had her mewing like a gull in flight. 'Enough?' he said, leaving her. She smiled at him, her eyelids drooping in that instant drowsiness coition brings.

Palinor got up, padded barefoot round the bed, and got in beside Joffre. 'Our turn,' he said. 'I'll show you something else.' He kissed the boy hard and turned him face down on the crumpled sheets. Afterwards, rolling over, he said, 'Now you do that to me.' Then for a while they all slept, the lingering heat of the afternoon lulling their sleek bodies. When Palinor woke, he found Dolca lying beside him wide-eyed, with a tear flowing down her right cheek. 'Do you think we have deserted you?' he murmured. 'Give me your hand.' And he showed her how with oil and honey, with a sliding palm and a greedy tongue she could accomplish for both of them a resurrection of the flesh, till satiety was overcome by ecstasies of lust.

Much later, after nightfall, when they were at last hungry, and the servants went, walking weak-kneed and as though drunk, in search of food, Palinor put on a cloak over his nakedness and went out on the colonnade. The moonlight was casting molten silver over the moving column of water he had raised up. At the far end of the colonnade Beneditx's window was lit, and the grid between the panes made it appear like a large lantern in which Beneditx's head, bowed over his books, was centred like the flame. 'I could teach you a thing or two about triangles,' said Palinor, softly, and he returned to his room, where Joffre was setting out a late supper on his table and Dolca was bundling up an armful of sheets musky with the blended odours of oil, honey, blood, semen and sweat.

23

It was dusk when Severo reached Ciudad, and the night
watch were closing the gates. They held them half open
for him and greeted him as he rode through. It had
been very hot in the city; the streets still brimmed
with the heavy warmth. Lights were lit in windows,
and he glimpsed families sitting round their tables.
Drinkers at a tavern had carried their mugs into the
street and stood around under a lantern hanging
in a tree. Someone called, 'Bless you, Holiness!' as
he passed, in so light a tone it was impossible to
judge whether it was mocking or no. Severo half
lifted a hand from the pommel of his saddle in
reply. A girl's laugh cascaded from an unlit upper
window, and he saw Rafal look up.

They had to knock to be admitted to the courtyard
of the cathedral palace, but as soon as they entered an
anxious clerk came running. 'There is someone to see
you, Holiness.'

'So late?'

'He won't go away; he sits waiting.'

Severo sighed. He was tired, and he wanted to sit
quietly, thinking over the day, thinking of Palinor's
words.

The visitor was sitting on a bench outside Severo's
cell, leaning against the wall. He was wearing monastic
habit, and his hood was up, deeply shading his face.
But when Severo appeared he stood up and threw
back the hood. 'I think you are expecting me,' he
said.

'No,' said Severo.

'Cardinal,' the man said quietly. 'You must be expecting me.'

'I am not,' said Severo. 'State your business.' He looked hard at the intruder. A tonsured head; a puffy face, with the colour and texture of raw dough. The eyes were deep set, and glittered coldly at him, like marcasite.

'We have heard . . . It has been reported to us that you have a particularly impious and contumacious heretic on the island. And that you have not promulgated an edict of grace. You have not handed him over to your local Inquisition for examination. You have spirited him away somewhere out of sight. Frankly, you *must* be expecting me, or someone like me. I am Fra Damaso Murta. I have plenipotentiary powers. I am a special inquisitor.'

'You wish me to put my own position in front of you positively, instead of simply carping negatively at yours?' said Palinor. He and Beneditx were walking along the covered walk – a tunnel of green leaves, lovingly trained by the gardeners. Alongside it ran a little runnel from the fountain, which had been simply a tumbling water last time Beneditx stepped this way, but was now a sequence of tiny fountains, making fans or weaving water jets in interlacing patterns, so that the sound of water filled the air, and the bright little displays with the sunlight behind them sparkled, and cast moving patterned shadows on the path between the shadow columns of the overarching vines. 'I am not sure I should agree to that.'

'Why not? Why ever not?' asked Beneditx.

'I do not understand faith,' said Palinor. 'But I have a kind of respect for it. There are people in Aclar for whom a position based on faith is like a red rag to a bull; they try at once to drag it down. I believe my position to be very strong – unanswerable, in fact. But I do not wish to proselytize, least of all here, on a theological island! I do not seek to persuade you as you have sought to persuade me.'

'I seek to persuade you still. I invite you to expose your own arguments to the possibility of refutation.'

'At your own risk?'

'Certainly. Do not hesitate,' said Beneditx, though he felt a touch of chill.

Nevertheless, Palinor did hesitate. They reached the end of the walk and turned before he said, 'Well, to start with, I do not find the world around me puzzling in the way you do. I am not amazed to find that things move, things change, things operate as causes or arise as effects. Whereas you assert that these things are so mysterious they must have some cause – you call it God – which is outside the material universe, I am content to think that material things have material causes, and things contrived, like fountains, shall we say, have causes in human ingenuity and human will. Your attempt to prove otherwise seems nearly scandalous to me.'

'Scandalous? What do you mean, Palinor?'

'First you say that nothing moves without a mover. Then you say that after all there must be something which moves without a mover, else the process could not start. This is an argument whose conclusion contradicts one of its premises. But, Beneditx, much more important is another difference between us. Living as you do, here on Grandinsula, you are surrounded by belief; it seems to you that disbelievers must prove their point. But logically, you must see, this is not so. It is always a person who proposes something for belief who must prove it; the burden of proof must lie with those who suggest that in addition to what we can see and feel around us, there is a God. And even your philosopher saint, I think – you will

191

correct me if I am wrong – agreed that things which can be explained by fewer principles should not be explained by more.'

'But it seemed to him obvious that there could be no explanation of the world around us without postulating God. He needed even to discuss whether so self-evident a proposition could be demonstrated.'

'Your proofs all call God into the issue to be an *explanation*,' Palinor said. 'But God is a useless explanation – he explains too much. Potentially he explains everything, and to explain everything is to explain nothing.'

'I do not understand you.'

'You can explain one thing in terms of another. I can explain the behaviour of fountains by saying it is a law of nature that water flows in such a way; I can explain the growth of vines by saying that all plants reach towards the light, and the orderly curve of these tendrils above our heads by saying that the gardener tied them thus. These explanations refer to something else, something else in the material world. But if you explain by reference to God, you explain too much. God's will could indeed explain why water flows downhill; but it would equally, and likewise, explain why it flowed uphill, if it did. It will explain every state of affairs, and would equally explain any conceivable alternative state of affairs. But for that precise reason it cannot therefore explain why water flows downhill and not uphill; it makes no distinction between what happens and what does not. I cannot see, therefore, how one could use what happens as evidence for God's existence.'

'Give me time to think,' said Beneditx. 'That is a new idea to me.'

'Beneditx, do you require me to come to believe in a weak God, or a strong one?'

'What do you mean, my friend?'

'A weak God – such as an explanation for a falling stone, or the excellence of a bird's wing for flight – or a strong God, such as the God of Abraham?'

'They are the same. The difference is only that one might reach, by pure unaided reason, your "weak" God; knowledge of the God of Abraham is given us through revelation. A man like you, who has not received revealed truth, is not expected to know it.'

'And is a man like me allowed to enquire why the God of revelation is admirable? Is he not depicted to us as both crazed and vengeful? Did he not set an apple in front of a man and woman, and then punish them horribly for eating it? And did he not, with injustice that surpasses that of the grossest human judge, punish also many millions who did not eat, merely for being descended from Adam, who did? Why should I not conclude that this God is less than human, rather than more?'

'The bitten apple is only a figure. All men are sinful, and have deserved hell.'

'But what would you say to a human judge who justified punishing a man for a crime he had not committed on the grounds that although he was innocent of what was alleged against him, he had done something else?'

'You must have in mind that God is God of the New Testament as well as of the Old.'

'Ah, yes. Who is mollified in his unjust vendetta by a sacrifice of innocent blood . . .'

'Hush, Palinor!' cried Beneditx. 'These are great mysteries. Where were we when he laid the foundations of the earth? When all the morning stars sang together, and the sons of God shouted for joy? Have we entered into the springs of the sea? Have we walked in the search of the depth? Can we say, hath the rain a father? Or who hath begotten the drops of dew?'

Beneditx was standing stock still, with tears pouring down his face.

'I spoke because you told me to speak; I will hush since you tell me to hush,' said Palinor. 'I did not mean to distress you. And you have retreated now, I think, where I cannot follow you.'

'Take off your shoes,' said Beneditx. 'For this is holy ground.'

'What do you mean by trespassing in our fields?' demanded Sor Agnete. 'This is a holy cloister, and our seclusion is surrounded by holy vows. All who have lawful business here come by the gate.' She was standing facing Jaime, leading a little group of novices and the two gardeners, all with stout sticks in their hands. He had been seen from the window of someone's cell, talking to Josefa and Amara.

'I did not mean to intrude upon a nun,' said Jaime, blushing. 'I wished only to speak to . . . her.' He pointed to Amara.

'Are you not ashamed to persecute the child with vulgar curiosity? To afflict her with cruel stares that drag her down again, that make of her a thing?' Sor Agnete's indignation and contempt rang in her voice.

Josefa said, 'Sister, he knows her; he has had dealings with her before; he says that she made those scars he wears . . .'

'Come and explain yourself,' said Sor Agnete. She led Jaime back down the grassy path below the orchard trees and made him wait in the gatehouse. Later, he found himself talking to the abbess.

'Why did you not come openly, if you meant no harm?' she asked him.

'I have been forbidden to come; I have been forbidden even to think of her,' he said, miserably.

194

'Who has forbidden you?'

'His Holiness, the cardinal. But Mother, I cannot obey him! I have tried, believe me I have tried! But in the night, or as I work in the fields, the thought creeps back to me. It is like a raging fever, Mother, a craving like the need for water in the heat . . .'

'Tell me about it,' she said. He told her how he had stopped the blow from Galceran's blade, that would have killed the child. How the others had thought he had been wrong. He told her what he had done about it, how he had brought the child into Severo's care. How he had been dismissed. How he had struggled to keep from remembering any of it, often in vain, and how he had at last heard a rumour, reaching his village through tavern talk, that there was a wolf-child being reared at Sant Clara. He said he had come, on foot. He had seen the mob at the gate, and had thought of beating on a drum to make them think soldiers were coming.

'What drum?' she asked him. 'Why did you bring a drum?'

He pulled a little drum from his pack, and held it out to her. 'It is a toy,' he said. 'I brought it for her. May she have it?'

'You puzzle me,' the abbess said. 'Why bring a drum?'

'I am married, now,' he told her. 'I have three fields and some olive trees. My wife will bear me a child in the spring. I made a drum for my child, and then I thought to make another for that other child.'

'Well, it was lucky you did,' she said, warming to him. 'You helped scare off that crowd of rascals. You know, of course, that you must obey the cardinal. That I must send you away and forbid you to return. As for the wanton thoughts that have tormented you, we will pray for you, that God will help you to think of other things.'

195

'It will be easier, now that I know she is cared for,' he said. 'Now I have seen her stand and heard her talk. But, Mother . . .'

'There can be no buts,' she said sternly. 'You must simply obey.'

'If ever she needs a friend,' he said. 'if ever there is something to be done for her in the world outside the cloister; if I could serve her, would you summon me?'

'Yes,' said the abbess. 'If there were ever any need, we would send for you. But now you must leave, and endeavour to do henceforward what his Holiness commanded you. You may give Amara the drum,' she added.

Searching for Joffre with an errand for him, Palinor found him on his knees before a crucifix on the chamber wall, praying.

'I haven't seen you pray before,' said Palinor. 'Is it a new thing?'

The boy blushed and got up.

'You needn't stop, for me,' said Palinor.

The boy said, 'Sir, is there for you such a thing as sin?'

Palinor smiled, laughed, nearly. Then he said gently, 'There are things one should not do. That self-love should keep one from. None of them bring joy. None of them have we done together.'

Joffre's grave expression lightened. 'What kind of thing is sinful in Aclar, sir?'

'Each man there would give a different answer,' Palinor said.

'And your answer, sir?'

'There are many things I would not do,' said Palinor. 'But no misdeed could be graver, it seems to me, than trying to increase one's own luminance by quenching the light shining from another man. There's a problem calling it sin, however, when it is committed most often by holy men, by revered teachers, priests, mullahs . . .'

The boy furrowed his brow.

'Leave sin to churchmen. They have the expertise,' said Palinor. 'And get me something to eat, will you? I am hungry.'

24

Severo sat facing Fra Damaso Murta across the table
in the cathedral refectory. Great though the powers
of a cardinal might be, they did not extend to
countermanding a special inquisitor. The prince of
Grandinsula, be he cardinal or no, could not defy the
Inquisition, without facing terrible anathemas from
Rome. And that would be a scandal among the people.
The simple people feared heretics as they feared
witchcraft; they gladly assisted inquisitors, in hope of
procuring their own salvation. And Severo had taken
the great vows to serve and obey the Church that are
laid on all the clergy, and had thought to live and die
without the least temptation to break them. He was
struggling to overmaster dislike of the man before him,
and do what he had decided, overnight, and in prayer,
to do. He was going to explain to the special inquisitor
why he had not proceeded in the usual manner, and
invite him to take an interest in the snow-child.

Fra Murta listened to the account of Palinor, to
the careful analysis of his position that Severo put
before him, with pursed lips. The expression made
his features, loaded with surplus fat, wobble, so that
he looked like a pig.

'You are too scrupulous, Holiness,' he said icily. 'Of
course an atheist is a heretic.'

'I have understood from the best scholarship available to me that there is some doubt whether knowledge
of God is innate,' said Severo. He paused, in case his
opponent wished to contradict him, but Fra Murta

offered no comment. 'How would it be,' Severo continued, 'if there were available to us an absolute proof, worldly evidence of an incontrovertible nature, that the knowledge of God is inborn in everyone? Would that not be a missionary weapon of great power? Would you not like to have such a thing?'

'What kind of evidence do you mean?' asked Fra Murta.

'Suppose there were a child reared outside human society, who had never heard a word spoken in any language. Suppose such a child were taught to speak in careful seclusion, so that it could not accidentally learn the truths of religion; and then suppose one were to ask it what it knew . . .'

'Such an experiment would be forbidden,' said Fra Murta. 'It would outrage charity. I could not approve it. Never forget, Holiness, that the purposes of the sacred Inquisition are merciful.'

'But what if this forbidden experiment had occurred naturally?' Severo asked. There was an expression of deep interest in the glittering eyes of the other man, which he failed to dissemble by toying with the quill and paper before him on the table. 'In fact, it is extremely lucky that you have come, Fra Murta, for now there will be two of us to witness what occurs,' Severo continued, and gave him an account of the snow-child. About the providential coincidence of the child and Palinor's arrival, about what arrangements he had made, and why.

'I must ask your forgiveness, Holiness,' said Fra Murta. 'I was too hasty in ascribing your slowness in this case to slackness, or even to reluctance. There are some bishops, I blush to tell you, who regard the duty to pursue heresy with repugnance, and who not only fail to assist the Inquisition but even obstruct it. It is not at all unheard of . . . Indeed, as I need hardly tell you, it was the disgraceful tardiness in the bishops'

Inquisition against heretics that led to the duties and powers of inquisition being given to the mendicant orders of monks, my order among them. That led to our powers to override the local clergy. You will forgive us for supposing that you too were slack or recalcitrant; the reports that reached us in Rome were garbled.'

'I am familiar with the origin and extent of your authority, Fra Murta. As to confusion about the present case, I am not surprised at it. I have proceeded with the greatest possible discretion in regard to the atheist, and in sworn secrecy over the child. My reasons are obvious to a man of your intelligence.'

Fra Murta bowed. 'I cannot wait to see this phenomenon of nature,' he said. 'How long since, Holiness, did you consign her to the care of the nuns of Sant Clara?'

'It is now many months ago. Some progress has been made. I am not sure if it is yet enough.'

'But shall we not go at once and see?'

'I think I should warn the nuns that we intend to come; they may need to prepare her for a visitation of strangers. I will take you there in, shall we say, a fortnight? Meanwhile, the island is full of shrines that a man of your piety will no doubt wish to visit.'

As soon as Fra Murta had left, Severo called Rafal. 'Have that man watched,' he said. 'I want to know of every inch of ground on which he sets foot; I want to know just where he is day and night, and every person to whom he has spoken, even to give a good day. Discreetly, mind, and by no-one of clerical appearance. Go and hire me a couple of footpads.'

Beneditx was praying. 'Out of the depths have I cried unto thee, O Lord, Lord hear my prayer. Let thine ears be attentive to the voice of my supplication . . .'

When he had finished, he rose and went to find Palinor. He had one last dart to throw. Palinor was not in his chamber. Beneditx flinched slightly at finding himself with Dolca. The girl was heavy-lidded, and Beneditx, who had not noticed her at all at first, was suddenly finding her disturbing. He longed for the peace of the Galilea.

'He is below,' she said. 'In the workshops.'

Beneditx descended the stairs into the warren of coopers' shops, weaving shops, potters' shops, carpenters' shops and suchlike, full of noisy workers, men and women, whose crafts produced the wealth of the Saracen's House. Palinor was deep in conversation with the blacksmith, and showing him drawings. 'Really?' the man was saying. 'Would it work?'

'Perfectly,' said Palinor. 'Look, we put a wheel in the waterfall, and we take a drive off like this . . .' He frowned slightly when he saw Beneditx, but he came at once, saying 'Later' to the smith. They ascended again to their airy colonnade.

'What were you doing?' asked Beneditx.

'It would be possible to make the water drive a hammer for the smith. He would be relieved of a considerable part of the labour, and could use both hands to work the metal. I was discussing it with him.'

Beneditx had never given one moment's consideration to smithy work, and was nonplussed. 'Is the work hard?' he asked.

'You have only to watch it, to see,' said Palinor, sitting at the little rustic table and clapping his hands for Joffre. Joffre brought nuts and apricots and a jug of wine, and left them, padding silently away on bare feet.

'You make out a good case for doubt,' said Beneditx. 'Before you came I would have thought that unbelievers were all frivolous – merely people who wished to be relieved of the duty to good conduct that belief imposes – but you have taught me otherwise. I see that doubt may be as deep, as serious, as belief. But there is a deficit in your arguments, just the same. It is one thing to be an unbeliever, to think that the proofs of God are not sufficient; but that would leave the matter in doubt. You would be maintaining simply that you did not know. How can you go further and say, "There is no God"? How can you defend a claim to negative certainty, which of all things is the hardest to prove?'

Palinor was silent for a while. Then he said, 'You are right, Beneditx, in saying that to claim to know for certain that there is no God would be a preposterous claim, so vast is the universe, so puny our understanding of it.'

Briefly, hope and relief spiralled in Benedtix's heart. 'Will you answer to the name agnostic, then?'

'No. Not in the sense you defined – that an agnostic is one who thinks that one day or if something happened he might be convinced. For I think that it is *in principle* impossible to know whether there is a God or not. I know therefore with immovable certainty that I shall never know that God exists. Likewise I shall never know that he does not. Such knowledge is always, and in principle, out of reach.'

A sort of coldness ran in Beneditx's veins. 'Why do you say that?' he asked.

'Have you seen the little fishes that swim in these clear streams?' asked Palinor. 'What do they know of the air? As they are immersed in water and can know only water, so are we immersed in space and time and can know only our universe. But your God is outside both space and time and beyond the universe. Perhaps, if he exists, there are dim reflections of him in the material world, as, for the fishes, there are green reaches of the water shaded by trees. But knowledge is a firmer, clearer thing, and for us not possible.'

'But God has revealed himself to us, so that we do know him, though it be not by human means . . .' Beneditx spoke urgently, but as if to himself.

'No, my friend. For the difficulty in this knowing does not lie with God, but with us. It arises out of the very nature of the tools we have for thinking with, for knowing with. Our minds are sunk deep in the waters of space and time. Look, I will show you something, as you showed me the mosaic.' Palinor clapped his hands for Joffre, and Joffre brought him a broken lantern, that had been hanging above the stair. Working delicately with his long dark fingers, Palinor extracted a pane of glass from one side of the lantern. It was a greenish gold colour, and full of little bubbles. Before he had freed it, Joffre brought him also a handful of flowers.

Palinor laid the flowers on the ground. Then he put a white blossom in his wine-cup on the table and said to Beneditx, 'What colour is that?'

'White,' said Beneditx.

Palinor held the glass in front of the cup. 'What colour is it now?' he asked.

'It looks golden,' said Beneditx, patiently, 'but it is still white.'

'You know that only because you saw it without the glass,' said Palinor. 'Close your eyes for a moment.' While Beneditx closed his eyes, Palinor switched the flower, taking a different, large one from the bunch. He held the lantern pane in front of the flower, and said 'You can look now. What colour is this one?'

'White?' said Beneditx. *wrong*

Lifting the glass away, Palinor showed him a golden flower. 'Shut your eyes again,' he said. This time, when Beneditx looked again, there were two flowers behind the pane. 'Which of these is blue?' asked Palinor.

'The smaller one is darker,' said Beneditx, un-happily. 'So I expect it is that one.'

'Alas!' said Palinor. 'The darker one is red. Now, what colour is the smaller one?'

'Red,' said Beneditx.

'How do you know?'

'You told me yourself.'

'But I might have been lying,' said Palinor, laying down the pane. The smaller flower was blue. 'To trust me and to know are not the same thing at all. You may believe your scriptures, Beneditx, and they may be true – but still you do not and you cannot know what lies outside space and time. You cannot, I cannot. Nobody can.'

'And this is what you mean when you say that you are an atheist?'

'Yes. It is not quite what you mean by the word, I know, but the only alternative you offered me was to name myself as one who could in principle be convinced, and I know that I am one who in principle cannot be. Further, I know that all those who say that they know that God exists are mistaken. They can know no such thing.'

It was of his opponent that Beneditx thought first. 'This might cost you your life, Palinor.'

'But will you tell me to bend my conscience in order to save my life? If I am the fragment of dark glass that the great craftsman set to be a shadow in the picture, to be the obverse of a sparkle in his golden sky, why do you strive so to alter the pattern, to tilt me into the light? You are a man of faith, but is faith more than doubt? Or is it also part of a whole, each part being necessary, but none more necessary than another?'

25

Severo found Fra Murta's company unpalatable, and was relieved when the path narrowed as it began to ascend the pass to Sant Clara and they had to ride single file. Until then the friar had maintained a continuous stream of nauseating conversation, retailing the huge numbers of heretics who had been flushed out by various stratagems used by the brotherhood of itinerant inquisitors of which Fra Murta was one. Severo did not doubt the Church's right, the Church's duty, to crusade against heresy, where heresy was a problem; on Grandinsula any heretics kept their heads down, and he thought it best to leave them to their own damnation. But it was one thing to accept that there must be steps against heresy, and another to relish them. After listening for some miles to an animated account of how many had been 'relaxed' – that is, handed over to the secular powers for execution – and how many at the last minute had offered confessions and repented in exchange for being garrotted before being burned, Severo offered a rebuke.

'The shedding of blood is a terrible thing, in any circumstances, Fra Murta.'

'My name is Damaso, Holiness. And yes, of course, naturally. But the Church is innocent of the blood of these recalcitrants. The Holy Inquisition merely discovers heretics; they are handed over to the civil power to dispose of. Any blood guilt is on the hands of the civil power.'

Severo reflected grimly that on Grandinsula the civil

power in question was vested in him. 'Fra Murta, has it ever happened in your extensive experience that a person accused of heresy has been found to be innocent?'

'Once. The woman's accusers all owed her money. We kept the names of the accusers strictly secret, of course. But when we asked her to name any enemies she had, she listed them all. We admonished her and released her. That was the only time I can recall. Of course, heresy accusations are nearly always denied vigorously at first. Later they are admitted.'

The narrowing path brought relief to Severo. Instead of this distressing conversation and repeated invitations to call the man Damaso, he could ride ahead in blessed silence, hearing only the murmuring winds in the branches and the innocent birdsong, spurring his horse lightly whenever the clopping hooves of the horses behind him seemed to gain on him. He tried to calm himself. What the child said was in the hands of God, and God was merciful.

He was welcomed with the usual semblance of joy at Sant Clara. A posy of wild flowers stood on the windowsill of his room in the guesthouse, overlooking the sea. A ewer of warm water was ready for him, and a jug of wine. He felt suddenly and irrationally ashamed – like someone who has unwittingly trodden in filth and brought it into a friend's house on his shoes. The creature whom he had brought with him, who was even now settling into the room next to his, should have been kept away from this kindly house. Severo took a grip on himself and offered a silent apology to his God for such a twinge of loathing for a fellow churchman. He wondered what was happening to him; instead of the calm progress through life which he had been able to achieve these many years, he seemed to keep needing to rein in his feelings, turn himself round, calculate a new course, like an inexperienced navigator in stormy waters. He recited a psalm to himself before going across the garden to interrogate the snow-child.

'Is this she?' he asked. She was standing facing him and Fra Murta at the other end of the long refectory table. That ugly young novice stood just behind her, and the sisters were all ranged in the shadows, sitting along the walls of the room. He was staggered by the change in the child. In his mind's eye he had expected the howling, scratching, raging creature he remembered. A thing that could not really be questioned, that bore witness in its every sound and movement that it knew neither God nor man. He had expected Fra Murta to be confronted with what Jaime had called blackness. But what he saw now was a slender, bone-thin child wearing a clean shift, standing straight. Her fingers were laced together, and she wove and wound them restlessly. Tendrils of dark curling hair hung round her narrow face and shaded her brow. She seemed – he was thunderstruck – a pleasing young girl. Then suddenly she worked her jaw convulsively, moving it in an exaggerated sideways slide, suddenly wolfish, an appearance which as rapidly disappeared. Watching her, Severo discovered that he had not expected his experiment to work, that he had been deceiving himself, and that he was terrified now of what she would say.

'Amara,' he said to her, 'do you remember me?'

She shot him a darting, piercing, discomforting glance from under her dark brows, her fringe of hair. He asked again, and she said, 'Not know you. Not like him.' She looked fleetingly at Fra Murta. Severo pressed his lips firmly together. He could not afford to smile.

'Amara,' he said, 'do you remember living in the mountains?'

'Snow there. Yes,' she said. 'I go there more. Soon.'

'Who was with you in the mountain cave?'

'Wolf. Young wolfs.'

'Who did you then think created you, looked after you, as the nuns do now?'

'Wolf.'

He tried again. 'Was there any spirit, anything all around you, unseen, but that you felt?'

She scowled with an effort, it seemed to him, of thought. 'Cold,' she said.

His relief was immense. She was not going to say anything to comfort Fra Murta.

Fra Murta now joined in. 'What was above you, in the mountains, my child?' he asked.

'I not your child,' she said, scornfully.

He tried again. 'What was above you in the mountains, Amara?'

'Sky,' she said.

'Was the sky empty? Could you feel something there that helped you, cared for you?'

'Like wolf?' she said. 'Wolf in sky?' She emitted her startling, barking laugh. 'Nothing in sky.'

'She does not understand us,' said Fra Murta. 'They have not taught her enough language. Teach her some more.'

'Fra Murta,' said Severo, standing abruptly. 'You overreach yourself. It is not for you to command this sisterhood. Withdraw with me, and help me decide what is to be done.'

As they left her he heard the soft voice of one of the nuns behind them, comforting the child. 'It is all right, Amara. You answered well. You did well, child, we are proud of you . . .' It was true, he thought. The poor creature had done well. To the immense question they had put to her she had given a clear answer. The answer was, 'No.'

26

Sor Agnete, the abbess, and Sor Eulalie were in conference together. It was not exactly an official conference;
that would have needed the whole sisterhood, everyone who had taken the final vows. But these three
were old friends. They had been together so long. The
world they had renounced had vanished behind them,
and the years had flowed steadily in the unchanging
channels of Sant Clara. The sisters who had admitted
and instructed these three lay now in the little church-
yard below the abbey. And Severo had left such dismay
behind him that in their distress the three friends
needed to talk together before uttering a syllable to
the whole convocation.

'What is to be done?' asked the abbess.

Sor Agnete looked out of the window into the cloister
garden. There below her sat Amara, playing with her
drum. Josefa, half visible sitting in the shade of a tree,
was sewing expertly, with swift jerky movements of
her needle. It had for some time now been possible
to combine watching over Amara with other tasks.
Amara did not beat her drum or tap a rhythm on
it, though she had been shown over and over. She
picked up a handful of tiny pebbles and cast them
at it, making a meaningless rattle, a random sound
like a burst of rain against a pane of glass or a little
avalanche under a foot on a rocky surface. She seemed
to like this inchoate sound.

'We were too simple,' said Sor Agnete. She was
in the grip of moral anger. 'I never imagined that

the experiment we were asked to carry out was not genuine. Had the possibility crossed my mind that his Holiness was not in good faith, I would have dismissed it. But now he has his answer, and he rejects it. We are to retain the child until he has a different one!'

'He is wrestling with that other man,' said the abbess. 'And perhaps he does not realize, as Fra Murta certainly does, that the longer we keep her here the more certain it is that her answer will be contaminated.'

'Contaminated?' asked Sor Eulalie. 'What do you mean, Mother?'

'With knowledge. Contaminated with worldly knowledge of God. She lives amongst us; God is our everyday concern. Sooner or later, one of us will forget her vow, let a word slip, answer a question carelessly. Sooner or later, when nobody is looking, she will wander into the chapel . . .'

'She is blessedly free from curiosity,' said Sor Agnete.

'But we thought we were doing a work of charity towards her that would come, by and by, to an end; that the cardinal would receive her back from us in a gentled state and find a place for her. And it seems to us now that we may be her prison keepers for ever.' The abbess spoke quietly, as if thinking aloud.

'She hates confinement. She likes neither our food nor our company. And how should these things seem good to one who cannot in the smallest degree understand or share our purposes?' said Sor Eulalie.

'Besides, there is Josefa,' said Sor Agnete.

'Yes,' said the abbess, 'there is Josefa. We received her, but she is shut out of her rightful progress here. Until the child is gone, Josefa cannot proceed to her fuller vows. She is in limbo. Sor Agnete, remind me what you spoke of some time back, in regard to the strangeness of the child . . . I told you to keep such thoughts to yourself.'

'I had wondered, Mother, if the child was strange because she had been abandoned to the wolves or if, perhaps, she had been abandoned to the wolves because she was strange. I know that sometimes the poorest people cannot think what to do with crazed or maimed children. They cannot afford them. But Mother, I think now there is nothing wrong with Amara. I think, on the contrary, she must be fully sharp-witted, or she would not have been able to learn as much as she has.'

'But you see, Sisters,' said the abbess. 'If the child had been abandoned when she was already speaking, already hearing those around her . . . then the whole experiment would be pointless. She would already have some idea of God, gained in the usual way.'

'But Mother, the difficulty seems to be the opposite. She answered that she did not know God,' said Sor Eulalie.

'She said that she was not aware of something above her and around her in the mountains. And his Holiness and his companion answered that we should teach her some more and better speech. But if we could show that she had been in human society long enough before she was with the wolves, then if she understands better and her answer shows knowledge of God, it will not prove that she has that knowledge inborn, only that she has remembered fragments from her earliest life through later vicissitudes. Then there would be no point in this experiment; then we could teach her to know and love her Saviour; then we could let her depart.'

'We did not promise not to try to discover more about her,' said Sor Agnete.

'No; we promised enough, but not that. We are not bound beyond our promise,' Sor Eulalie agreed.

'But how could one find out?' Sor Agnete wondered.

'She must have been abandoned either as a babe, above a dozen years ago, or as a tiny child, say ten years since. And we don't know where. To whom could we write for intelligence? And is it likely that the perpetrator of such cruelty would readily admit to it?'

'People do reclaim their abandoned children,' said Sor Eulalie. 'They don't mean to be cruel. They leave them out in public places in hard times, for some more prosperous person to raise.'

'Amara is not absolutely friendless,' said the abbess. 'We will send for Jaime. We will see what he can find out about her.'

'It is a matter of great interest,' Fra Murta said. 'I thank you for letting me share in it. By and by the wolf-child will be a great and powerful example to all who hear heresy condemned. She will define the limits of good faith, beyond all possibility of doubt.'

'You think her answer will change? I heard her say "no" to our questions.'

'But she did not understand us. When she does, she will surely say yes; she knew her creator by brute instinct, even among the brutes.' The path had widened out again on the final miles back towards Ciudad, and the two men were riding side by side. 'However, that will take a long time. Meanwhile, I should declare an edict of grace. And you should deliver the atheist to me for questioning. That is what I was sent here to do.'

'Does your work please you, Fra Murta?' Severo enquired.

'It pleases God,' the man replied.

'Some might prefer to please God in other ways,' Severo said.

Fra Murta said, 'I have met heresy. I know its power of evil as others, perhaps, do not.'

'Was some friend of yours entrapped by it?' asked

Severo. He supposed he ought to try to understand the man.

'I myself was ensnared!' cried Fra Murta. 'And the trap that ensnared me was my very desire to know the truth! I stood at a roadside husting, when I was but a green youth, hungry for the word of God, and an evil man poured poison into my pure heart – and what glittering poison, too! Talk of the spiritual church which had replaced a worldly one, which acknowledged no obedience and allowed foul unchastity full rein because sin could not touch the souls of the elect! Into this mire I fell full deep and was with great labour rescued and set right by the love of an inquisitor. As he did for me, so would I do for others, while I draw breath.'

Severo rode with a heavy heart. He had been entertaining a thread of hope that it might be possible to buy Fra Murta off; it was widely believed that inquisitors were avaricious, driven by greed for the fines paid by penitent heretics; but that did not sound likely in view of Fra Murta's last effusion. Severo's duty as a loyal son of the Church was clear. Fra Murta came to him on a mission from Rome. Severo's power was sufficient to obstruct him but not without long and grave repercussions. Besides, even a cardinal obeys Rome. Outside that allegiance chaos lies. And, thought Severo, whatever was he thinking of, even considering foiling a servant of the Holy Inquisition? Could he be one of those contemptible people who gladly obey until the first moment obedience becomes difficult? For he was realizing that his unspoken desire to save Palinor presented the first difficulty his faith had ever occasioned him – beside which penance and celibacy and vigils and plain-living were nothing – mere bagatelles.

'Preach an edict of grace by all means,' he said. 'But as to the atheist, the question of whether he falls within your competence is the very question at issue. I will meditate further on that.'

Fra Murta looked daggers at him but only bowed his assent.

In the days and weeks that followed, Severo's watchers enabled him to follow the friar's progress. Fra Murta went on foot from parish to parish round the island, preaching. He kept away from Ciudad at first. He declared his time of grace, inviting heretics to accuse themselves, to come forward, to accept punishment, lenient punishment, and escape the terrible fate that would fall upon those who were wicked and failed to confess. He had a golden tongue, and the people flocked to hear him. He whipped them to a frenzy of remorse and hatred of heresy. Tears flowed freely, and storms of prayers ascended. And in the quiet parishes among the olive groves and terraced fields, in the tall churches that crowned the little towns on the wide plains, every nook and cranny was searched, and here and there a heretic was found – found and forgiven with tirades of gratitude to the presiding saints.

27

It had happened everywhere. The women wept, sometimes. The men shrugged. They had had no choice.
The harvest had failed, the child had been faulty –
lame, blind, lacking. The little fields and the orchards
belonging to so many could not support such burdens.
Or the child had simply been one too many. Jaime had
a friendly face; people answered his questions. Was
it a brother he was seeking, or a sister? They cast
back their minds, tried to remember for him. Angelina
had abandoned a child, some dozen years back . . .
yes, a girl. What had become of the babe? Why, Pere
and Jacinta had picked her up and reared her. As a
servant, of course, a playmate and handmaiden for
their daughter. Jaime would find her at the house in
Camino da Granja.

Everywhere he asked, he found the abandoned
children. If it was a sin to abandon babes, it was
not one that the Church was much agitated about;
very much less sinful, one would conclude, than
heresy. People often left a token with the child – a
trinket, a coin, an embroidered kerchief, so that later
the foundling could be identified, perhaps reclaimed.
Mostly the parents would keep their mouths shut,
Jaime gathered, watching from a distance and silent
unless there was a risk of incest. Once or twice he
was told of a quarrel between parents who wanted
a child back and the foster family who had rescued
and fed it. The priest had appealed to the bishop for a
ruling. Once he heard a tale of a boy claimed back when

his elder brother died; girls, however, once abandoned, seemed to be gone for good.

There was a way of doing this. A child would be left at dawn on the church steps, with a little salt, if it was a baptized child. Someone would see it there and take it in. Jaime heard of a woman given public penance for leaving a child at dusk, in winter. By morning it was dead of cold, and there was outrage at her callousness. Had she left it in daylight none would have blamed her. But wickedly, because it was a child of shame, she had tried to leave it under cover of night.

Eventually, Jaime went home and talked to his mother. 'It's often done, Jaime,' she told him. 'If you weren't such a dreamer you'd know these things. It isn't cruel; not so cruel as dragging a whole family down to starvation. Often the child does well out of it – it's a wealthier house that picks it up than the one it was set out from, you see. Do you know Leonor? She has five looms – five – going all day every day, and her women are all girls she picked up at the church door. You can hear them chattering and laughing together at the open door as you go past – and what a quantity of cloths she brings to market!'

'But they are slaves. They can never marry.'

'Is that such a terrible thing? You could not have married if you hadn't found a patron.'

'Mother, why did you rear me, then? If there wasn't enough patrimony for me and my brothers . . .'

'Why do you think?' she said, crossly. 'Do you want me to tell you I love you – a great grown lump like you with a wife of your own to coddle you?'

He smiled at her. 'I shan't find what I'm looking for in the plain,' he said. 'I must look in the mountains, where things are wilder. I might be gone some time. Help Fransoya look after the babe, won't you?'

'I'll help her all she lets me, son,' Jaime's mother said. 'You know yourself how little that is.'

'It is enough. It would be more at need.'

'Son, you know what you are looking for, don't you? A slut of some kind, a girl with a reason not to expose the child on the church steps. A secret act. Perhaps an intention that the child would die. Most likely something you won't get told by anyone, and you won't get thanked for asking. You take care of yourself, son.'

'Yes, yes,' he said. 'I shall take my leave of Fransoya and the boy and be gone in the morning, Mother.'

So Jaime walked out of Sant Jeronimo the same hour that Fra Murta walked in.

Amara had discovered a new game. 'What you thinking, Josefa?' she would ask.

'Of the sea,' Josefa might answer.

'Sea not here,' Amara would say triumphantly. 'We go now?'

Every time, Josefa was pleased that Amara could ask for the sea – that she could speak of something not present before her eyes. If she was asked in her turn what she was thinking of, she usually said 'meat', but sometimes said 'mountain', or 'snow'. Once she said, 'Running. Running far,' and sulked for the next hour, pacing to and fro in the haybarn. She could not be used to help Sor Blancha with the sheep or the three goats, because these creatures were terrified of her. She seemed now so little, so seldom wolflike to the nuns that it was astonishing that the sheep knew any difference between Amara and another guardian, but they did.

Josefa was slowly being driven crazy by the endless meaningless patter of handfuls of grit cast on the little drum.

The people of Sant Jeronimo packed into the square. A stand of boxes had been made halfway up the church steps, and the bell was clamouring brazenly for everyone's attention. Fra Murta looked grave. His hands were tucked into the wide sleeves of his habit, and his head was bowed. The crowd was eager. Fra Murta was something new; and last time an itinerant preacher had come he had urged instant repentance, and there had been a fine show. All the notorious sinners had repented and come forward for forgiveness, and Juanita had caused raptures of approval from the crowd by asking loudly to be forgiven what she had done with Pablo, and Petro, and Benito, and Tomas, and . . . naming just about every respectable man in the town.

But heresy turned out to be nothing like so much fun. It was a sin which one could commit without realizing it. It could be a mistake. One could be cast into eternal fire for something from which not a twinge of pleasure had been derived! Fra Murta assured the uneasy crowd that error was more likely to entrap proud and clever people than those of simple minds, but he had surely got it wrong; everyone knew that errors were more likely in the less learned!

They had thirty days, he told them, to come forward and confess. And they were under a duty to denounce any of their neighbours who had committed any crime against the faith. 'If any of you,' cried Fra Murta, 'has known or heard say that anyone, living or dead, present or absent, has done or uttered or believed any act, word or opinion, heretical or suspect, erroneous, rash, ill-sounding, scandalous or heretically blasphemous, you must come forward! You must reveal it to the tribunal within six days! Are you uncertain what deeds should be denounced? These are the crimes of heretics, my friends. They blaspheme; they keep familiar devils; they practise witchcraft; they make pacts with the devil, and by his means have fair-weather harvests and children who escape infection. They mix sacred and profane objects, and will steal the consecrated host for foul purposes; they marry in holy orders and solicit women in the confessional; they commit bigamy. They say there is no sin in simple fornication, or usury, or perjury, or that concubinage is better than marriage. They insult or maltreat crucifixes and images of holy saints; they disbelieve or doubt articles of faith, and continue in excommunication, refusing to be reconciled, they have recourse to astrology, they possess forbidden books, as for instance, works of Mohammedan sages, or those of perfidious Jews, or the Bible in a vulgar tongue. They keep friendship with other heretics, and say that those who confess to the Inquisition are innocent martyrs or confessed only through fear – my friends, such sinners are so loathsome in the sight of God that they bring misery, misfortune and disease on all who harbour them. You must cast them out! Denounce them, even if they are your mothers and sisters, your cousins, your masters, or your priest! Anyone who comes forward and confesses, provided he denounces to us all other offenders known to him, will be given mercy, will be given a light penance and restored to the bosom of the Church. But anyone who is denounced not having confessed has cause to fear! Think well then, people of Sant Jeronimo. I leave you to think; but I will return tomorrow to hear what any of you have to say to me!'

The people were sick with fear when he left them. The priest of Sant Jeronimo rang the church bells at nightfall and gathered the townspeople in the nave. He told them that anyone who confessed would not be released till they had named others, and those others would be taken up and likewise released only when they had given names.

'We shall be engulfed all alike, sinners and believers,' he said, 'and so nobody must confess or name a single person to the inquisitor. If nobody speaks a single word, we shall all be safe. And you must confess your sins of heresy to me. I will punish and absolve you.'

'But he will not be satisfied unless he has someone denounced,' said Tomas, the cobbler, a man who could read. How could his illiterate neighbours tell if his three books were by Mohammedans or Jews?

'We will tell him that no such crimes have ever been heard of amongst us,' said the priest. 'But we will tell him that we have heard that there is a heretic at Alquiera, who is using witchcraft to deform the water and to work iron without labour of human hands. He will leave us then and go after larger fish to fry.'

Jaime camped at night. He slept under a cowhide, propped on a crossbar between two low forks made of branches. He had a jar of oil to soak and soften his stale bread, some olives, some salt fish. The mountains gave forth abundant fresh water. How far might a wolf range? he had wondered, and concluded that the heights above Sant Jeronimo were the best place to look. Among the great swelling masses of the mountains, the high woods, their trees dwarfed and thinned, the lush pastures that the high valleys cradled, up there in the cool air, where water flowed freely and the land was never parched. There from the spring to the autumn the flocks and herds fattened and prospered, and the shepherds and drovers lived like hermits, cutting fleeces and making cheese. There were dozens of little encampments where they lived the summers through. The children stayed with the women in the hot little towns below.

A shepherd told Jaime something that caught his attention. That was a tale of a stolen lamb, that had been found alive in the wolf's lair, curled up among its cubs. The shepherd thought the wolf had taken the lamb living back to the den to feed the cubs, and then the cub scent had got on to the lamb's wool before she killed it and confused her. Certainly the lamb, restored to the flock, had spread terror among them, and had had to be reared by hand, because its mother rejected it. But beyond this, Jaime could hear nothing that helped.

Lower down the slopes the charcoal burners worked, felling and sawing, levelling their sites, and ringing the hearth circles with stones, stacking the timber with an ancient elaborate skill. When a mound was ready, it was sealed with clay and gravel and set alight by dropping burning morsels through the smoke hole at the apex. The pitstead burned for many days, and they watched it, adding more burning tinder, or closing the air-vents between the stones. They were easy to find, though they worked in the deeps of the upland woods, because of the thin bluish columns of smoke from the burning that ascended above the treetops from their camps. And they were easier to visit; they brought their wives and children to the high woods with them, and baked bread in makeshift clay ovens, and usually had some to spare. Children ran around the workers and were scolded only for touching axe or saw, or playing too near the heat of the smouldering pitsteads. A visitor was welcome – another voice, a different face, some news from the world below.

But the *carboneros* were scattered all over the mountain ranges, living and working in families, maybe hundreds of tiny groups. None of them had ever heard of abandoning a child up here in the woods, instead of waiting till winter and taking it to the church door. Such a thing would be an outrage, they told Jaime. Up here in the woods anything could happen to a child left out alone. It would not be found for many days, if ever. It would die of cold, or have its eyes taken out by an eagle, or fall from a precipice, or be taken by a wolf . . .

'Didn't the Mulet family lose a child to a wolf?' said a woman Jaime was talking to, to her companion.

'That's what they said had happened,' the older woman answered. 'The poor mite was mauled, certainly.'

'Do you know of a child that vanished utterly, that might have been stolen and not harmed?' Jaime asked. Nobody did. Guided by the smoke on the distant hillsides, the spread of haze in the clear air, he thanked them and moved on. His wanderings were taking him further and further away from Sant Jeronimo, from the reaches of the mountain pastures that were worked by men of his own town and from the spot where the wolf-child had been found. He had lost hope of success. And then he came upon a larger encampment of burners – they had better than a dozen hearths working, and had cut a wide swathe through the woodlands, taking every oak for a mile or more through the forest. He realized at once that they were strangers, for they spoke with the slight tang of easterners. They were pirates – no landowner had given them a licence to fell and burn, and not for nothing were their fires damped down in daylight and vented at night, and their sites all tucked into a towering fold of the precipice, often wreathed in cloud. Jaime made himself out to be escaping from some scrape with the authorities in the town below, and they accepted him and let him buy his supper by bringing loads of small kindling, working his donkey to and fro between woodcutters and pitstead.

At dusk they were busy, fanning up the fires and adjusting them. A sheep roasted with succulent fragrance on a spit in the middle of the camp – he did not ask where they got it – and a young girl with bare dirty feet strummed for them on three strings and sang a wild shapeless song. They gathered to eat by moonlight, feeding their children with scraps of fat meat offered on the tips of their knives. Jaime remembered a bottle of wine in the bottom of his pannier, and going to fetch it found it had been stolen. It was already open and going from hand to hand, which did not stop them thanking him for it, handsomely. He chose his moment carefully, between song and song, and asked his question, worn into limpness by his hopelessness of an answer; and there he heard the story that kept him sleepless all night, that had him loading his blanket into his empty panniers and leading his donkey away down the mountainside when dawn was at its first and thinnest illumination and his companions of the night before were still sleeping soundly all around.

Rafal brought Severo reports from the men he had set to watch Fra Murta. There was no comfort in them – Fra Murta had not been seen visiting prostitutes or taking bribes. He had been preaching his edict of grace from end to end of the island, with inflammatory zeal. 'It is the same everywhere, Holiness,' Rafal told him. 'The quiet, pious folk stay silent, and the miscreants tear their garments and repent and offer to accuse their neighbours . . . What makes them flock to hear him and willingly obey him, when their own priests can barely harry them so far as church on holy days?'

'When he is so loathsome, you mean?' asked Severo. Rafal hung his head.

'He must be a good preacher,' said Severo. 'And he is something new. And they are afraid. They are promised safety in heaven and on earth if they pray loudly and denounce others.'

'Can't you do something, Holiness?' Rafal said.

'What would you have me do? He is within his powers. Let him make one mistake – one step too far, however tiny, and I will send him packing. But he will be very careful. He knows I am his enemy, and watchful.'

'Forgive me, Holiness. You seem always to be his friend.'

'He better understands me than you do, it seems,' said Severo, sighing. 'Leave me now; I have work to do.' He returned to his writing. The documents curled and were held down with seals, with his psalter, with his inkstand. He read and signed doggedly. '*Severo, miseratione divina episcopus Grandinsulensis, Salutem . . .*' When he heard footsteps approaching his door, he bowed his head and wrote faster, hoping to finish one more fiat before the interruption. He expected a clerk with another bundle of placets from the scriptorium, but instead Beneditx entered.

He was dusty from the road and casting off his outer cloak as he stood there. Severo swept the work aside and, standing, reached out his hands, smiling at his friend.

'Have you convinced him?' he asked.

'No,' said Beneditx. He sat down on the edge of Severo's bed and sank his head in his hands. 'He has convinced me.'

28

'They are not sure how long ago – twelve, thirteen, fourteen years back. Their lives are unchanging; one year is the same as another to them.'

Jaime stood in the cloister garth, talking to the abbess. He came now as a friend, and only Sor Agnete lingered nearby, overhearing.

'About the right time, then. Go on.'

'She came from the valley somewhere, of course, but she didn't say and they didn't ask where. She was heavy with child, and it had taken her days, they thought, to climb to their region. She begged for food, and they made her work for it, kneading dough, carrying water. They speak of her with contempt – as a slut.'

'No wedding ring? Of course not. Go on.'

'It seems the charcoal burners have known this to happen repeatedly. A girl comes up to them from one valley, before it shows too much; she swells and gives birth in the mountain, and then takes the babe and goes down into another valley where nobody knows her. She might expose the child, or she might pass herself off as a widow. They reminded me that the sierra is called "the widow maker".'

'I thought that was because men died of their exploits there.'

'So did I, Mother, but it seems there is this other reason.'

'Go on.'

'Her time came, and she was delivered, lying on the

forest floor a little way from the camp. The woman with her was alarmed and went for help. When she returned with others, they found the woman dying and alone. But they saw a wolf, or they think they did, slinking off, moving above them on the open face of the mountain. Two of them could remember this.'

'So we have found her origin? And it does not help us; if she was stolen in her first hour of life, then the cardinal is right, she can have heard no word of God . . .'

'The story fits Amara, Mother,' said Jaime, 'in every way but one. The woman bore twins; both were taken. There should have been two of her.'

'There is still faith,' said Severo. 'Hold fast to faith . . . can't you?' But Beneditx shook his head. An expression of desperation transformed his familiar face.

'I am punished,' he said, sombrely. 'Bitterly punished. Simple faith was for others, Severo; I knew better. Reason carried me to the limits of reason's possibility, I prided myself to think how far that was. God with his gift of faith stooped almost into the pit to reach the understanding of my fellow men, but I ascended scales of understanding and extended my grasp towards him! I was founded on reason. And now the mounting block is kicked away from under me, and without it I cannot mount and ride. I have no strength to gain the saddle of the fine steed that bore me once so proudly! I am falling into the pit.'

'God will see you falling,' said Severo bravely. 'He will unfurl the ladder of faith and lower it to where you stand, be it at the gates of hell . . .' But he was sick at heart.

'Pray for me,' said Beneditx.

'We will pray together,' said Severo.

'I cannot pray,' said Beneditx. 'I am afraid the whole sky is empty, and no-one hears our voice . . .'

'I have done this to you,' Severo said. 'I set you to this task, and when you asked me to take it from you, I would not, but set you on to it again. I am to blame.'

Beneditx shook his head. 'No, Severo. Each of us must take the blame for his own state of mind. And how could we know what the atheist might say? We had never heard such words spoken and were warmly wrapped with the cloak of faith. I had no idea of the force of the wind. But, for example, how could one answer . . .'

'Do not tell me what he said,' said Severo. 'Or I too might lose my footing. We will pray together, now, all night. That void you speak of, that unanswering empty sky, is your God for this hour, and you will pray to it, if none other be there for you. Come, I command it.'

Face down, side by side on the marble floor before the high altar of the cathedral, the two men lay in the deepening darkness. The clergy sung vespers and retired, the candles lit by the faithful below the images of the saints guttered one by one into darkness. At some time in the long hours between vespers and prime, Severo's outstretched hand reached the outstretched hand of his suffering friend and held it.

In the morning Severo did two things. He sent Beneditx home. 'Back to the Galilea, Beneditx. Finish that treatise on the knowledge of angels. Finish it in peace.'

'But what will you do with Palinor?' Beneditx asked.

'Think of him no more,' said Severo. 'I command you not to think of him.'

When Beneditx had gone, Severo sat reflecting. He was appalled to think of the damage he had done; heart-sick at the misery into which Beneditx was cast. What had he thought he was doing, trying to outmanoeuvre an inquisitor, who should have had his fervent support? How had he come to value the safety of a blasphemous heretic above that of a great doctor of

theology? Sunk in self-loathing, he reproached himself.
How had it happened that he, Severo, had spent his
whole life in the service of the Church and then failed
in diligence the very first time something was asked of
him that he found difficult?

In an impulse of remorse and rage, he enquired
where Fra Murta was to be found, and learning that
he was now promulgating his edict of grace in the
streets of Ciudad, he sent for him and gave Palinor
into his hands.

'Were you always alone, Amara? Did you have a
companion in the snows?'

It seemed most likely the other babe had died – was
it not incredible enough that either one had survived
such rigours? But the abbess was asking, just the same.
A lingering hope that perhaps the snow-child was not
one of those hapless twins but someone else, someone
who got lost late enough to take human knowledge
with her . . .

'Yes,' Amara said. 'Me, and her. Two of us, long
while.'

'What happened to her?'

'I killed her,' she said.

'Holy Mother of God!' said the abbess, breaking for
the first time her solemn oath. 'Why?'

'Not remember why,' Amara said.

29

Fra Murta arrived at Alquiera at midday. He had a band of pious laymen with him, carrying staves. They prayed as they rode, incanting strings of invocation. Fervour burned in their noonlit eyes. They found Palinor drowsing in a hammock on his balcony, with a book upturned on his belly and his hand dangling, slack fingers trailing on the marble pavement as his hammock swayed.

'Get up!' said Fra Murta, standing over him, taking the book. His eyes narrowed as he saw it was St Augustine's *Civitate Dei*. Palinor opened his eyes and stared sleepily at the dark-clad figure looming over him.

'Who are you?' he asked, whereupon Fra Murta's stout fellows tipped him out of his hammock and pinioning his arms forced him to his knees at Fra Murta's feet. Holding him down, they pummelled him with feet and knees. Joffre came at a run and hurled himself on his master's assailants, but he was easily beaten back. He came again, half blind with blood from a running cut on his forehead and screaming. Suddenly forcing himself half-upright and looking round, Palinor cried, 'Stop, Joffre!' and the boy stood back against the wall. Palinor was being manhandled down the stairs.

At the foot of the stairs Fra Murta met with a hold-up. The estate servants were massed in the courtyard, standing several deep at every door, solidly filling the archway. The blacksmith stood below the doorway arch, in front of the crowd. He just happened to be holding his forge hammer. At his shoulder stood the butcher, who happened to be holding his boning knife. Fra Murta's men were heavily outnumbered. They dropped Palinor and came to a halt.

'I have a warrant to arrest this man on charges of heresy,' said Fra Murta, loudly. 'Excommunication awaits any who obstruct me.'

'Show us the warrant,' said the blacksmith.

'My friend, you wouldn't know an Inquisition warrant from a receipt for pudding,' said Fra Murta scornfully. 'Stand aside.'

'Not until we see your papers, Brother,' the blacksmith said. He swung his hammer idly as he spoke. Muscles rippled in his massive arms.

Fra Murta held out a parchment. At once a little clerk darted out from under the blacksmith's arms, took it, and retreated. The crowd murmured. 'What does it say, Mattheo?' the butcher called out.

'It is a warrant,' said Mattheo, reluctantly. 'It arrests him to stand question.'

'Does it say he is to be beaten by ruffians?' asked the blacksmith.

'Not a word about that,' piped up Mattheo.

'A blow for a blow, then – huzzah!' shouted the blacksmith, and he led a surge of the crowd forward to set upon the gang Fra Murta had brought with him. There was an ugly zest to it. Palinor struggled towards the well in the centre of the yard and scrambled on to the windlass cover above it. 'Hear me!' he shouted. 'Hear me!'

The mayhem was suspended for a moment. 'Thank you,' Palinor said. 'But take care not to share my danger. If the warrant is good, I must go with this man sooner or later. Ask him to let me put a shirt and mantle on, and let him go with me.'

Thus it was that Fra Murta rode back into Ciudad with a tatterdemalion escort of bruised rough-arms, caked with drying blood, black-eyed and broken-nosed, sore-buttocked and groaning in their saddles, and bringing a man riding in a clean shirt of fine linen, wrapped in a deep blue mantle and crowned with flowers.

Behind them as they rode, the blaze of sunset dropped behind the mountains, and the road ahead was cast into shadow. The walls of the city could be made out a distance before them, built in battlemented shadow and overtopped by towers and spires whose uppermost tips stood high enough to burn with the fiery touch of the last fingers of the sinking sun. Suddenly a river of light ran out of the gate towards them, flowing to meet them along the curve of the last mile. A few more minutes' riding, and faintly there came towards them voices – a great choir of voices singing.

Fra Murta was riding alongside Palinor. Ahead of them the river of light divided, resolving itself into the spectacle of hundreds and hundreds of torches, carried by singers who stood lining the roadway left and right. To Palinor, whose nerves were stretched tight by fear now, they seemed the strangest vision. They were clad in dark garments that obliterated their bodies in the shadows. The torches they carried cast lurid light upon their heads and faces – their faces floating, of the hue of molten metal in the furnace, their tresses curling like the lick of fire – their eye-sockets pools of shadow, and in their eyes leaping flamelets of reflected torches, echoing their neighbours' light. Left and right they lined the roadway, singing and crossing themselves as the riders passed.

At the entrance to the city the riders were confronted by a narrow street so packed with torch-bearers that it was hopeless to think of riding forward; uneasy at the ring of fire, the horses snorted, and started. With a word to the gate-keeper, Fra Murta turned aside.

Coaxing the horses up the steps, they rode up on to the city wall and began to move along it. Below them the streets of Ciudad were mapped in fire. Plumes of light moved slowly in every alleyway, flowed in every street, massed in every square, fusing in blazing pools. The roofs between were quagmires of shadow, the churches were shapes of darkness, their outlines flickering in the moving illumination from below. A sonorous bell from the cathedral tolled relentlessly, and the spires and pinnacles and gargoyles of the cathedral appeared as in a mist, faintly through the smoke, smelling of tar and lit from below like the miasma of a bonfire. The voices brimmed in the streets below and overflowed, reaching the riders from many directions, unsynchronized and blended together, deep voices, and the soaring notes of boys, tune and words alike indecipherable.

As the turns of the wall brought them round nearer and nearer to the cathedral, the singing resolved itself, the voices of the vast crowd in the cathedral square sounding together. The riders dismounted to descend to the cathedral cloister. Palinor made out the words of the endlessly repeated singing: *Jesus, remember me, when you come into your kingdom* . . .

'What is that they are singing?' he asked Fra Murta.

'It is the prayer of the Good Thief.' Fra Murta told him. 'He who repented at the last minute.'

'And what is happening? What festival is this?'

'It is a day of special prayer. Of petition for a special intention. The Inquisition is empowered to offer strong indulgences to everyone who takes part. Every person in that crowd has fasted all day today, and will carry torches and walk in pilgrimage, going from church to church all night.'

'And what are they praying for?'

'For you,' said Fra Murta.

'For me?'

'That you may escape the fire.'

Palinor stood speechless, staring at the enormity of the myriad moving lights below him. 'That I may escape?' he said at last, extending a hand to encompass the scene below.

'The fire in the next world, we mean,' said Fra Murta grimly. 'The fire in this world you have no chance of escaping.'

30

'The child has been forgiven,' said Pare Aldonza. The elderly chaplain was trying to comfort the abbess. The old lady was trembling and tearful. Her clouded eyes watered, and her gnarled hands shook on her sticks.

'But . . . murder!' she said.

'Yes; she has been forgiven murder. Old friend, collect yourself. The cardinal baptized her after the time of her captivity. She has been baptized in the blood of Christ, washed in the blood of the Lamb, and stands spotless in the eyes of her saviour. No sin can follow her across the water of Jordan. You know all this well. Be calm. Remember your faith in the Lord Jesus.'

'Murder!' the old nun said. 'We have given house room to a murderess.'

'No!' he said. 'Her sins are all forgiven her. *Confiteor unam baptisma, in remissionem peccatorem;* come, say it after me.' He looked around the room at the white-faced company – Sor Blancha, Sor Agnete, Sor Eulalie . . . A deep affection for his charges lurked beneath his reverent demeanour. It cohabited in his heart with some degree of scorn for those whose innocence was protected by retreat from the world. The nuns were God's daughters, no doubt, for they were like children who still lived in their parents' house.

'I acknowledge one baptism, for the remission of sins . . .' They chorused the words after him.

'How many times have you said this?' he asked them. 'But this that you ask me now is what it means.'

234

They were abashed. 'I am ashamed of my lack of faith,' said the abbess. 'I was distressed, and I have led my daughters into my own error. You must give me penance, Father.'

'There, there,' he said, so far forgetting himself as to pat her gently between the shoulder blades. 'Do not distress yourself. We will all pray to the Apostle Thomas each day this week. And be of good heart – we are all forgiven in Christ's death and resurrection. We are all forgiven everything.'

A sudden inspiration possessed him. 'I too have been at fault,' he said. 'Because we are forbidden to teach the child, it does not mean we are forbidden to bless her. Bring her to chapel after terce.'

The cell in which Palinor was confined had no window. It was deep in the cellarage of whatever building it was, and the floor was puddled with water, which ran down the bare stone of the walls. There was filthy straw on the floor, only the foulest water to drink, and no bucket or any other kind of privy. After a day and a half, however, Joffre and Dolca, who had walked the distance from the Saracen's House, arrived and brought a little comfort: clean straw, good bread, a bottle of wine, a shirt, and the cardinal's copy of *Civitate Dei,* retrieved from the pavement below the hammock.

After three days Fra Murta suddenly appeared, standing outside the massive bars which closed off the opening of the cell, and said, 'Admit that once you believed in God like everyone else and that from that belief you are an impious renegade, an apostate and a traitor to the truth.'

'No,' said Palinor.

'Very well,' said Fra Murta and disappeared with brisk steps.

Next came a blacksmith, who fitted a great neck-iron

to Palinor – two jailers held him down while it was done – and to the neck-iron a heavy chain of shackles, padlocked to a bracket in the wall.

After that Fra Murta came every two days or so and asked the same question – 'Admit that you once knew God like everyone else and that you are a renegade, an impious traitor . . .' Palinor refused to admit it, and later the blacksmith came and removed a shackle from the chain. The bracket in the wall was low down, and soon Palinor could not stand upright. Meanwhile, the jailer often denied admittance to Dolca and Joffre, sometimes for hours, sometimes for days together, while the prisoner went hungry and thirsty, and his filth fouled the unchanged straw on which he crouched. By and by, Fra Murta had *Civitate Dei* removed, on the grounds that it was blasphemous for a heretic to read the words of a father of the Church; then he forbade tapers, on the grounds that one who would not see the light of God deserved no other light.

Joffre found a room above a stable for himself and Dolca. They counted out the money that Rafal had paid them when he hired them – very little of it was spent. It would sustain the two of them and Palinor, they reckoned, for some weeks if it was carefully hoarded and doled out. They kept their heads down, not wanting to attract any attention, afraid at first even to bribe the jailer, in case Fra Murta had them driven away for good, dreading the day when they would have to apply to Rafal for more money.

Joffre did ask Dolca, hesitantly, if she would like to take a few coins and go – look for work in a place of safety somewhere . . .

'And leave him?' she asked, her voice becoming shrill at once. 'You go if that's what you want. But I won't!'

'Anyone would absolve us from duty to a heretic. But it's the last thing I want,' said Joffre. 'I needed to know what you thought.'

'Thank God you did not mean it,' said Dolca. 'It would be the end between us if you did, after what he taught us.'

'My dear, my dear,' he said to her, 'you do realize, don't you, that a heretic does not fear hell? That he has led us into sin?'

'Look at me, Joffre,' she said. 'Meet my eyes and tell me that you repent, and desire to do it no more.'

He could not. So they stayed, tending their master whenever they were allowed to. Palinor had given Joffre a task which he performed every day, every day going to the wharves and shipyards. At night the two slept clasped together close, lying face to face, aching for the lack of another warm body between them or behind them.

Doggedly, repeatedly, Palinor said, 'No.'

Josefa and Amara were playing in the meadow, making garlands of flowers. It was a cool and dewy day of a kind that Grandinsula sometimes had in early autumn, when a second flush of wild flowers seized the chance to bloom before winter. Sor Agnete, coming up through the fields to fetch them, was struck by the sight – two grown girls, romping like children. Josefa was laughing, and Amara was pelting her with flowers. The game must have grown out of an attempt to teach Amara numbers, for Sor Agnete heard her saying, 'One, two, three, five, eight . . .' as she threw the wilting blooms, and Josefa's 'No, no' was accompanied by 'Three, four'. Sor Agnete was a little mollified by this, since before she heard it she had been wondering how Sant Clara had managed to let Josefa run wild, to let her so lack dignity. Well, she had borne the brunt of the struggle with Amara, after all.

Sor Agnete came up to her, panting slightly from the scramble up the terraced fields. Josefa was covered with bits of leaf and petal; her hems were wet with dew, her head-dress askew. No matter; it was Amara Sor Agnete had come for, and as though Amara had known it was a special day, she had crowned her dark head with flowers.

'Come, Amara; we have something to show you,' Sor Agnete said.

They made a funny little procession down the path, with Sor Agnete leading and Amara in between, saying, 'One, three, four, two, five . . .' to herself as they went.

Terce was over, but the sisterhood had lingered in the chapel to see Amara blessed. Pare Aldonza stood waiting for her before the altar. She seemed at first unwilling to enter and came through the dark doors only when Josefa took her hand and led her. Then she looked around her. At first she was drawn to a painting of St Jerome, which hung just inside the door on the southern wall. She stared at it for a long time and ignored Josefa's nudging and Sor Agnete's softly repeated, 'Come.' The saint was praying, and the wild creatures of his desert hermitage were shown lying at his feet or crouching nearby. A lion, a serpent, a wolf . . .

'Come, Amara,' called the abbess, and they succeeded in diverting her and leading her up the aisle. Pare Aldonza smiled at her and raised his hand to make the sign of the cross over her; she raised her eyes to follow his gesture, and her features suddenly twisted into their wolfish form; she rolled her eyes back in her head, shrank away from him, and uttered a long piercing whimper. Then, breaking away from Sor Agnete and Josefa, who each tried to hold her, she fled, taking to all fours before she was half way to the door.

Josefa ran after her, and Sor Agnete after Josefa, and the sisterhood after both of them. Amara stood in the sun in the middle of the cloister garden, facing them, and said, 'Bad place. I not go back in.'

'It is not a bad place, Amara; it is a holy place,' said Pare Aldonza. 'But no-one will make you go back there till you ask it. I will bless you here, under the open sky.' He raised his hand again. He made the sign of the cross, and she followed the movement of his hand quite calmly.

'*Dominus vobiscum. In nomine Patris, et Filii, et Spiritus Sancti,*' he said. He told her that every one of the sisters prayed for her every day.

'Pray?' she parroted.

'They ask for good things, for you, child.'

'Meat?' she asked.

'And other good things. That all your needs may be met.'

'Kind,' she said gravely. 'They kind.'

Sor Agnete looked on, deeply troubled. Amara had not played that wolfish trick for many weeks, months. Something had upset her. And now she stood demurely, evincing knowledge that prayers said for her meant kindness, though she did not know what prayer was. Her mind was neither light nor dark now, but dappled, like the sun in a deep forest . . . but what had upset her? Sor Agnete returned to the chapel alone. She stood where Amara had stood. The child had been watching the priest's hand; Sor Agnete raised her eyes, reconstructing . . . Above the altar, behind where Pare Aldonza had been standing, hung the great crucifix. It was a masterpiece, painted long ago and given to Sant Clara by a wealthy merchant who had wished to marry the foundress, the Blessed Alicssande. When she had taken vows and retreated to this lonely place, he had found the most precious thing he could to give to her.

239

The figure of Christ was painted on the wooden cross, on a golden ground. He was wearing a loincloth of many folds, painted in darts of deep blue. His hanging body had a Byzantine twist to it, and his leaning head was surrounded by a blazing halo. Daggers of light shone out of the wound in his side. His flesh was painted in that gold-green colour used by eastern icon-makers. A little green border of putrescence outlined every painted orifice, every weal and wound, and the great nails in his hands and feet stood out of brimming pits of crimson blood.

Sor Agnete had prayed in front of this crucifix many times a day every day of her life for twenty years; but now she realized for the first time, sinking in dismay, that if you did not know it was an image of love, if you did not know it portended God's infinite compassion, his mercy for mankind, if you did not know of the resurrection and the life, what you would see, enshrined at the heart of Sant Clara, above the altar, in the holy sanctuary, would be an image of a man viciously tortured and horribly done to death.

Amara not like

240

31

'It is a horrible picture he paints, Holiness,' said Fra
Murta. The two men had met at the door between
the cathedral and the cloister and were standing in
the cloister walk. 'Of a country where the truth has
no defenders. Where the poor and ignorant are at
the mercy of every charlatan, for each man makes
up his own mind about the truth. Where there are
many religions, and all can set up and preach and
enlist followers, like so many vulgar peasants bringing
produce to a market and each setting up his own stall.
Where one town can have three or four bishops, each of
a different stamp, and people change churches as men
change horses, several times in a journey. If this priest
will not marry you, another will, he says. Neither hope
of heaven nor fear of hell is called into the balance to
support the rulers of this place, for any citizen may
entertain neither! He says I overstate the force of both;
most people he says, keep the law in this world for
reasons of this world, and his country has a civil force
of law-keepers. I asked him if there were not often riots
and disputes, wars almost, between the followers of
one religion and another, and he answered that this
sometimes happened. There is quite often disorder,
he says, and uproar in the streets, but this is usually
about the fortunes in a game of some kind played
between teams of citizens, about which feelings run
higher than over the truths of religion. He speaks most
proudly and obdurately of the freedom with which
each man forms his own conscience there, which I find

is like the freedom of the blind to fall into the pit.'

'Is this all?' said Severo wearily. 'We have heard him talk of his country many times before. Certainly it has strange and perhaps outrageous customs; that does not make him a heretic.'

'I think it might be enough,' said Fra Murta. 'We burned a woman on the mainland once for describing the world after the Second Coming and filling it with a foul debauchery of every woman with every man, saying that "no marriage nor giving in marriage" meant a disgusting free-for-all, a universal orgy, and trying to start it at once, to bring about the end of the world.'

'Your poor crazed woman was however, advocating wicked conduct. The atheist has advocated nothing; he has kept silence on his views and on the customs of his country except in answer to questions.'

'I think he might have disseminated his vile views to his servants.'

'What do they say?'

'They will tell me nothing. Their loyalty smells. After all they have not been with him long.'

'Their loyalty *smells,* do you say?' said Severo, appalled.

'It smells of witchcraft. He has bewitched them!'

'It is not a proof of heresy that a man has loyal servants,' said Severo coldly.

'We should put him to the torture. That will have him confessing fast enough.'

'I thought that torture was a matter of last resort in the most contumacious cases,' said Severo.

'In theory, yes. In practice, its undoubted, reliable efficacy leads to its use very frequently . . .'

'Fra Murta, let us understand one another. You come to me with a special commission from Rome. I know how precious to the Holy Father the Sacred Inquisition is, as I know that you will return to Rome when your mission is complete and that you have the ears of powerful people there. I am sure that you would fearlessly carry out your duty to report any obstruction you had encountered in the course of your inquisition. But I too have friends in Rome. Should any abuse of process occur, any regrettable error in the conduct of investigation, anything which vitiated the soundness of the verdict against a heretic, although this is a remote island, a report of such a thing might nevertheless be made in Rome. If one were ever to encounter an inquisitor who used his great powers with anything less than the most perfect circumspection, one might think it one's duty to report the circumstances in the most high places.'

Fra Murta bowed slightly. 'We will both do our duty under God, Holiness,' he said. 'I will take matters no further without consulting you further. But this is a most obdurate case. Did I tell you that he has threatened me?'

'He threatened you? Whatever could he threaten you with?'

'He said if ever his countrymen should discover what had become of him in this island, their revenge would be terrible beyond comprehension . . .'

'Not a very immediate threat, then.'

'He said, if his country were nearby, then his people would fight to keep him from falling into my hands, but as it was, his country was far off.'

'Where does he come from?' wondered Severo, *sotto voce*. 'Fra Murta, have you ever heard of Aclar?'

'I have heard of hell,' said the friar.

Severo stood at a table in the library. A great bookcase lined the wall on his right, and the volumes of patristic teaching were ranged in it. The keeper of books had brought him maps – all the maps they had. The scrolls of vellum lay spread out in front of him, kept flat by the keeper's dusty hands.

'This one is thought to be the best, Holiness,' the keeper said. The map showed Jerusalem in the middle, haloed and marked in red ink on the dark brown, stained parchment. An extensive faded blotch of black ink represented the Mediterranean, hatching showed mountains, and little cities were drawn all over it like tiny coronets, shown bunched within their battle-mented walls. Rivers wandered over the surface, webbing it as with spider work. The map was annotated with blocks of writing in a meticulous tiny hand. The world was a great disc, surrounded by a river running round its rim; the corners of the vellum were filled up with angels. Within the ring, in every country depicted, swarmed beasts and birds of fabulous appearance, every one labelled and named.

Severo leaned eagerly, closely, over the map. He found the Garden of Eden, and the Tower of Babel and the little burning bush from which God spoke to Moses; he found Constantinople, and the lands of the Great Khan, and the Pillars of Hercules, and Ultima Thule. Red letters denoted the Pyramids, the Hanging Gardens of Babylon, the tomb of Mausolus, the Colossus of Rhodes, the temple of Diana of the Ephesians, the statue of Jupiter at Athens, the lighthouse at Alexandria. Gold letters pointed up the cave of St John's revelation on the island of Patmos, the mountain of the Ascension, the Sea of Galilee, St Peter's at Rome, St James at Compostella. Porphyry and silver marked the whereabouts of every fragment of the true cross. An arrow marked the line set out by a lodestone. He could not find Aclar. Neither, when consulted, could the keeper of books. They both scanned for some time, reading every word on the surface of the great map, in vain.

At last Severo straightened and sighed. Then some-thing struck him. 'Where is Grandinsula?' he asked.

'Not shown, Holiness,' the keeper said.

'Why not?'

'Well, we are a small island, Holiness, and nothing of great importance has happened here.'

'Where was this map made, then?'

'Here. In this very library, I believe.'

'Ah,' said Severo, baffled. 'And when was it made?'

'Long ago, Holiness. In a time of wisdom, but before my time.'

That night Severo was visited in his cell by Rafal, who knocked quietly and entered. 'You found something?' Severo asked him.

'Not much, Holiness. I asked on every ship in the harbour as you told me to, without any success. But then I thought of the taverns where the seamen drink. I wrapped my cloak over my soutane, Holiness, and sat in a corner with a wine bottle in front of me and several wine cups, and I soon had talkative company. You do not think this was wrong of me, Holiness?'

'No, no, Rafal, it shows enterprise. Go on.'

'Still nobody had heard of Aclar, Holiness. But at last there was a drunken captain – very drunk, I'm afraid, Holiness, and I dread to think how he will spend the dineros I had to give him for his news – who told me something.'

'He knew of Aclar?'

'Not really, Holiness. But he remembered something. He remembered long, long ago – he was a young man at the time – he was serving on a ship which was tied up at Genoa, or at Livorno, he really could not recall whether it was Genoa or Livorno, and they were tied alongside a ship with curious rigging. He said he and his fellow seamen were very struck by something about this rigging. He told me all about it, Holiness, and at great length, but I'm afraid I didn't understand a word of it – something about keeping ropes from slackening. Anyway, as well as this business about the rigging, the ship was curious in another way – it didn't have galley slaves. It just had crew. They all worked, he understood, and would all get paid. So his captain took fright and moved his berth across the harbour. He didn't want the wretches in his own ship to get mutinous ideas, I gathered. The point is, Holiness, that my drunken friend thought he could remember asking one of the sailors on the other ship where he hailed from and being told he was an Aclaridian. That's all. Just that one word, "Aclaridian". And from some twenty years ago, as far as I could reckon.'

Severo sat for some moments in silence. Then he said, 'Thank you, Rafal. You serve me well.'

'Holiness, there is just one other thing. It probably doesn't matter, but . . .'

'Tell me.'

'I quickly found out that being asked about Aclar was no novelty. Someone has been at the harbourside repeatedly, coming repeatedly for many months, asking the question before me. From the description of him, I think it must be Joffre, the atheist's servant.'

'Hmm,' said Severo. 'That's a relief, I rather think. I feared for a moment it might have been some agent of Fra Murta's.'

32

The abbess had been carried out into the garden as soon as the chill of the morning softened and set under the fig tree. She could no longer stand, nor even really sit, but was laid tenderly in a hammock in the open air. Pare Aldonza had absolved her from her duty to hear office, and while the work of the nunnery went on all round her, she simply lay quietly – not at ease, for her bodily condition prevented ease, but calm. Now and then one of the sisters came out to her, bringing drink or a little bread and cheese. She ate like a bird these days, but drank plentifully, water mixed with wine. All her daughters in God were gentle with her now, even the ones she had no love from before; she well knew why.

They were full of pity for her blindness. And yet it was not true that she could see nothing; the world of the garden in which she reclined was full of blotches of colour. That soft swaying cloud of green was the fig tree, which gave her shade, and the pale, shimmering watery colour that flowed around it was the sky. The earthy colours which bordered the garden in a blurry ribbon were the walls of her abbey, painted newly in deep terracotta wash some time back – not long since, so no wonder they were bright. Sor Agnete said it was twenty years ago, but she must be wrong. The world was a bowl of earthen pottery colour, in which fishes of soft hues floated and swam.

When people came near, she saw them as soft grey outlines if they stood between her and the light, not

247

at all otherwise. Pare Aldonza brought her communion after mass, and sometimes he came and sat with her for a few moments in silent companionship – there was nothing to say. She knew he was anxious; he was afraid that the sisters would elect Sor Agnete to take her place and he thought Sor Agnete had no time for him, and would ask the cardinal for a younger chaplain. The abbess knew that the sisterhood would choose Sor Eulalie and that Sor Eulalie would ask for a younger chaplain. She knew these things without any ripple of disturbance to her mind; they belonged to another world and did not concern her.

There were many hours of quiet. She could hear the distant sound of the hours being sung only when they left the chapel door open. She took no notice of it. She was no longer sure whether she had entirely given up praying or whether she prayed all the time. She slept a good deal. And awoke, once, to find a hovering shadow before her. Someone; she could not tell who. The visitor stood so still, so long without speaking that she thought perhaps it was death, come for her. But at last the shadow did give voice – Amara's husky, unaccented tones.

'Mother, why I kept here? Why I prisoner?'

Recalled abruptly from the drifting limbo in which she floated, the abbess said, 'They wanted to know what you would say, child.'

'Not like it here,' Amara said. 'Closed in. Want to go.'

'I know what you mean, Amara,' the abbess said. 'I too would like to go, now. But we must wait until we are called.'

'Wait how long?'

'I don't know how long,' said the abbess. 'Soon, I hope. I would greatly like to talk to my mother again. What about you, child? What are you longing for?'

'Being far,' Amara said. 'Going far. And snow lonely.

248

No speaking.' She took a long time to find each cluster of words. And the abbess seemed to be asleep. Amara wandered disconsolately away.

Severo woke in the middle of the night, sweating. He had been dreaming. His dream remained with him, clearer for a few moments than the ghostly outline of his window, a lilac grid admitting shadow to the total darkness of the cell, clearer than the damp and tangled bedsheets which appeared when he fumbled for a tinder-box and lit a candle. He had been dreaming an example – the example of the Saracen chess-player. The books of moral theology studied in the Galilea were full of examples. The students read and debated them. This one was the story of a Saracen prince. There came through his country a Christian knight, on his way to the Holy Land in fulfilment of a vow. The vow was a promise the man had made to God: if God would heal his daughter, he would build a church in Jerusalem and give money to feed ten poor men and women at its western door every day for thirty years. The Saracen prince was impressed by the virtue of the Christian's intention and declared that he would not detain him nor hinder the fulfilment of a vow to Allah. Indeed, he would contribute gold himself, to feed the poor of Jerusalem more lavishly. However, the prince had a passion for the game of chess and could find few worthy opponents and, finding that the knight could play well, he detained him day after day at his court, always saying that after one more game he would escort the man to his ship and let him embark. At last the knight caught the plague which was the scourge of the Saracen's court and died without fulfilling his vow. The question was, what part of the sin of the broken vow could be laid at the door of the Saracen prince?

Severo could remember excitable debate about this.

He could remember – what pain it gave him! – Beneditx's youthful face alight with enthusiasm, propounding some particular view of the matter. He could no longer remember what line Beneditx had taken, and he no longer cared, for he knew the answer now. With what biting remorse he knew the answer! How easily he could have put Palinor on some ship or other, and forgotten about him! Yet he had detained him, not, as he now realized, out of a desire to be guided by providence, or any such thing, but because he wanted to talk with him; he wanted a worthy player on the other side of his private board. And now see what followed. He was enmeshed in consequence, all of it terrible, all of it his, Severo's, fault. As for that impulse of blind anger in which he had given Palinor into the inquisitor's hands – what was it but the rage of a stupid child who upsets the board on which he is losing a game? Gnawing at his knuckles, Severo waited for the sickening miasma cast by the dream to fade, and it did not. After an hour he rose, wrapped himself in an ample cloak, drew a fold of it over his head, and went out.

A huddled mass of wretched-looking people were sleeping in the street outside the Inquisition prison. Moonlight gave them faint visibility where they lay under tattered coverings, as close as they could lie to the dying embers of little charcoal fires. They looked like the bottom right-hand corner of the great judgement scene in the cathedral, showing the damned piled upon the damned. Severo stepped carefully over prostrate bodies, not wishing to wake anyone. The prison watchman would not admit him until he thrust his hand through the grill and showed his ordination ring, worn by every priest. Then the door was opened for him and closed behind him.

The place was in total darkness, and full of an overpowering stench. The watchman led him, holding his elbow, many paces down a sloping corridor and some greasy steps. The stench thickened. At last there was a clank of keys, and Severo was pushed into a cell. The floor was awash with some dreadful liquid, and Severo slipped, and found himself sitting on straw. The cell was full of a rough and painful breathing.

'Smells bad, doesn't it?' said the watchman.

'*No worse than my conscience,*' Severo thought. 'Bring lights,' he said.

'He isn't allowed them,' said the watchman. 'More than my job's worth.'

'Bring a light for me,' Severo said. 'I need to see.'

'You won't like it,' said the watchman, shuffling away.

He was right. The lantern, when it appeared, showed Palinor lying askew, held by the neck. There were no shackles left in the chain, and his neck-iron held him tight to the soaking and mouldy wall. He was held just too high to rest his shoulders on the ground. The sodden straw beneath him was foul with excrement, and he was covered with weeping sores.

Severo let out a great bellow of rage. 'Get this iron off him!' he cried.

'I wouldn't dare, Father,' the man said, 'and that's the truth.'

Severo produced his great cardinal's ring of office.

'Holiness,' the man said, trembling, 'I have done nothing except under orders . . .'

'Get that iron off him!' cried Severo.

'Sir, it needs the blacksmith . . .'

'Fetch him!'

'He has gone home, Holiness. It cannot be done until morning . . .'

'By morning you will be in irons yourself, if he is not freed.'

The blacksmith was sent for. Severo sat on the stinking straw, waiting. It was indeed nearly dawn before the blacksmith arrived. He had a great axe with him. 'Close your eyes and tilt your head as far forward as you can,' he said to Palinor. Then he swung the axe high above his head and brought it down with speed and force between the man's head and the wall. The bracket was severed, and Palinor fell forward on his face. His shoulder blades had rubbed raw against the wall.

Severo leaned forward and lifted Palinor, propping him in his arms. Looking up, he saw a young man and woman standing beyond the grille, holding hands like children.

'Do you serve this man?' he asked.

'When we are allowed to, Holiness,' the man said. 'We have not been let in for many days.'

'Why not?' asked Severo.

'Against orders,' the watchman said. 'Holiness, I implore you, do not take this man from the prison. Consider the scandal, Holiness. The people will think their cardinal is a heretic-lover. The inquisitor will go berserk, Holiness, and find a way of punishing me. I'll find the prisoner a dry cell with a window and a bed, I'll let his servants come and go, I'll find clean water . . .'

'At once,' said Severo. 'Do these things at once.'

Later, he said to Palinor, 'Listen to me, my friend. If for one moment you admitted to Fra Murta that you have ever believed in God, at any time in the past, then you would be lost. You would be punished as a renegade, and I could not save you. But if you were to tell him that though you never were a believer in all your life before, you have suddenly come to believe now; if you told him, for example, that an angel had visited you in prison, and the knowledge of angels had convinced you, then I would baptize you, and you would be beyond his reach.'

'No angel has come,' said Palinor, wearily.

'Listen: if there is no God, but you behave as though there were one – what do you lose? A few transitory pleasures in this world. Whereas if there is a God, in behaving as he desires, you gain eternal happiness and avoid eternal pain. Surely a prudent man should behave as if there is a God, simply to avoid so great a risk? Dissemble; invent that angel. If there is a God, he will not blame you for so innocent a deception, since it leads you to do the right thing . . . What would you stand to lose?'

'My integrity,' said Palinor. 'The nearest thing I have to what you would call a soul. And besides, it is my right to entertain my own beliefs.'

'How can a man claim a right who does not believe in God?' said Severo, miserably.

'I claim it, not because there is a God, but because I am a man,' said Palinor.

33

'Torture,' said Fra Murta, 'is the only way to break the will of an obdurate man.'

'What you call obduracy is the conduct of a man following his conscience, which is his conscience though it be mistaken,' said Severo.

'You cannot exculpate him with that, Holiness,' said Fra Murta. 'For a false conscience does not bind.'

'I would have thought that any man was bound to follow his conscience – how else can he suppose himself to be doing right?' said Severo.

'There are mighty authorities on my side in this,' said Fra Murta. He had a habit of staring very brightly and directly at Severo as he began to speak and looking away thereafter. He was always looking away from anyone who answered him, Severo noticed. Now he turned his head away and stared out of the window of the chapter-house in which the two of them were seated, conferring. 'For example, the great Augustine says that a sin is a word, deed, or desire contrary to God's law. But a false conscience is not in accordance with God's law. Therefore it cannot be sinful to ignore a false conscience.'

'But . . .'

'The Apostle Paul, in his epistle to the Romans – I can give you the exact reference if you require it – has written, "Let every soul be subject to higher powers," and in his commentary on this passage St Augustine says that we should not obey a lower power contrary to the commandment of a higher power, just as we should not obey the proconsul if his order is contrary to that of the emperor. And a false conscience is inferior to God. Need I go on, Holiness?'

'To the contrary,' said Severo. He was choking with hatred, struggling to contain himself and level his tones. 'Consider Romans 14:23. I will remind you: the text says, "For all that is not of faith is sin." And the commentary says, "That is, it is a sin in conscience, even if it is good in itself." But a conscience which forbids that which is good in itself is false. Therefore, the text teaches that such a conscience binds.'

'God is merciful,' said Fra Murta. 'More merciful than a temporal lord. But a lord does not hold his servant blameworthy in something which he did by mistake. Therefore, in God's sight a man is much less obliged by a mistaken conscience.'

'The holy Damascene,' said Severo, 'after whom you are yourself named, Fra Murta, wrote that "Conscience is the law of our understanding." But to act contrary to a law is a sin. Therefore, it is also a sin to act against conscience in any way.'

'Are you telling me,' said Fra Murta, 'that a man can stand up before us defending any blasphemous belief and any foul conduct by saying that his conscience commands it? If a mistaken conscience binds, then one who has fallen into error sins if he follows his conscience and sins if he does not. But a merciful God would not allow us to be so perplexed. A man is bound to follow his conscience only when it commands him to do what the Church teaches is right.'

'Think again,' said Severo. 'Someone who has a false conscience, but believes that it is correct, clings to his false conscience because of the correctness he thinks is there, and strictly speaking clings to a correct conscience but one which is false accidentally, in so far as this conscience which he believes to be correct, happens to be false. We should say therefore that he is bound by a true conscience, but accidentally by a false conscience.'

'You have a most delicate intellect, cardinal,' said Fra Murta. 'What a loss to the Inquisition that you did not elect to become a friar! Confronted by a man in the grip of a false conscience we should seek to change it. And if reason fails we should use force. One hour in the torture chamber will change his conscience like wax in the fire. You must allow this.'

'You have yet to convince me that a false conscience does not bind a man so long as it remains.'

'It seems to me,' said Fra Murta, glancing at Severo, and looking away again, 'that the false conscience I must seek to change may not be only that of the atheist but that of a churchman with too tender a regard for heretics – I had nearly said for heresy. One who acts according to conscience and sins against the law of God sins mortally. For there was sin in the error itself, since it happened because of ignorance of that which one should have known.'

'But that is the very question under dispute!' cried Severo, exasperated. 'This argument goes in a circle! Should he have known of God, or might he in good faith be ignorant? That was the very matter for which the wolf-child's testimony was independent evidence. And she said "No", Fra Murta.'

'She did not understand the question. We should ask her again.'

'Very well, then,' said Severo. 'We will ask her again. And keep your hands off him until we have her answer, do you understand?'

The nuns were sitting round their long refectory table, their hands folded neatly in their laps. Even the novices were there, even Josefa. Only one chair was empty, and that was the great chair at the head of the table, the abbess's. She was asleep under the fig tree, and there was no point in waking her. She might be able to understand her daughters' deliberations – who could say? – but she could not answer their views, or enunciate her own. Like her dreaming soul, her authority was adrift and for the moment was nowhere. The sisterhood was holding a quiet conclave, to decide upon urgent affairs. Agitation fluttered in the air of the room; the sisters were like passengers of a vessel at sea, summoned to the deck because the captain was overboard and asked to sail the ship.

'There are two questions,' said Sor Agnete. She was sitting well down the table, far from that empty chair, in which, in truth, she longed to sit. 'First a petition from Taddeo Arta . . .'

Josefa gasped, half rose from her chair, and subsided. Clearly this was the first she had heard of it.

'. . . He says that he understands his daughter has not yet taken final vows, and he requests that she be returned to his household. He says that his young wife is sickly and cannot look after the children properly. He needs his daughter's care of her stepsisters, one in the cradle and the other now first walking. He offers money.'

Every face in the room turned towards Josefa. 'Oh, please!' she said, beginning to cry, copiously, 'Oh please . . . please . . . I beg you . . . Oh . . .'

'Please what, child?' said Sor Eulalie. 'Please release you, or please retain you?'

'Please let me stay!' cried Josefa.

'Have we ever sent a sister away against her will?' someone asked.

'Only for gross turpitude,' said Sor Agnete.

'There, there, girl,' said Sor Blancha. 'Of course you can stay.'

'We must think, though,' said Sor Agnete. 'If this Taddeo appeals to the cardinal . . . It would be easier if

257

she had taken the final vows. Then any release would be unthinkable.'

'Why doesn't she take them right now?' said Sor Blancha.

'Is she ready?' asked Sor Lucia. 'Our other three novices are more diligent. Has Josefa even so much as started on the contemplative life?'

'She has worked hardest of all!' cried Sor Blancha. 'And with never a word of complaint!'

'Work, certainly!' said Sor Lucia. 'But prayer, Sor Blancha?'

'You are not fair!' cried Sor Blancha. 'We have laid on her the drudgery of care night and day for a . . . a thing like an animal; you have been praying all day, while she has been struggling in dirty straw and sharing misery with that poor savage creature, under obedience like you, and do you now turn up your nose at her?'

'No, I do not, Sor Blancha. But I point out that Sisters of Sant Clara have chosen the part of Mary, who sat at the feet of the Saviour . . .'

'While Martha in the kitchen made the meal,' said Sor Blancha. 'Have a care what you say about the Marthas, Sister. Remember that the food you eat here has been the product of my work with farm and flock these many years. And who prays well when they are hungry?'

'What will become of us if we fall out, when the abbess is unable to rule us?' said Sor Eulalie. 'If there are many mansions in heaven, surely we can manage more than one kind of virtue in Sant Clara! And doesn't it say in St John that the Lord loved Martha?'

'Come, Sisters,' said Sor Agnete. 'Let us not argue over such a matter as this. If Josefa takes her final vows this day, is there anyone who does not welcome her among us? Speak now, or for ever hold your peace.'

No-one spoke. Into the silence Sor Agnete continued, 'There is another matter. The cardinal is coming to question Amara again.'

'I don't understand this,' said Sor Blancha. 'He wanted to know what she said, and she said "No". So now he comes again – will he keep her here until she says "Yes"? Is that the idea?'

'I have never understood how she can answer questions about God if she doesn't know what the word means,' said Sor Eulalie.

'It is a cruelty to keep her here, like caging a bird, or tethering a young horse,' said Sor Blancha.

'But we are deeply sworn,' Sor Agnete said.

'Must I make a confession, before I take final vows?' asked Josefa.

'Yes, yes, of course,' said Sor Coloma.

'And in confession we are forgiven great sins as well as little ones?' said Josefa.

'Yes, Josefa. Yes, you know this,' said Sor Coloma.

Sor Agnete was looking at Josefa with a shrewd understanding.

Josefa sat on the little painted chair in her cell and looked through her window-grille at the shining sea. By and by, she took to her knees and attempted prayer. It is a terrible bondage that chains those who need to those who give help. Soon the comforter needs the sufferer as fiercely as ever the sufferer needed the comforter. Helplessness is addictive, like poppy water, and it is the helper who needs to drink on and on. Josefa contemplated life without Amara with a limitless dismay. She had barely courage enough to think about it. But she knew an equal dismay in thinking about Amara's life, locked up for ever in the narrow compass of Sant Clara and kept from knowing what was happening all around her – forever locked in and forever locked out. And Josefa understood love;

she had been loved until her mother died. She knew by unconsidered instinct that love involves letting go. She was afraid of the cardinal in a way – had she thought he would know of her perfidy, she would have been terrified. But he would not know. She would sin, and confess, and be forgiven, and enter the safety of a nun's life, making a new vow that she would never break. She crossed herself, rose, and went to find Amara, to coach her; to teach her what to say.

At vespers that evening the sisters admitted Josefa irrevocably to their community. Pare Aldonza heard her confession and led her to the altar rail. She knelt, and Pare Aldonza blessed her novice's ring and heard her speak over the words that locked doors for ever – every door in Sant Clara except the one to heaven. She was wearing a wedding veil; Sor Berenice had stitched it with a border of white flowers. It had been ready for many months.

The cardinal brought a large party with him to Sant Clara. He wanted witnesses. He wanted Fra Murta to be wrong-footed in public. He wanted no more saying 'Teach her further' and rejecting what she said. She had convinced him: there was no innate knowledge, just a simple duopoly of faith and reason. He was going to cite the child's answer in his own defence against the sniping there would undoubtedly be when he protected Palinor. But with her help he would be invincible. The atheist was not a heretic, only a man who had not encountered revelation and who had failed to ascend by his own unaided reason.

Therefore Severo brought to Sant Clara with him the father provincial of the two orders of friars, three canons from the cathedral, a holy hermit, four parish priests, and the prefect of the western quarter of the island, besides two august teachers from the Galilea.

He had thought of commanding Beneditx but was not sure if it would be kind. And there was also, of course, Fra Murta and some private chaplain of his. And Rafal. Severo barely noticed Rafal. The cardinal's party filled the little chapter-house. They had all been told the child's story, and they were full of pleasant curiosity and excitement. Here was something different: something to talk about for the rest of their lives! They had not been told that the question had been asked and answered already; they were flattered to be called to the great occasion.

Led in before them came a young woman. She wore a simple white dress, pinned chastely at the neck. Her dark hair fell to her shoulders, curling softly and held back from her face with a simple band of white ribbon. She was barefoot. The cardinal saw with interest how the terrible strangeness was ebbing from her. A certain vacancy in her expression, a certain sliding evasiveness of her glance was all that was left of it. She did seem very frightened, as she took in how many people thronged the room around her. She cringed slightly, and he heard her teeth clash. The nuns standing behind her murmured to her.

'Do not be afraid, little maid,' he said to her gently. 'We only want to ask you some questions.'

She glanced at him and away again, and nodded.

'When you were in the mountains,' he asked, 'were you alone there? Was there any other presence, to your senses invisible, but . . .'

'Kindness,' she said.

'What?'

She spoke slowly, tonelessly, with her eyes shut. 'I had a friend,' she said, 'not seen. I was despised and rejected of men, but when I would have died the spirit moved the wolf and made her foster me. The mountains where I lived had a maker. I had a protector, though I not know a name for him.'

261

'Amara!' Severo cried at her. 'Did anyone tell you to say this, or do you know it of yourself?'

'Who could tell me?' she answered. 'Could the wolf speak? Nobody there but me. The silence taught me.'

And so Fra Murta won his victory without, himself, speaking a word. Those who saw how the cardinal wept, copiously and silently, tears which filled his eyes in the chapter-house and continued while he blessed the child, while he visited the abbess and gave her the last sacrament, while he mounted his horse and rode away among his companions, took them for tears of joy.

34

Palinor was afraid. Fra Murta had taken him from his cell and with two hefty servants was marching him through the prison. He had said, 'Now is the time when you will admit the truth.' The prison, it turned out − Palinor had not seen enough of it to realize − was a friary, complete with church, cells, and garden. They descended. Below ground level was a vaulted crypt of wide extent, divided into chambers. Some were workshops, some were storerooms. He did not see the warren of foul little dungeons where he had been held before, though he thought they were in the same building somewhere − he did not remember having drawn a single breath of the open air when Severo had him moved.

They marched through a little side-chamber where at a long narrow table four or five clerks were sitting, diligently writing. A grille above their heads admitted daylight, and they had each a candle-lamp. Immediately beyond this little scriptorium was a door, standing wide, and through it Palinor was half led, half thrust. He felt a moment of relief: the room had an open grille in the door and was in earshot of the scribes. Then his eyes widened as he took in with terror and disgust the purposes, visible in blades, spikes, levers, straps and pulleys of the mechanisms in the room.

One of the scribes rose behind him and came in. He went to the corner of the room and sat on a little stool. He unbolted and lowered a wooden flap in the wall.

It dropped to an angle that formed a writing surface for him. In the little cubby-hole that opened behind it was an inkwell and quill. The scribe dipped his quill, and held it expectantly poised above his vellum.

'Let her go?' said Sor Agnete. 'Let her go where? Where could she go?' Nobody offered an answer.

Sor Agnete went upstairs to the cell where the abbess was lying. Sor Blancha was with her, trying to feed her a thin gruel, a spoonful at a time. Sor Agnete stood at the foot of the bed. 'The cardinal said we could let Amara go, Mother,' she said, 'but where? Where can she go?'

The abbess seemed to be asleep. She was breathing so lightly she might have expired in the last few moments since Sor Agnete spoke. But after a long pause, she did answer, in a difficult whisper that the two nuns leaned forward to hear.

'Ask Jaime,' she said.

News spread fast enough on Grandinsula, being always in short supply. When Palinor rode out of view, escorted by the prefect, Lazaro and Miguel and their friends assumed that he was on his way home. He disappeared as completely as any embarked traveller, and only Esperanca remembered him. She had her reasons in her dream of gold, and also in her unreasonable love of her son. Rescuing Palinor was the only thing in the least remarkable he had so far achieved. The news that Palinor was still on Grandinsula, and in the heretics' prison, was a terrible blow to her.

'So much for your hope of riches, my poor Esperanca,' said her neighbour, suppressing a smile. It would after all be very vexing if Esperanca became suddenly rich. Who would mend clothes for nearly nothing if that happened?

Esperanca's welcome in nearby houses cooled a good

deal, and a certain number of unkind remarks about heretics and the danger of dealing with them were heard on the square, when families took a stroll in the cool of the evening.

'I'll not believe he is a heretic!' Esperanca wailed when the door was shut at night, and there was only Lazaro to hear her. 'He seemed so kind and lordly. How could he be one who eats babies and casts spells that sicken cattle? I'll never believe it!'

The torture audit lay on Severo's desk. He came upon it without warning, among the papers for the day. It was written in a steady legible hand, closely covering the page.

Prisoner shown the devices.
DIXIT INQUISITOR. 'Do you wish to confess?'
PRISONER. 'What have I to confess? What have I done?'
INQ. 'You know what you have done.'
Prisoner stripped and bound.
INQ. 'Do you wish to confess?'
PRISONER. 'What would you have me say?'
INQ. 'That you have known God from your first hours, and that you have perfidiously deserted him.'
PRISONER. 'I will not confess that. It is not true.'
Cordeles and garrotes applied to prisoner.
INQ. 'Confess. We will release you at once if you confess.'
PRISONER. 'No.'
Three turns. Prisoner voids his bowels. Prisoner screams.
INQ. 'Do you confess?'
PRISONER. 'No.'
Mancuerda applied to prisoner. All cordeles attached to maestre garrote. Three turns. Prisoner screams.
PRISONER. 'Don't. Don't. I cannot bear it.'

INQ. 'Do you ask for mercy?'

PRISONER. 'Yes, yes!'

INQ. 'Only confess and you shall have it.'

Prisoner sobs. Three more turns.

PRISONER. 'Stop, aah! stop. All right, anything. *Screams.* 'Anything, only stop.'

Ropes slackened.

INQ. 'Say it.'

PRISONER. 'Say what?'

INQ. 'My disbelief is but a lewd pretence.'

PRISONER. 'No. How can you do this? Have mercy.'

INQ. 'I will have mercy on your poor misguided soul. Confess, and we will send you to the judgement seat a penitent, for whom a mansion is prepared in heaven. Remain obdurate and you will go straight to hell.'

Ropes wound five turns. Prisoner faints. Revived with cold water. Doctor summoned.

INQ. 'Why do you make me continue? I am distressed to see such suffering – I, who only mean you well. But make no mistake, yours is a special soul, and I hunger and thirst to save it. You are a great prize, and I will have your confession, though your limbs are bare bones before I get it. Look how you bleed. Have pity on yourself and confess now.'

DOCTOR. 'Enough now, Fra Murta. He must not expire.'

INQ. 'One more attempt. Three turns.'

PRISONER. 'I believe in God. I lied when I denied it.'

Ropes slackened. Prisoner carried to his cell. Torture suspended.

To the truth of the above, I, Petro Llop, clerk, etc. etc., in nomine Domini, etc. etc., set my hand in witness.'

Severo staggered to the basin set in a corner of his cell, and vomited. When he had thrown up all there was, he was still doubled over and retching. Rafal must have heard him, from the next cell, for he came to help. Severo refused the offer to summon a doctor.

'No, Rafal, I am not ill, just horrified.' He gestured at the papers on the table. Rafal picked up the top one, glanced at it, and went pale.

'Could you not have stopped him, Holiness?' Rafal asked.

'It was my duty rather to assist him,' said Severo. 'I relied on the snow-child to outwit him, and she changed her tune. I don't know why, something went wrong. I believed her when she answered the first time – what can have gone wrong?'

'Someone at Sant Clara breaking their vow to you, Holiness?'

'Surely not. I trust those women both for sense and sanctity.'

'Then perhaps . . . No, perhaps not.'

'What were you thinking? Anything that might cast light . . .'

'She was captured by shepherds. And then spent time in a cage until Jaime prevailed on you to rescue her. Perhaps she heard God named during that time?'

'And if she did, the answer she made is void – it would not prove innate knowledge! Rafal, go at once! Find horsemen. Ride to Sant Jeronimo and find everyone who was involved, and get them here fast . . . Why did I not think of this before? I was so besotted with the thought of the child bringing proof . . .' Severo was looking and speaking wildly, and Rafal was alarmed.

'Holiness, it's only a slim chance . . .'

'Anything!' Severo cried. 'Quick, Rafal! On your way!'

35

'She could be an ice-keeper,' said Jaime. He had come with a plump, rosy-cheeked little boy riding in his donkey pannier, and he himself looked prosperous; he was filling out, losing the slenderness of youth and the expression of intense attention to the world that he had once had. The little boy ran around in the cloister garth and chased a hen that had wandered from the farmyard.

'What is an ice-keeper?' Sor Agnete asked.

'We cut snow in winter,' Jaime told her. 'We pack it into pits where it stays unmelted under a roof of reeds. Then on summer nights it is carried down the mountain in baskets of straw and sold. Someone has to stay up there, to keep the reed roofs in good order – you get a melt-down very quickly if the wind takes off the reeds, and it can blow hard up there when it's warm and still below. She could do that, couldn't she, if I showed her how to fix the reeds?'

'Is such work paid for?' asked Sor Agnete.

'We don't use money much between ourselves,' he said. 'There is a good hut at the Sant Jeronimo ice-pits. The men who come for the ice would bring bread, and savours, and a jug of wine. Now and then someone goes up and cuts firewood, to keep a stove burning in winter. She would be welcome to the job – everyone hates it. The loneliness drives people crazy.'

'How can we be sure she will be all right?' demanded Sor Eulalie. 'Mightn't she come to harm up there on her own?'

'I'll go up myself every week or so,' said Jaime. 'I'll keep an eye on her.'

The two nuns glanced at each other. 'Why should you take this on yourself, Jaime?' asked Sor Agnete.

'If I hadn't stayed Galceran's hand . . .' he said. Then, seeing their blank expressions, he simply shrugged and said, 'I am willing. She will need warm clothes.'

'Come back for her in a week,' said Sor Agnete. 'We will have clothes and shoes ready to go with her.'

It took Rafal three days. And of course he couldn't find everybody. He missed Jaime, for Jaime was on the road from Sant Clara. He brought Galceran, and Salvat, and Juan's younger brother – Juan ran away and hid somewhere rather than be hauled in front of a cardinal. And Old Luis was dead. One or two others presented themselves whose account was vague; Rafal thought they were eager to share the journey, riding good horses, and gaining importance in the eyes of their cronies, not to speak of eating well, for he would, of course, have to sustain them from the cardinal's bounty for three days at least – the journey each way and the time in Ciudad. Rafal's nerves were drawn taut as tentered linen; he could not stand their cheerful conversation, and he rode a little ahead. But they sobered up as Ciudad came in sight and the prospect of the cardinal loomed nearer.

The cardinal spoke to them gravely. He told them that matters of vast importance hung on the answers they might make to him. He asked them to remember the capture of the wolf-child and what they had then done and said. Had they mentioned God to her?

He amazed them. They stood, nonplussed, glancing uneasily at each other, Galceran, it seemed, almost laughing, for he spluttered and covered his face with his great beefy hand.

'Did we what, Holiness?' he asked recovering himself.

'Do you think you might have mentioned God to her?'

'We didn't exactly talk to her, Holiness,' the man said. 'She wasn't friendly.'

'Could you have talked about God amongst yourselves in such a way that she might have overheard you?'

They looked at the floor. They shuffled their feet. Galceran answered, and his voice had taken on the unmistakable tones of a man talking to a child. 'We, er, don't talk about God much, Holiness. Not much at all. Can't remember when he last came up, in fact. Can you, Salvat?'

Salvat coloured and shook his head.

'When you found her, you didn't ask her where she came from? Or tell her to thank God for her rescue, or wonder aloud if she had been baptized?'

'It was like overpowering a wild beast, Holiness, not like meeting a sweet little child. She drew blood; we were covered in wounds and scratches,' said Galceran.

'We might have cursed her,' observed Salvat. 'We might have sworn at her, Holiness. Is that the sort of thing you mean?'

'You might have used curses that name God?' he asked.

They seemed relieved, pleased almost, to understand him at last. 'We might have done that,' said Galceran. 'I expect we did, Holiness. I'm almost sure of it.'

'Yes,' said Salvat. 'Old Luis knew a blasphemy or two. He was always taking names in vain, and she bit him deep and hard, I remember. I bet he cursed her.'

Severo returned to his cell. It was a desolating thought that the child might have learned of God through curses – poor outcast soul! Not that he believed it. Whatever it was that could be learned from being the object

270

of cursing, it was not, surely, the existence of an ever-loving creator. But he could tell Fra Murta that a creature who had been cursed in God's name had heard of God. He had his little troop of witnesses. The experiment was void, and he would do battle with Fra Murta again on freshly chosen ground.

He was too late. Lying on his desk was a fresh pile of papers, and on top of the pile was another document penned in the careful hand of Petro Llop. 'Audit resumed,' he read.

> *'Location: prisoner's cell. Prisoner unable to walk or stand.*
> INQ. 'You must repeat within one day a confession made under torture, or it is invalid.'
> PRISONER [groans]. 'Of course it is invalid. I will not repeat it.'
> INQ. 'If it is not true, why did you make it?'
> PRISONER. 'You know why! But if you only knew how eagerly your cardinal, and his friend Beneditx, have been seeking my free consent to their religion! And all is lost now; you have lost the game for them. For if I say now that I believe in God, how will anyone know whether what I say is sincere or said through fear?'
> INQ. 'I cannot answer for others. I have no difficulty in believing what you say. Repeat your confession.'
> PRISONER [groans]. 'What if I will not?'
> INQ. 'We shall resume the *mancuerda*.'
> PRISONER. 'You'll be sorry for this! The captains of Aclar are not usually savages, but they would be so outraged and revolted by this, if ever they found out what you have done to me, that they would have scream for scream and tear for tear.'

INQ. 'You'd be surprised how often we are threatened
with ridiculous revenges.'
PRISONER. 'God rot you in hell!'
INQ. 'Who is to rot me? We have you, I think! Now,
God be praised! We have you.'

To the truth of the above, I Petro Llop etc. etc., put
my hand . . .'

36

'I cannot save you once you have confessed,' said
Severo. He was standing beside Palinor's pallet. 'I
thought I could make something of the fact that the
child had been cursed. It isn't watertight, of course;
she couldn't at first have understood a word of human
speech, but Fra Murta doesn't know that, and I have
witnesses to the cursing . . .'

'I don't understand a word you say,' said Palinor,
speaking painfully. 'One of us is demented, and I
suppose it is more likely to be me.'

Brought up short, Severo remembered that from
beginning to end Palinor himself had not known about
the snow-child.

'Don't try to save me now,' Palinor went on. 'I don't
want years of crawling like a spider. Only . . . I am
hideously afraid of the fire. Is there a better way than
that?'

'I can make sure you will be dead before the flame
reaches you,' said Severo. 'Is there anything else I can
do for you?'

'When they fished me from the sea,' said Palinor, 'I
did not at first realize what had happened; I thought
I was still myself, and I promised to reward them; I
promised them gold and rubies. Such a debt ought to
be paid; will you see to it for me? Don't forget.'

'No; it shall be done,' said Severo. 'Are you sure
there is nothing else?'

'This isn't ancient Athens,' said Palinor. 'You can't
sacrifice a cock, but would you offer a prayer for me?'

273

'You cannot think it makes any difference! But I will do penance for you and pray for you every day of my life remaining.'

'It makes a difference to you, if not to me,' said Palinor. The ghost of a smile hovered on his gaunt and pain-racked face. 'Don't spare yourself the penance!' Then, as Severo, openly weeping, rose to go, he said, 'Ah, friend, I should have swum the other way for your sake, as well as for my own!'

Outside the prison a few bystanders were lurking, drawn by a ghoulish curiosity. Among them Severo recognized Palinor's servants. The boy looked at him with passionate reproach, and the girl with unbridled hatred. He gave them his heavy purse, but it did not lighten his tormented conscience.

On his way through the cathedral cloisters, Rafal accosted him.

'I cannot serve you any longer, Holiness,' the man said. 'I am leaving. I no longer believe in God.'

Severo looked hard and long at the familiar, unobserved, modest features of his chaplain. He saw that Rafal was trembling – was he trying to elect the path to the fire? Severo did not answer him, he merely clapped his hands. Two servants and a clerk in minor orders came running to his command.

'Bind this man hand and foot; gag his mouth,' said Severo, wearily. 'Take him at once to the quays and cast him into whichever ship is the next to slip hawsers and set sail, wherever it may be bound. Pay for his passage; I don't mean him to be enslaved.' To Rafal he said, 'To return will be the death of you.' To the astonished clerk, he said, 'Come with me. You are now my chaplain, and we have jobs to do.' Then he walked on.

When Beneditx returned to the Galilea, he declined to occupy his old cell. There were darker, remoter caves, deeper and higher on the cliff-face across which the monastery straggled and towered. He sat in darkness, silently. At last his confessor, an old colleague, rather a stupid man, Beneditx had thought when he was teaching him, ordered him on pain of sin to return to a cell with a window and resume the treatise on angels. Just as Beneditx now found it hard to eat – food was like ashes in his mouth – so he found it hard to think; thoughts were like cold ashes in his mind. Of course he still believed in angels – how else could the movement of javelins after they left the hand of the thrower, the movement of water, the unfurling of leaves be explained? In a world full of mysteries, and in which one should never explain with more entities what could be explained with fewer, there was no alternative to angels. What Beneditx no longer believed in was the beneficent purpose with which he had always relied on angels to operate; now he feared they might have malign purposes, or none.

The monks and priests at the Galilea were full of concern for Beneditx. Though they did not know what had happened to him, they knew the dark night of the soul when they saw it. It was a country some few of them had suffered in and struggled home from. They tried to cheer him by taking every opportunity to praise him, to mention his achievements, admire his scholarship. They meant well, but they made it worse. Beneditx was humiliated. His faith turned out to be less efficient, less sufficient, than that of the stupidest peasant woman. It was not enough without the help of reason. It did not reach down to the point to which he had fallen.

He could kneel, and he could wind words through his mind: 'Out of the depths have I cried unto thee, O Lord; Lord, hear my prayer. Let thine ears be attentive to the voice of my supplication . . .' On the far side of space and time, his God could not hear him. Beneditx

275

had failed to save Palinor, whose probable fate haunted him at night, after the last bell, the last hour of prayer in the Galilea, when all fell silent and the lamps were all extinguished. He had deserved to fail; he could not even save himself.

He opened the book at the marker he had put in it to hold his place, many months ago, when he had closed it and gone with Severo's messenger to Ciudad. It was a volume of St Thomas – *De Veritate*. 'Should morning knowledge in angels be distinguished from evening knowledge in angels? It seems not,' he read. 'There are shadows in the morning and evening. In the angelic intellect, however, there are no shadows, for as Dionysus says, angels are very bright mirrors . . .'

Beneditx left the pages unturned, set down his quill, and gazed out of his high window. The vale of the Galilea in all its beauty spread out before him, and he could watch the day move across it in a changing panorama of light and shade from dawn to dusk. Once he had seen the world drawn very fine and thin, transfused with the presence of God, a bright immanence giving all things solidity and meaning. God did not merely exist, but was present in every atom of his creation, so that every sight and sound was a sacrament, the flight of the smallest bird was a blessing. Now the world had come to seem a brutal and purposeless chaos, wholly contingent, not a noble building but a tumble of stones.

Where was comfort to be found? Once it had flowed unfailingly in the exquisite liturgy performed in the Galilea, where the voices of the boys of the oblate school soared so that he used to think the vault must be full of angels, hovering, hushed and envious. The liturgy was like a garden now, where he used to walk as of right, a son of the house, and which now he was cast out from, so that every beauty increased his sense of pain and loss.

Once there had been consolation in Scripture. Beneditx used to open the psalter at random, finding always comfort and joy abounding. Now he opened and read: 'In the morning thou shalt say, "Would God it were even," and at even thou shalt say "Would God it were morning."'

How high he had once aspired! He had desired the knowledge of angels, in whom there was no difference between morning knowledge and evening knowledge – in whom knowledge of the world as it was created in the mind of God, and knowledge of the world as in reality it was were one vision, one knowledge, one seamless whole – like an angel he had sought a knowledge without shadows, holding up to the creation a very bright mirror. And now the mirror of his soul was so fouled and darkened that neither morning nor evening could be distinguished from the black onrush of night.

37

Severo was keeping vigil, lying face down before the altar, praying. He was consumed with bitter remorse, for Palinor and for Beneditx, who had both asked him to be set free and then been shipwrecked because he had refused them. In the darkest hour he rose and went to the great Bible that lay always on a golden lectern before the high altar. He opened it, at random. But there was no such thing as accident – the hands of angels, so he had believed, directed the fall of the page. The volume opened at Isaiah, chapter seven. 'Ask thee a sign of the Lord thy God,' he read. 'Ask it in the depth or in the height above. But Ahaz said, "I will not ask, neither will I tempt the Lord."' Severo did not need a footnote, nor to turn a page, for his mind to jump to the words in the Gospel of Matthew: 'Jesus said, "It is written also, thou shalt not tempt the Lord thy God."' And at last he understood what he had done. He had thought to use the snow-child to entrap his God.

Trembling, he returned to his prostrate position before the altar. He could not pray for what he desired now, for what he longed for was that he might not believe in God; that he might walk out from the darkness into a clear morning, in which the sky was empty and things had no meaning but simply were; in which one might be able to hate suffering without trying to believe that it could be just or could be corrected later. His God refused his unformulated prayer, but weighed him down with presence all night long and would not go away.

Palinor lay awake. This was not only because he was in pain, but because it seemed improvident to spend any of his last moments asleep when an eternity of unawareness lay ahead, and these were the last moments of consciousness before morning. Not one he could look forward to. He did not know what means Severo would take to kill him before the fire, but he didn't expect it to be pleasant. For a while he let his thoughts wander amidst memories of his wife and son. He wished he had not sent Joffre with messages to talk to sea-captains who might in some distant harbour encounter a ship from home. This far-fetched attempt to save himself had not worked, and he thought his wife would sleep easier at night, his son grieve for him less mordantly if they never knew what had become of him. Well, after all, there was little likelihood they would ever know. He remembered a phrase in St Augustine, which had been his only available reading for so long, about the City of God, which he took to be located in the next world: 'There our being will have no death, our knowledge no error, our love no mishap.' In that world, if he had understood the saint correctly, suffering would be transfused with moral meaning and converted into joy. In the last hour before dawn he longed to believe this, and he even attempted a prayer, attempted in his mind to knock on the doors of the great silent universe, and shout, 'Is there anyone there?' Nothing answered him, and as the light of morning slowly flooded his cell, he wondered ruefully why it is those who believe most passionately in a merciful deity who are themselves most murderous and cruel.

When Josefa embraced her, Amara stiffened and clenched her teeth. She permitted herself to be held and kissed, however. Jaime stood waiting, carrying her bundle. The nuns were nearly all standing in the gatehouse to see their fosterling go; all but Sor Blancha, who was sitting by the abbess's bedside, reading to her from the Book of Revelation. The abbess had been ill for so long that the book was nearly at an end.

'I, Jesus, have sent mine angel to testify unto you these things in the churches. I am the root and the offspring of David, and the bright and morning star . . .'

'It has been dark here for too long,' said the abbess. 'Even so, come, Lord Jesus . . .' Sor Blancha started up in alarm.

It was not safe to make so large a pyre in the city streets, and so the burning was to be held at a crossroads, some miles outside Ciudad, on the plains. The people came from far and wide to see the heretic burn; nobody could remember anyone being burned alive in living memory, although one or two who had fled had been burned in effigy some time back. The workshops were empty, the markets suspended, and the labourers given 'Sunday grace' to flock out to see it.

Severo's clerk had bribed the executioner with a king's ransom to garrote Palinor before lighting the fire, but the inquisitor watched him so closely that he did not dare to. Even so, Palinor did not die the death that Fra Murta had purposed for him, for at the cost of the whole of the gold that Severo had given her, Dolca had procured in a back street in the Jewish quarter a little brick of dark brown sticky substance which emitted when ignited an instantly lethal, invisible fume, and when Palinor was already stripped naked and bound to the stake, she climbed wailing upon the pyre and kissing his feet, thrust it among the faggots below his heels.

38

Jaime took Amara first to Sant Jeronimo. He stood her
in the midst of the little square in front of the church,
and as people came and went, he told them about her.
'This is the new snow-keeper, friends. Her name is
Amara, and she will belong to my mother's household
from now on.' Various of his neighbours stopped to
talk and to look at the strange young woman, standing
so stiffly and looking askance at everyone. Those who
had seen her as the wolf-child seemed not to recognize
her now, and Jaime saw no reason to tell her true story
and every reason not to. It was simpler to give her out
as a servant, brought to look after the snow-pits, and
a parishioner like any other.
   'She doesn't look one straight in the eye,' said
Galceran. 'Is she a bit simple, Jaime?'
   'Only timid,' said Jaime. 'She's had a troubled
childhood.'
   'Haven't we all?' said Galceran. 'Well, it doesn't
matter in a snow-keeper anyway.'
   When dusk fell and the evening softened, the people
of Sant Jeronimo came out of their houses, linked arms,
and walked for an hour round the squares and streets
of the town, calling to each other, talking and stretching
their legs, eyeing each other's sons and daughters,
matchmaking, striking bargains and taking the air.
Jaime and his brother and his young wife walked
with Amara and named her to as many people as
possible. Then in the morning Jaime loaded a

string of four donkeys, and they began the ascent.

They climbed all day, at first through the woods of pine and holm oak, and then on narrow ledges zigzagging across the face of the bare rock, through rags of thin cloud, and into a region of scrubby thyme and bushes of thorn and rosemary, and then still higher, to the towering platforms that the mountain thrust up towards the sky. They passed a solitary charcoal burner somewhere halfway up or so, and then saw nobody moving on the precipitous face of the mountain except themselves. Towards evening they reached the snow-pits, which in winter had been on the melt-margins of the snow fields but now were some six hundred feet below the shrunken summer extent of the mountains' winter mantle.

Jaime unloaded the donkeys, opened the hut, and showed Amara her quarters – one tiny room with a shelf for a bed and a stove. He busied himself making a fire for the night and setting out the food his mother had packed for them. There were already stooks of reed in rows behind the hut and Jaime's donkeys had carried up more of them. He showed Amara how to spread them in a conical fan over the top of the ice-huts, and told her how thickly she must keep the ice covered. He showed her how to throw wet straw on her stove to make a smoke column to summon help if she needed it.

She hardly answered him, only nodding and copying when he asked her to do so the tasks he showed her. Between them they repaired the coverings of the three pits; then as darkness came down on a blazing sunset, they slept, Amara on her bunk, Jaime rolled in a blanket outside. He did not sleep deeply, in the biting cold and under the bright stars, and in the morning he took his leave.

'You won't mind being alone, Amara?'

'No,' she said, and stood and watched him out of sight.

Once he had descended over the shoulder of the nearest bluff, and could no longer see or be seen from the place where he had left her standing, she turned and began to climb the other way, ascending. Almost at once she scrambled, moving on hands and feet on the steep inclines, to a dizzy viewpoint commanding a wide prospect of the island across the inland plain. She saw without curiosity a thread of smoke, white in the clear light of morning, rising far off in the direction of Ciudad, ascending and expanding like a flower on a narrow stem. She turned her back and climbed higher.

Some hour or so later she was skirting the persistent snow which cloaked the uppermost crests. In the valleys the warmth of summer lingered into a balmy autumn, but here it was sharply cold. A recent snowfall covered the grey, glazed, older surface lightly, and she could see clearly, making a diagonal across the face of the slope above her, the footprints of a clawed and four-footed creature – a wolf-spoor. She clambered onto the cold white carpet and began to follow it.

When the light glorified and enriched at evening, she was still climbing. In the fine air she moved slowly and breathed rapidly. A western prospect opened out, across the whole range of lesser jagged crests and out to sea. The sea shone golden in the descending sun, and she saw, likewise without curiosity, dark specks on the expanse of water, spread out all over the plains of the sea – ships under sail. There were hundreds and hundreds of them, darkening the dimpled water like bees swarming on a honeycomb, as though a great nation had embarked in fleets and was bearing down on the island.

Amara looked at the approaching host for a

moment only. It was already too late to return to the snow-keepers' hut before darkness, and the wolf-spoor had petered out some way below. Only the last of the summits still rose above her, but she continued to climb, further into the unbroken solitude of the inviolate snow.

THE END

A DESERT IN BOHEMIA

Jill Paton Walsh

It is 1945. Somewhere in Central Europe, in the aftermath of violence and confusion, a terrified and bloodstained young woman, Eliska, emerges from the forest to take refuge in an apparently abandoned castle. Soon she is joined by others – the idealistic Jiri, the sinister Slavomir and his partisans, and Count Michael Blansky, who is the castle's ancestral owner.

But the war has changed things forever. In a storm of ideological change, the existing order and the aristocratic heritage of ten generations are brushed aside by the arrival of Communism, and Count Michael must join the flood of refugees, if he is to survive. He leaves behind a legacy which will entangle those involved for the next forty years in more ways than they can possibly imagine.

As divided post-war Europe unravels around them, they must make what they can of lives buffeted by circumstance. For many, individual freedom is at best problematic. For better or worse, communities are destroyed, families uprooted, and the ties of trust, friendship and duty which bind them together are broken down by the implacably irresolvable forces at work. Told through the eyes of nine characters who live through the forty years between the end of the war and the fall of Communism, *A Desert in Bohemia* is a complex and enthralling testament to the power and powerlessness of the individual in challenging times.

NOW AVAILABLE AS A DOUBLEDAY HARDBACK

0 385 60121 2

A SCHOOL FOR LOVERS

Jill Paton Walsh

'AN INGENIOUS CELEBRATION OF MOZART . . . AN
ENTERTAINING DANCE THROUGH SELF-DECEPTION TO REAL
FEELING . . . ARTFUL IN THE BEST SENSE, ENRICHED BY FINE
DESCRIPTIVE WRITING'
Guardian

Against the idyllic background of a labyrinthine country house in
need of restoration, two friends are dared by their manipulative
tutor to try to seduce the other's lover. As the two young women in
question restore the paintings and revive the gardens of the
mansion, they are pursued unobserved. In the absence of their
lovers, each begins to weaken . . .

All too soon, idealistic love is beset by misunderstanding and
irrational desire. And what begins as a game soon becomes a far
darker pursuit . . .

'AN ELEGANT AND WITTY TRIBUTE TO THE GENIUS OF
MOZART . . . THE BEAUTY AND GRACE, ARTIFICE AND SKILL
OF THE WORK . . . A CHARMING RENAISSANCE CONCEIT'
Opera Now

'PACY NARRATIVE, STRONG VISUAL SENSE, DIRECTNESS OF
TONE, CLARITY OF STYLE'
Times Literary Supplement

'A LIGHT, WITTY NOVEL ABOUT THE RISKS OF FALLING IN
LOVE. THE NOVEL WORKS AS SHAKESPEAREAN COMEDY, AN
OPERETTA WITH MAJESTIC SETTINGS, QUICKSILVER CHANGES
IN EMOTION, AN AMUSED BUT SYMPATHETIC TONE AND THE
BELIEF THAT YOUNG LOVE IS TOO NAÏVE AND TRANSITORY
TO BE TRAGIC'
Financial Times

0 552 99646 7

BLACK SWAN

GOLDENGROVE UNLEAVING

Jill Paton Walsh

'THIS IS A BEAUTIFUL NOVEL AND AN ENDURING ONE'
New York Times Book Review

Once a year cousins Madge and Paul visit Goldengrove, their
grandmother's idyllic Cornish home. But one year as Summer turns
to Autumn and as they are drawn from childhood to maturity, their
seemingly indomitable grandmother turns to Winter, and the
precious moments of innocence begin to be swept away . . .

Years later Madge, now living at Goldengrove, reflects on her own
grandchildren and the events and revelations which disturbed the
tranquillity of her childhood, as current events begin to strike
echoes from the past. Against a stunning Cornish backdrop,
Goldengrove Unleaving is a lasting tale of innocence and beauty
amidst the calm and storm of changing lives.

'AN EXTREMELY GOOD STORY, MARVELLOUSLY TOLD. AS THE
STORY GATHERS MOMENTUM, THE DEEPLY UNDERSTOOD
CHARACTERS, THE GOLDEN ATMOSPHERE, THE SMALL
CHANGE OF EVERYDAY PLEASURES AND AGELESS TRAGEDIES
ARE ALL PUT OVER WITH SUCH NEWLY SEEN IMMEDIACY AND
SUCH CONTROLLED MASTERY THAT THE READER IS CARRIED
ALONG LIKE A SURF RIDER ON THE CREST OF A WAVE,
KNOWING IT MUST SOON BREAK'
Times Literary Supplement

'WRITTEN WITH AN INTENSITY OF FEELING AND CARE, WITH
A WOOLF-LIKE AWARENESS OF THE INSTANT'S SENSATION: A
STORY ALL IN THE PRESENT TENSE BUT WITH A REMARKABLE
SENSE OF AN OVERSHADOWING PAST'
Guardian

'PATON WALSH DOESN'T TIDY UP THE BLIGHT FOR WHICH
MAN WAS BORN. SHE'S TOO WISE TO ATTEMPT ANSWERS
ABOUT GROWING, LIVING, DYING, ETHICAL CHOICES. SHE
EXALTS THE MYSTERY, THE UNKNOWING ITSELF'
New York Times Book Review

Winner of the Boston Globe-Horn Book Award.

0 552 99655 6

BLACK SWAN

A SELECTED LIST OF FINE WRITING AVAILABLE FROM BLACK SWAN

THE PRICES SHOWN BELOW WERE CORRECT AT THE TIME OF GOING TO PRESS. HOWEVER TRANSWORLD PUBLISHERS RESERVE THE RIGHT TO SHOW NEW RETAIL PRICES ON COVERS WHICH MAY DIFFER FROM THOSE PREVIOUSLY ADVERTISED IN THE TEXT OR ELSEWHERE.

☐	99313 1	OF LOVE AND SHADOWS	Isabel Allende	£6.99
☐	99820 6	FLANDERS	Patricia Anthony	£6.99
☐	99619 X	HUMAN CROQUET	Kate Atkinson	£6.99
☐	99824 9	THE DANDELION CLOCK	Guy Burt	£6.99
☐	99686 6	BEACH MUSIC	Pat Conroy	£7.99
☐	99767 6	SISTER OF MY HEART	Chitra Banerjee Divakaruni	£6.99
☐	99587 8	LIKE WATER FOR CHOCOLATE	Laura Esquivel	£6.99
☐	99770 6	TELLING LIDDY	Anne Fine	£6.99
☐	99801 X	THE SHORT HISTORY OF A PRINCE	Jane Hamilton	£6.99
☐	99848 6	CHOCOLAT	Joanne Harris	£6.99
☐	99758 7	FRIEDA AND MIN	Pamela Jooste	£6.99
☐	99737 4	GOLDEN LADS AND GIRLS	Angela Lambert	£6.99
☐	99807 9	MONTENEGRO	Starling Lawrence	£6.99
☐	99718 8	IN A LAND OF PLENTY	Tim Pears	£6.99
☐	99817 6	INK	John Preston	£6.99
☐	99810 9	THE JUKEBOX QUEEN OF MALTA	Nicholas Rinaldi	£6.99
☐	99777 3	THE SPARROW	Mary Doria Russell	£6.99
☐	99819 2	WHISTLING FOR THE ELEPHANTS	Sandi Toksvig	£6.99
☐	99788 9	OTHER PEOPLE'S CHILDREN	Joanna Trollope	£6.99
☐	99720 X	THE SERPENTINE CAVE	Jill Paton Walsh	£6.99
☐	99646 7	A SCHOOL FOR LOVERS	Jill Paton Walsh	£6.99
☐	99655 6	GOLDENGROVE UNLEAVING	Jill Paton Walsh	£6.99
☐	99673 4	DINA'S BOOK	Herbjørg Wassmo	£6.99
☐	99723 4	PART OF THE FURNITURE	Mary Wesley	£6.99

All Transworld titles are available by post from:

Bookpost, P.O. Box 29, Douglas, Isle of Man IM99 1BQ

Credit cards accepted. Please telephone 01624 836000, fax 01624 837033, Internet http://www.bookpost.co.uk or e-mail: bookshop@enterprise.net for details.

Free postage and packing in the UK. Overseas customers allow £1 per book (paperbacks) and £3 per book (hardbacks).